MAHU BLOOD

NEIL S. PLAKCY

mlrpress
www.mlrpress.com

Published by
MLR Press, LLC
3052 Gaines Waterport Rd.
Albion, NY 14411

Visit ManLoveRomance Press, LLC on the Internet:
www.mlrpress.com

Cover Art by Victoria Landis
Editing by Kris Jacen

ISBN# 978-1-60820-306-2

Issued 2011

Dedication

Like so many of my books this is for the man who turned out to be someone to watch over me: Marc.

Acknowledgments

A writer needs an ohana, a family and a community, in order to put out a book—and I've been lucky to have a very supportive ohana during the years of the Mahu series. Christine Kling, Sharon Potts, Mike Jastrzebski, Miriam Auerbach and Vicki Landis all critiqued parts of this book, and their help has been invaluable.

Cindy Chow once again provided yeoman service by reading the manuscript and pointing out so many mistakes I'd made about Hawai'i, though any remaining errors are my fault, not hers. She has been a wonderful tutor into the intricacies of life in the Aloha State.

Kimo has a number of favorite mystery writers I consider my friends, including Anthony Bidulka, Deborah Turrell Atkinson, Greg Herren, James W. Hall, Joe DeMarco, Joe Pittman, Les Standiford, Pat Brown, and Vicki Hendricks. James O. Born always provides me with a couple of great lines, including, in this book, "Don't worry, it's not my blood."

For their personal support I am grateful to my mother, to Eliot Hess and Lois Whitman, Fred Searcy, John Spero, Steve Greenberg, Eileen Matluck, Andrew Schulz, Elisa Albo, and Lourdes Rodriguez-Florido. And as always, gratitude is due to my other colleagues in the English department at Broward College's South Campus for their support and encouragement, and to the college's Staff and Professional Development program, which has allowed me to attend conferences and conventions.

For professional advice and encouragement I want to thank Wayne Gunn, Stacy Alesi, Ware Cornell, and my fellow members of the Florida chapter of Mystery Writers of America. David Currie and Sarah Byrne offered the use of their names (and in Sarah's case, her singing voice) for characters here. Lynne Barrett first gave me the idea, so many years ago, of bringing all the characters together at the end of the book for a big luau.

A big mahalo to Laura Baumbach and Kris Jacen, for all their help in bringing the Mahu books out in new editions.

And of course, the biggest thank you goes to the ohana closest to my heart—Marc and Sam, who give me love and make me laugh every day.

In the Kingdom of Hawai'i

The alarm went off at six, and my boyfriend Mike rolled over and mashed the snooze button, then yawned and looked at me. "Morning, sunshine," he said.

I pulled the pillow halfway over my head and said, "I'm going back to sleep."

He stood, scratched his balls, then grabbed the covers from around my neck, snatching them down. I was left laying there on the mattress, naked and cranky.

"Come on, Kimo, get up. You've got to get in the shower and get your uniform on."

"Just say no to polyester." I held up my fingers in the shape of a cross.

It was Hawai'i Statehood Day, the third Friday in August, and every available officer and detective had been pressed into duty along the route of a parade sponsored by a group called Kingdom of Hawai'i. They believed that the takeover of the islands by the United States in 1893 was illegal, and agitated for independence and the return of the Hawaiian monarchy.

My partner, Ray Donne, and I had been assigned to duty at the Iolani Palace, the last home of Queen Lili'uokalani, where she was kept under house arrest following her overthrow. The department wanted to make a show of power, so uniforms were required, even from those of us who worked in plainclothes.

I dragged my sorry ass out of bed and into the shower. While I was in there, Mike came into the bathroom, still naked, and stood over the toilet, pissing noisily. I love Mike, and I find his naked body very sexy—but I wish he'd pee in private. He's an only child and doesn't understand the concept of personal space that you learn when you grow up with two older brothers.

He flushed the toilet, which caused a cascade of frigid water to stream out of the showerhead. "Oops, sorry," he said, when I yelped. "I always forget the shower does that when I flush."

I opened the shower door and grabbed for him with soapy hands.

"It's a work day," he said. "Go on, finish your shower so I can get in there."

A half hour later, I was dressed and ready to head out, while he stood in the bathroom, a towel wrapped around his waist, brushing his teeth after his shower. "I'm going," I said.

"Gimme a kiss." He puckered up, toothpaste foaming.

I leaned in, but at the last minute dropped my head and nibbled at one of his nipples. He yelped and pushed me away.

"Watch out. I could pull you in for assault on a uniformed officer."

"There's only one letter difference between uniformed and uninformed."

I flipped a vintage Hapa disk in the CD player of my Jeep and headed to police headquarters downtown to the gentle rhythm of Barry Flanagan's ukulele and the smooth tenor of Keli'i Kaneali'i. I found Ray, and we joined dozens other officers for a ride over to the Iolani Palace in O'ahu District School buses. The mood in our bus was light-hearted, as if we were a bunch of kids on a field trip.

I knew a lot of the men and women on the bus with us, and though we joked around together, some of them didn't like the fact that I am gay or that Ray was a pretty recent mainland transplant who'd jumped into a detective slot, based on his experience in Philadelphia, without spending time on the streets of Honolulu. We got along with the detectives and uniformed officers we worked with, but in big groups of cops, I think we were both a little uneasy.

The ride passed without incident, though, and Ray and I took up our position on South King Street, about a block from the palace. We were supposed to stand there as the parade went by and be on hand in case any trouble erupted.

Kingdom of Hawai'i, or KOH, had promoted this march to the palace from the Aloha Tower, on the harbor about three blocks away. The group, one of many which advocated greater autonomy and a return to traditional rule, appeared to have a lot of money, especially for advertising.

There had been rumors that there would be violence at some point. No one was clear on who would be responsible. Would it be KOH? Or a group opposed to them? And what form would that violence take?

Despite the lack of information, the police department took the threats seriously, and the streets between the Aloha Tower and the Iolani Palace were lined with uniformed cops.

My mother had gotten interested in KOH because her grandchildren were an ethnic mix, and she wanted to protect their rights under whatever new laws were enacted. She had formidable organizational skills, honed by managing a strong-willed husband and a household of three boisterous sons, and she had helped out with several smaller rallies over the past few months.

I meant to call her the night before to see if she would be marching but got caught up in processing a guy who killed his girlfriend with a buzz saw, so chatting with my mom slipped my mind.

Ray and I found some shade under a tall, broad-branched kiawe tree, and by ten a.m., the first vanguard of the parade reached us. A marching band from Kapalama High, one of the Kamehameha Schools for native Hawaiians, led things off, with the state song, *Hawai'i Pono'i*. They were followed by a group of musicians who chanted, banged drums and shook rattles. Male and female hula dancers in full regalia danced in front of a convertible carrying Ezekiel Kapuāiwa, a man who claimed to be a direct descendant of the royal family. His red and yellow feathered cape fluttered in the light breeze as he waved like a beauty queen.

The parade went on for blocks. A convertible passed, blasting Israel Kamakawiwo'ole's sweet, light tenor. I spotted my mother, wearing a bright red *holoku*, a sort of formal mu'umu'u, walking with my two of my nephews, both wearing aloha shirts and shorts, with kukui nut leis. We waved at each other.

I had a momentary pang of regret as I watched them. My mother was so proud of her grandsons, who were fifteen and thirteen, and they both looked so handsome marching beside her. Even though gay men and women are having children in record numbers, I didn't think I would. That meant I'd never see my own son walking beside her or my father. I felt my eyes getting moist, and I looked up to the sky so that no one would notice.

As I did, I saw a bright flash from the roof of a building across the street from us. Then three shots erupted under the blare of the music, one right after the other, as if from a semi-automatic weapon. The screams began as the last shot reverberated in the humid air, which smelled of plumeria blossom leis and automobile exhaust.

I reacted instinctively, checking to make sure there was no gunman on the street. The crowd erupted in chaos, so I couldn't have seen a shooter if he'd been a hundred yards away.

My mother and my nephews were about half a block ahead. I hurtled toward them, Ray right behind me, as my mother pushed back toward me with the boys. "You OK?" I asked when I reached them.

"Everybody's all right." My mother's face was flushed, and she was out of breath. A couple of strands of her black bouffant had come loose and were plastered against her forehead.

The boys' eyes were wide with fear, and I didn't blame them. The street looked like a scene from a disaster movie, people screaming and pushing. Ray took my mother by the arm, and I pulled the boys close to me. We started down the block toward a building with a low roof stretching over a plaza.

My mother already had her cell phone out, calling my father. "I'm fine, Al. The boys, too. Kimo's right here." Her voice shook, which meant to me that she wasn't all that fine, but she's a strong woman and I knew she'd bounce back.

I heard my father shouting as she held the phone away from her. "I'll come home as soon as the streets clear out," she said, when he paused to take a breath. "I want to stay away from the crowd."

She listened and then handed the phone to me.

"Yes, Dad, Mom's fine. The boys are good, too. They're not little kids, you know. They're young men. They won't let anything happen to their *tūtū*." I winked at my nephews as I spoke, and I saw Keoni, the younger, wipe his eyes with the back of his hand. Both of them stood up straighter.

I slapped the phone closed and gave it back to my mother. "You've got the right idea, Mom. Stay here a while. Where's your car?"

"At the garage by the Aloha Tower," Jeffrey said. He had just gotten his learner's permit and was already memorizing every street and turn. "I know how to get back there."

"Good. I'm counting on you and your brother to look after your tūtū, okay?"

They both nodded. "Jeffrey, you're in charge. Keoni, you're second in command. But you both listen to whatever your tūtū says."

My mother's cell rang as we reached the building, where a crowd had already gathered in the wide lobby. "It's Liliha," she said, looking at the display. My oldest brother's wife and Keoni and Jeffrey's mother, Liliha was a helicopter mom, hovering over everything her kids did.

I took the phone from her and flipped it open. "Hi, Lili. Everybody's fine. The boys were very brave. I'm proud of them. Mom'll get them home as soon as the streets clear. I've gotta go, though. Love you."

I flipped the phone closed before my sister-in-law could get a word in. My mother looked relieved, and my nephews laughed as I turned the phone off and handed it back to my mother.

"Gotta get back to work, Mom." I leaned down and kissed her cheek and pulled the two boys in for hugs. "You guys stay in here until the police have the area under control."

Ray and I walked back out to South King Street, where people pushed and shoved, children cried and a woman screamed and clutched her arms around her chest. Uniformed cops struggled to gain control, but no one was paying them much attention.

The sun blazed around us, and heat rose up from the city street in shimmering waves. "I think I saw something, on the roof of that building over there," I said to Ray, pointing at a six-story office a block away, back near where we'd been standing. "I want to check it out."

"Right behind you, partner."

We maneuvered our way to the building where I'd seen the flash. A Korean security guard stood in the doorway, trying to organize the swarm that sought shelter in the building. One of the benefits of wearing a uniform is that you never have to show a badge to prove who you are; the crowd parted as Ray and I squeezed into the jammed lobby.

Elderly women in mu'umu'us and young men in tank tops talked and argued and called family members on cell phones. Men and women in business suits and young moms pushing strollers blocked the elevators, so Ray and I entered the stairwell and started climbing.

"If there was somebody up there, he's long gone," Ray said, from behind me.

"Yeah, but maybe he left something behind. Or maybe I'm seeing things."

"Always a possibility."

When we reached the sixth floor, we stopped in front of the door to the roof to catch our breath and listen. We couldn't hear anybody outside, just a murmur of crowd noise from below.

I drew my gun and tapped the door open. Hearing no response outside, I swung it wide and stepped out into a shooting stance. We could see most of the flat roof and the short parapet that wrapped around it, but there were a couple of air handlers that someone could hide behind, so we split up and crept around each one.

It was sweltering up there, without a hint of breeze, and the sweat dripped down my back, gathering under my arms and pooling around my waist. I felt foolish—but better to be a living fool than a dead hero.

Within a couple of minutes, we had established that the roof was empty. "If you were going to shoot at the crowd from up here, where would you set up?" Ray asked.

I pointed to the South King Street side of the building. "Over there, I guess."

We walked across the single-ply membrane roof, feeling our feet settle slightly into the sun-softened material. It didn't look like anyone had been up there, and I was about to admit that it had been a trick of light when I glanced down at the ornamental cornice above the front entrance.

It stuck out from the building a foot or so, with a flat part on the top. Shining up at me in the morning light was a round piece of bronze-colored metal. It was hard to tell without field glasses, but I thought it was a spent rifle casing.

"Down there," I said, pointing. "What's that look like to you?"

"Looks like we need a crime scene team out here."

As I was about to make the call, my radio crackled, and dispatch notified us that we'd been assigned to a homicide. From our vantage point, I realized that the crime scene we'd been called to was right in front of us. A few hundred feet away I saw a body laid out on the street, two uniforms standing guard over it.

My problems had gotten a lot bigger than a sweaty polyester uniform.

"We're right on it," I told the dispatcher. Ray remained on the roof until I could get a uniform up there to replace him, and I took the steps in the dark, damp stairwell two at a time, swinging around the turns in my eagerness to get outside.

The security guard had the lobby organized by the time I got there, leaving a narrow aisle from the elevators to the front door. People clustered at the front windows, talking and pointing at the police activity outside.

The two uniforms guarding the body were Lidia Portuondo and Gary Saunders, and I'd known them both for years. Lidia, a slim woman who wore her dark hair in a French braid, stood over the body of an elderly woman in a flowered *holoku*. I realized with a shudder it was similar in color and style to the one my mother wore.

Saunders, a big blond guy with more brawn than brains, kept the curious at bay. As I walked up, another pair of uniforms arrived, and I dispatched them to relieve Ray.

"What have we got?" I asked.

"Saunders and I were stationed over there." Lidia pointed a few hundred yards in the opposite direction from where Ray and I had been posted. "We heard the shots and started crowd control. When we heard the women screaming, we came over to take a look."

A group of older ladies, all in *holokus*, stood a few feet away.

"We discovered the victim, saw the blood and the bullet holes, checked for vital signs and called it in." She looked at me. "How'd you get here so quick in this crowd?"

I told her where we'd been posted and then leaned down to take a look at the woman, careful not to touch her until the medical examiner's team and the crime scene guys arrived. The streets were jammed with protesters and police, so I figured it might take them a while.

Blood had pooled on the pavement under the woman, who looked to be in her sixties or seventies. She was Hawaiian, with a shock of white hair and skin a couple of shades darker than mine. A small handbag made of quilted fabric lay by her side, where it appeared she had dropped it.

"Anybody else hurt?" I asked.

Lidia shook her head. "A bunch of the *kupunas* were shook up," she said, referring to the elderly women, "but none of them were hurt. We only heard three shots, and… well…" She pointed to the victim on the ground, where I could see the bloodstains from three separate bullet wounds.

Ray arrived, and I asked if he had any gloves on him. I'd been so obsessed with getting the uniform together that morning I hadn't brought any of the usual stuff I carried—evidence bags, rubber gloves and so on.

"Call me a Boy Scout," Ray said, handing me a pair. "Always prepared."

While Lidia filled him in, I picked up the woman's handbag. All she had inside were a pair of reading glasses, a wallet and less than a dollar in change. She didn't have any credit cards, family pictures or the rest of the usual debris we carry around with us. A Hawai'i state identification certificate, the kind people use when they don't have driver's licenses, said her name was Edith Kapana.

Like a license, it had her height, weight, hair and eye color, along with her address and ID number. She lived in what I thought was Hawaiian homestead land in Papakolea, a neighborhood clustered around the base of Tantalus, on the other side of the H1 freeway. Ray leaned down to take a look at her. "Who would kill an innocent old woman?" he asked.

"We don't know how innocent she was." I shivered again. Suppose Edith Kapana had been a random target chosen by someone trying to disrupt the march? My mother had been only a few hundred feet away; the shooter could just as easily have aimed at her and my nephews.

Though why three shots to the same woman? If someone really wanted to cause trouble, why not shoot randomly into the crowd? And if the shooter had a semi-automatic weapon, why fire only three times?

We left Lidia to guard Edith Kapana's body and walked over to the group of women who stood behind Gary Saunders. We introduced ourselves and began interviewing them, one by one. Ray has a lot more patience for that kind of thing than I do; he liked to empathize with witnesses, bond with them, while I just wanted to find out what they knew and move on.

The chattiest of the old ladies was a *hapa* woman of about Edith's age. *Hapa* means half in Hawaiian, and we use it as slang for anyone of mixed blood. Since I have Hawaiian, Japanese and *haole*, or white, ancestors, I could be called *hapa*, too. Maria Concepción Freitas looked like she had a lot of Hawaiian blood, and her last name connected her to the people of Portuguese ancestry who first came to the islands in the nineteenth century to harvest sugar cane.

Maria Concepción's hair was dyed an artificial black, and she wore more makeup than your typical Waikīkī prostitute. She started to tell Ray about her grandfather, who came to Hawai'i in one of the first waves of immigrants from the island of Madeira, but I interrupted and asked her to cut to the chase.

"Did you see anything today?"

"Poor Aunty Edith," she said, tears streaking her mascara. I doubted that Edith was really her aunt; "aunty" was a term of respect we all used for older women.

"You knew her?"

"Just to say hello," Maria Concepción said. "She was from the Big Island, but she lost her home, so she came to live here with family."

She had been walking a few feet from Edith when she heard the shots and saw Edith fall to the ground. "We could have all *wen maki*," she said, using the pidgin for dying. "Where da kine police wen dat wuz happen?"

Ray looked at her like she was speaking a foreign language, which to him, she was. He and his wife had moved to Hawai'i almost two years before, so Julie could enroll in a graduate program at the University of Hawai'i. He'd been my partner for almost as long, though he had yet to fully understand Hawaiian Pidgin, the polyglot mix of English, Hawaiian, Portuguese and Cantonese most locals grow up speaking.

I ignored Maria Concepción's jibe and asked how she knew Aunty Edith. She and the other women had met her at the community center in Papakolea or at Kingdom of Hawai'i meetings, and no one knew any reason to kill her.

The ME's team showed up as we finished our interviews. Edith had been shot three times: once in the head, once in the shoulder and once in the leg. The assistant ME's preliminary guess was that she had bled out from the wound in her leg, which appeared to have hit the femoral artery, but the shot to her head could have been the fatal one.

As they loaded Edith Kapana's body on a stretcher, the elderly women, led by Maria Concepción, began to wail again. While I ushered them toward a KOH-chartered bus, Ray volunteered to get us some beverages. Once the women were on board, Lidia helped me scour the area for evidence, but we didn't find anything.

Ray returned a while later with two bottles of cold water. I wanted to pour mine over my head, but instead I drank it in about three gulps. The crowd had dissipated by then, leaving the streets littered with paper fans, empty water bottles and signs on wooden sticks. Uniformed cops guided people back to waiting buses or toward the Aloha Tower. The usual street denizens harangued the trees as oblivious tourists wandered past, looking for photo opportunities in front of the Iolani Palace or by the statue of King Kamehameha.

Larry Solas, a crime scene tech I'd worked with before, showed up with another tech, and they took another look up and down the street for evidence. When they finished I led him upstairs and over to the parapet.

Larry, a skinny Hawaiian in an untucked aloha shirt, looked down at the cartridge, then out at the street. "You think the shooter was up here?"

"I don't know. I saw a flash of light around the time I heard the shots. We came up here to check it out."

He had to call in for some special equipment, and Ray and I went downstairs to interview the building security guard, an older guy in an ill-fitting dark suit with features that reminded me of Mike's Korean relatives. "You see anyone unusual come through this morning?" Ray asked.

The guard hadn't noticed anyone out of the ordinary, and he told us the fire exit at the back of the building was locked from the outside. "Here's the sign-in book," he said, pushing it across the wooden counter top toward us.

There were only about a dozen names, and we copied them all down, along with the offices where they'd been headed. "Things are slow this morning because of the march," the guard said.

"You keep a record of the tenants who come in and out?" I asked.

He shook his head. "Most of them, I know by sight."

We called Lidia and Gary in and asked them to go from floor to floor and ask about unusual or suspicious visitors, taking down names and contact information for everyone they spoke to. Then we went back up to the roof, where Larry Solas had found some trace fibers near the parapet.

"Looks to me like someone was lying flat here," he said, indicating what he'd found where. "But I can't say for certain the shooter was aiming at your victim."

Ray said, "She could have just been a sacrificial lamb. There's nothing like the death of a sweet old lady to bring up a public outcry."

By the time the bucket lift showed up, Lidia and Gary reported that none of the tenants they spoke with had anything to contribute, and I sent them out to clear the area around the front of the building. Larry rose up to the level of the cornice and collected the spent cartridge, and we all went back to headquarters.

I spent three years on patrol in polyester, but I couldn't remember ever feeling as uncomfortable as I did that afternoon, hitching a ride back downtown with Larry Solas. My hair was plastered down on my head, and my whole body felt slimy. And I couldn't shake a vision of Edith Kapana, lying dead on South King Street, and the knowledge that it was up to Ray and me to find out who had killed her.

We met with our boss, Lieutenant Sampson, as soon as he came out of a meeting with top brass. "You want us to work this weekend?" Ray asked him. "Go hard on this?" Ray was always up for overtime or special duty assignments, because he and Julie were building a nest egg for a house.

"You have any leads?" Sampson asked.

The lieutenant's a big guy, tall and broad-shouldered, and he favors polo shirts with khaki slacks rather than a shirt and tie. Today's shirt was a royal blue, with a polo player emblem. There was a loose thread on his sleeve, but I didn't reach over and pull it off. As the only openly gay detective working homicide, I had to be extra careful about stuff like touching other guys. Even a totally cool boss like Lieutenant Sampson.

"Not much." I laid out what we had: the witness statements, the list of tenants and visitors to the building, the forthcoming reports from the medical examiner and ballistics. Sampson fiddled with the toy cannon on his desk, flipping it back and forth as I talked.

"My budget is slammed, just like every other government office in this state," he said, "but I can authorize some overtime for tomorrow. I have a feeling the newspapers and TV stations are going to be all over this story, and the chief is going to want results ASAP."

He looked up at us, and I felt the weight of his trust and

the responsibility to find Edith's killer. "If you don't have any immediate leads, go home, get some rest. Let's talk at the end of the day tomorrow and see what you've got."

Sampson's mention of the media reminded me of how I'd been outed a few years before, the papers and TV stations hounding me for interviews. I didn't look forward to that starting up again, especially when we had so little to go on.

Hawaiian Homestead

I walked out to my Jeep, where I stripped off my uniform shirt and the T-shirt under it and flapped the air around me, trying to cool down. Leaving the headquarters garage, I switched CDs, and as Jake Shimabukuro's ukulele began to stream through my speakers, I had to remind myself to point the Jeep up toward Aiea rather than to Waikīkī.

I was having trouble thinking of Mike's house as my home, even after living there for nearly two months. When we met, I had a studio apartment a couple of blocks from Kuhio Beach Park, and he owned half of a duplex in Aiea, where he'd grown up. We dated for six months, broke up and stayed apart for a year, then got back together when a case forced us to work with one another.

After about a year commuting between his house and my apartment, Mike and I went to Maui for a sexy weekend. Late one afternoon at the beach there, Mike said, "It seems dumb for you to keep paying rent on your apartment, when I've got a whole house. What do you say you come live with me?"

We stood naked together in the incoming surf, our bodies pressed against each other. The sun glinted off the wave tops, and a couple of cormorants circled above us. It seemed like nothing could go wrong between us.

"I can walk to the beach from my apartment," I said, only half joking. "You want me to give that up?"

I'm no lightweight; I weigh a hundred-eighty dripping wet. But Mike picked me up in his arms as if I weighed nothing and said, "You bet your life I do."

There were arguments pro and con. If we lived together, we'd sleep side by side every night. We could have sex without making appointments, eat together as a routine rather than a special occasion.

But I loved my apartment, with its picture window that looked down Lili'uokalani Street to the ocean. I could roll out of bed and be in the surf within minutes. I was in walking distance of my favorite gay bar, and there was a convenience store at the corner that sold a Japanese candy I loved. And I didn't want to move into his house because I thought his parents didn't like me.

We considered selling his place and buying something else, but even with our combined incomes and savings, the cheapest house we could find was miles farther from the beach and from our jobs. After some soul-searching, I gave up my lease and borrowed a truck from my brother Haoa. I loaded it up with my clothes, my books and my athletic equipment, then drove it up to Mike's house.

It was an easy move but a tough transition. By Statehood Day, things were tense between Mike and me. I didn't feel like there was a single corner of the duplex that belonged to me. My books were still in their boxes, and though Mike had carved out space in the closet for my clothes, they were cheek by jowl against his, often getting mixed up.

Sometimes I thought I'd made a huge mistake, and other times I couldn't see myself anywhere but by Mike's side for the rest of my life. For the most part, I tried not to think about the situation. And between the demands of my job and keeping track of my family, that wasn't hard to do.

While I was stuck in traffic on the H1, I called my mother to make sure she and the boys had gotten home. Once the ban on using cell phones in a moving vehicle went into effect, Mike and I both bought Bluetooth earpieces with voice dialing, which we kept in the car. I stuck mine in my ear and said "Call parents."

When my mother picked up, I heard my father raging in the background, and though she told him to be quiet, I heard a tremor in her voice. "No more demonstrations for a while, okay, Mom?" I said. "I don't need to worry about people shooting you."

"Now you know how I feel about you being a police officer," she said, and I was glad to hear her feistiness returning.

Traffic eased, and I climbed the hill to Mike's house. When I got there, I shucked the rest of the uniform and took a long, cool shower. By the time Mike got home, I was standing in the living room in a pair of clean boxers, with a fan blasting cool air at me and a Longboard Lager in my hand.

"You get caught up in that riot at the march?" he asked, peeling off his aloha shirt while crossing the living room toward the kitchen.

"And how." I followed him, leaning against the wall as he got himself a beer. I told him about the flash on the roof, how the crowd had reacted after the gunshots.

"How close was your mom to the shooting?"

"Too close." We walked back to the living room, where he stripped to his y-fronts and stretched out on the sofa. "As soon as I could I rounded her and the boys up and got them out of the way."

He patted the sofa next to him, and I sat. Have I mentioned how handsome and sexy he is? Six-foot-four of muscle, body hair and sly grin? He has a dark mustache, and green eyes that look just a bit Asian.

"We didn't even know someone had been shot until dispatch called." I shook my head. "This poor woman." I could still see her, splayed out on the ground, blood flowing from her wounds.

Mike took my hand in his. "You'll find the guy who did it," he said.

I smiled at him. "Overtime tomorrow. Ray's psyched, as usual."

"We'll just have to make the best of tonight, then." Mike leaned over and kissed me. We ordered a ham and pineapple pizza, Mike's favorite, and then vegged out in front of the TV. I hadn't been surfing as much as when I lived in Waikīkī, and I promised myself I'd surf the next morning and work off the calories from the pizza and beer.

Around nine o'clock, Mike asked me for a foot rub, and I sat at the end of the sofa, his feet in my lap, rubbing them with shea butter. After ten minutes or so, he said, "I feel some slack key guitar coming on."

That was our little code. I swayed my hands in some vague hula-like movements, and he flipped a Keola Beamer CD in the player, trying to keep his parents on the other side of the wall from hearing what we were up to. We went into the bedroom and got a head start on working off those calories.

As I got home after my morning surf session, I saw Mike's parents getting into their car. We waved at each other but didn't speak. Because of the way Mike and I split up that first time, his father sees me as the guy who broke his son's heart and drove him to drink. His mother is more polite, but there's still a chill in her attitude.

I picked up the *Honolulu Star-Advertiser* from the driveway, and over a quick breakfast I read the first-page article on the shooting, the march and the mayhem that ensued after the shots were fired. There were the usual quotes from civic officials, who assured everyone that it was safe to walk the streets, as well as an outraged squawk from Maile Kanuha, a spokesperson for KOH, sure the shooting was motivated by the movement's enemies.

Mike woke up as I was finishing. We kissed, and he poured himself some cereal as I went into the bathroom. After a quick shower, I left for headquarters. He was at his computer researching a case of his own, and I promised I'd make it home for dinner.

Ray and I divided the sign-in book and the tenant lists Gary and Lidia had assembled between us. We cross-referenced them to anyone who'd been involved in Hawaiian nationalism based on group membership, letters to the editor of the *Star-Advertiser* and so on. It was slow, tedious work.

A woman on the office building's third floor had contributed to several groups, but Ray found she had a handicapped permit for her car based on a leg injury that required her to use a cane.

A guy at the advertising agency on the fourth floor had done pro bono work for one of KOH's rivals. He had no listed home number, so I jumped through a few hoops and found his cell number. When I reached him, he said he was on vacation in California, had been there for nearly a week. A friend of mine at Hawaiian Airlines verified his outgoing flight and his return reservation.

Every possible suspect either had an alibi or something else that ruled him or her out. By noon we were ready to get out of the office and drove out to Papakolea for background on Edith Kapana.

The address on her ID card was a ramshackle house on Hawaiian Homestead land—not a reservation for native people, like on the mainland, but something close. Civic leaders would tell you it was a way of preserving the land for descendants of its original inhabitants, but one of my teachers at Punahou, the private high school President Obama had also attended, had called it a modern-day ghetto, citing the socio-economic issues, including drug abuse and alcoholism, that were rife there at the time.

As we climbed toward the Cemetery of the Pacific, the houses around us shifted from well-kept gated properties to ramshackle structures clinging to the side of the mountain. Beat-up cars were parked by yards where hibiscus and bougainvillea ran wild. Though the government was taking steps to improve conditions, those initiatives hadn't reached the house where Edith Kapana lived.

It was only a single story, but it looked like several sections had been added on at different times, because the roof angles didn't match and the paint on each section was at different stages of fading. There was no doorbell, so we knocked.

A teenage girl came to the door, carrying a squalling baby on her hip. She was thin, with mocha skin, slack dark hair, and bags under her eyes. I introduced us and asked if she knew Edith Kapana.

"Aunty Edith? She *wen maki*."

"Yes, we know she's dead. That's why we're here."

The girl shivered. "I wen get all chicken skin when I heard."

As usual, Ray was baffled by the pidgin reference to goose bumps, but he nodded along. "How'd you know Edith?" I asked.

The girl, who told us her name was Leelee, shrugged. "She da kine *hanai tūtū*. Maybe year ago, her house on the Big Island get buss up, she come live here."

I could see Ray getting frustrated. "A *hanai* relative is one you adopt," I said to him. "Or maybe somebody you always think of as a sister or a cousin. So Aunty Edith's not her real grandmother."

"She real *kahiko*," Leelee said. "Always want to sit around, talk story." She hefted the baby on her hip. For a moment, he stopped crying and stared at us.

Leelee gave us permission to take a look around the room where Edith had lived, in what had once been the garage. "What was that she called her, kahiko?" Ray asked when we were alone.

"Old-fashioned. Someone who likes to do things the old way," I said, snooping around the piles of newspaper clippings and photocopies of legal documents on the desk. There was nothing much else in Edith's room other than some cheap furniture, a few books about Hawai'i, family snapshots thumb-tacked to the walls and a couple of photo albums.

"Doesn't look like anyone killed her for her money," Ray said.

I agreed. When we went back to the living room, Leelee said the house belonged to her uncle, but he was often drunk and didn't come home much. Her boyfriend, Dex, was at work, leaving her with the baby. I asked Leelee for Dex's full name, as well as her uncle's name.

"What you want that for?"

"We need to talk to them. My boss will look at stuff like that. You know how it is with paperwork. He wants every '' dotted and every 't' crossed."

Leelee looked like punctuation wasn't her specialty. She toed the carpet for a while, then said, "My uncle don't live here no more." She met my eyes. "But you can't tell da kine people from the OHA. Me and Dex, we don't qualify for homestead."

The Office of Hawaiian Affairs controlled housing on homestead land. "Don't worry, Leelee, we won't rat you out."

Her body relaxed. "Trale. Dexter Trale." She spelled it for us, though I could see it was an effort.

"Here's my card, with my cell number. You have Dexter call me, all right?"

She took the card, and the baby started crying again. I wondered if Leelee ever changed him—because he smelled ripe when we arrived, and he still did when we left.

"How old do you think she is?" Ray asked, as we walked down the driveway.

"Fifteen, sixteen."

"She looked pretty overwhelmed."

"I'll bet Aunty Edith helped her with the baby. She'll have to get some other aunty to help out now."

"You think we ought to call social services?"

"The baby didn't seem to be in any danger. Sure, Leelee's a kid herself. But half the people on this homestead are probably related to her. They'll help out. Hawaiians take care of their own."

We drove around the neighborhood, stopping to talk to anyone on the street, in yards or on porches. We didn't get the warmest reception; most of the time when the cops come to Papakolea, they're looking to arrest someone. People tried to ignore us, and when they spoke, it was only to me. Ray's white skin rendered him invisible.

It took a lot of persuading, but a few people admitted knowing Aunty Edith. Leelee's uncle was either Edith's nephew, her cousin or her husband's grandson, depending on who you talked to. There was general consensus that she had lived on the Big Island, somewhere on the slopes of Kilauea, until her house had been swallowed up by the *pahoehoe*.

"A kind of lava," I told Ray, as we walked back to the Jeep. "Real smooth, billowy. The rocky stuff is called *'a'a*."

"You're a fountain of information," Ray said. "They don't know how she's related, but they all knew what kind of lava knocked out her house."

"What can I say? They're Hawaiian. You know how the Eskimos have all those words for snow? We have a bunch for lava."

"I know the difference between anthracite and bituminous coal," Ray said. "And the name of the three rivers that come together in Pittsburgh."

"Good to know. In case it ever comes up."

We stopped at the community center, where posters for the KOH rally were plastered on the walls. Many of them read '*Ku I Ka Pono*: Justice for Hawaiians.' It was hard to disagree with a slogan like that—unless of course, you were not ethnically Hawaiian and that justice would come out of your pocket.

The community center was a simple two-story building with a set of steps up to the front door and a zigzag handicap ramp. We parked in the lot and took the stairs up, pausing outside to look at some pictures posted there.

Little kids performed at a hula recital, neighbors picked up trash along Tantalus Drive and senior citizens peered at computers. It looked like the center provided a lot of service to the community.

Inside, a group of elderly men and women drank coffee, nibbled on malasadas and talked story, with what sounded like the classic Hawaiian music of Alan Akaka playing in the background. Everybody shut up when we walked in; just the music kept going. I wondered if I should have left Ray in the car, but we were partners, and I'd had enough of being considered second-class myself, because of my sexual orientation. I wasn't going to do that to anyone else.

"Aloha," I announced to the room. I introduced myself and Ray. "We're investigating the death of Aunty Edith Kapana. Can we ask you some questions about her?"

The room remained silent. I went up to a grizzled old kupuna and said, "How about you, Uncle? You know Aunty Edith?"

Grudgingly, he nodded. He said his name was Israel Keka'uoha. "Aunty Edith, she good people, she like the kahiko way."

Yeah, I wanted to say, we heard that from Leelee.

"You watch," he said. "Wen Hawaiian people take over again, da kine police gon work fo' us."

At that, the room erupted in noise. Everybody agreed with the old man. They all wanted to complain about the sad state of Native Hawaiian rights, about past police abuse, about how we would have to look out when the Kingdom of Hawai'i was restored.

Patiently, Ray and I went around the room, listening to their litany of complaints. I told a few of them about the victim advocate's office, and I used my cell phone to get updates on a couple of cases.

The youngest person in the room was a forty-something woman with jet-black hair and matching fingernails. She was the caretaker of an elderly woman in a wheelchair, who spent most of the time we were there asleep. She said her name was Ellen Jackson and that the woman was her mother. "Nobody else will tell you," she said to me, in a low voice, "but Aunty Edith was making lots of *pilikia*."

I whispered "trouble," to Ray, then asked Ellen, "Pilikia for who?"

She looked around to make sure no one else was listening. "These boys, they sell *pakalolo*," she said, using the island word for marijuana. "They raise it up on the mountain. Aunty Edith threatened to call da kine police on them."

"You know their names?"

She shook her head. "But you can see them, hanging out on Tantalus 'round sunset."

I wrote down her name and phone number, and we continued talking to the kupunas. By the time we got back around to Israel, the mood in the center had thawed. I had a feeling there were a lot of hidden secrets out there, buried along the slopes of Tantalus along with the bodies of so many war dead. Just as the cemetery's caretakers protected the grounds, so the people of Papakolea protected their own secrets. Was one of them the identity of the person who killed Edith Kapana? Only time would tell.

I was thanking Israel when he shook his head and said, "Poor Aunty Edith." He looked at me to make sure I was paying attention. "Not many people know, Aunty Edith *hanai tūtū* to Ezekiel Kapuāiwa, too."

I remembered that Kapuāiwa claimed he was descended from Hawaiian royalty. "Really?" I asked. "He from the Big Island, too, uncle?"

Israel looked at me. "You *babooze*, brah?" he said, wondering if I was stupid. "He fo'real from *da kine ohana.*" He shook his head. "Aunty Edith, she love dat boy."

"What about you?" I asked. "What do you think of Kapuāiwa?"

"Ezekiel strange boy." He shook his head. "Sometimes I think he babooze, sometimes *lolo*. But if people want follow him, make things fo' real better for Hawaiian people, I say 'kay den."

I made a note of that. Israel turned back to his group, mumbling about da kine babooze police, and Ray and I went out to my Jeep.

In the parking lot, Ray said, "I thought it was going to get ugly in there at first." He looked out the window. "I felt like I didn't belong."

"If I went to Philly, I'm sure there are places I wouldn't belong."

"But you'd always know that you were in America. I don't even speak the language, like I'm in some foreign country."

"Out here, you are in a foreign country. The Kingdom of Hawai'i."

"Is there really a guy out there who should be king?" Ray asked as we drove back to headquarters.

"It's complicated. There are three different royal houses, and each one thinks they should be in charge. I guess we should figure out who the players are."

Though it was Saturday, our case was high-profile, and the reports from ballistics and the medical examiner were waiting when we returned to our desks. Ray reviewed them while I did some online research on the three lines that all claimed the right to rule the islands.

The House of Kamehameha ruled Hawai'i until the death of Kamehameha V in 1872. He died a bachelor, allegedly without issue, though there was a collateral branch descended from his eldest brother. Ezekiel claimed that that his great-great-grandfather was the king's illegitimate son, raised in secrecy on the Big Island in a hanai family. He based this claim on records he swore had been kept by his grandmother, who would have been Kamehameha's great-granddaughter.

I read more about the various houses, but it only made me confused. Who knew who should be king, if indeed Hawai'i should revert to a kingdom?

Ray's results were more concrete. The spent cartridge I'd noticed on the cornice matched one of the bullets recovered from Edith Kapana's body. She had been shot three times, as we'd seen at the site. Death was the result of massive loss of blood.

For an older woman, she was in good shape, according to the autopsy. Varicose veins, a slightly enlarged heart and some nutritional deficiencies. But for the bad luck of those three bullets, she could have lived another ten or fifteen years.

Ray and I had no good leads and no real reason to try and

stretch our overtime out. We called Sampson at home, and he told us to table the case until Monday.

Mike and I went out to dinner after I got home, and some of the tension I'd been feeling eased. He is truly my best friend, and I love spending time with him. And of course, sex always helps make things better, too. We cuddled up in bed and fooled around until we both drifted off to sleep.

When I announced I was moving in with Mike, my friend Gunter told me to put a dollar in a bottle every time we had sex during the first year. Then I could take a dollar out every time we had sex after that. The bottle would never be empty, he said.

I wasn't doing it, but if I had been, the bottle would have been filling up fast.

Monday morning, Ray and I met with Lieutenant Sampson, who leaned back in his chair, his snazzy bright green polo shirt stretching across his stomach.

Ray took the lead, filling him in on what we'd learned about Aunty Edith and KOH. "You think this was random?" Sampson asked. "Someone trying to damage this Kingdom of Hawai'i group?"

"Or the whole sovereignty movement. My mother has been volunteering for the group, and I know for sure she's going to back off, at least for a while."

Lieutenant Sampson raised his eyebrows, but didn't say anything.

"We're going to look into people who might have grudges against this group in particular or the movement in general. It's a pretty wide net, but you never know what we'll catch."

Back at my desk, I phoned Leelee, since Dex hadn't called me. There was no answer at her house. No answering machine, either, but I didn't expect one. I hung up and called an old school friend, Karen Gold, who worked at the local office of Social Security. "Can you give me a work address on a Dexter Trale?"

"Got a social on him?"

"No, just the name." I spelled it for her and heard her fingers clicking on her keyboard. "OK, here it is. He works for the Kope Bean." It was an island-based coffee chain, a local Starbucks clone. Ray and I often got our caffeine fixes from the downtown branch.

"Which store?"

She gave me an address, and I scribbled it down. "Mahalo, Karen. See you soon, okay?"

If we were going out, I wanted to see if we could hook up with someone from KOH. There was no number listed for the group, though, and the home number for Maile Kanuha, the spokesperson quoted in the *Star-Advertiser* article, was unpublished. I would have to call the reporter who'd written the article to get in touch with her.

I had dealt with Greg Oshiro a few times in the past, and he wasn't one of my favorite people. Of mixed Japanese and Hawaiian heritage, he was a big guy, tall and heavyset, with a fat belly always slopping over his belt. He had a dour expression, which I guessed came from working the police beat.

"News desk. Oshiro."

"Hey, Greg. It's Kimo Kanapa'aka. Howzit?"

"What do you want?"

He had written about a number of my cases and had the ability to turn even the most innocent information into something that sounds damning. He wasn't anti-police; often his articles seemed almost fawning. But he's had it in for me ever since I came out of the closet.

"I'm trying to get hold of Maile Kanuha. You got a number on her?"

"You working on Edith Kapana's murder?"

"Yup. You know anything about it?"

"Didn't you read my profile in yesterday's paper? Hers was another death in a long line stretching back to 1893."

"I read it. Maile Kanuha. Her number."

"Give me a quote for today's follow up story."

"This isn't a quid pro quo, Greg. If you don't cooperate, I'm sure I can find some reason to haul you in for obstructing an investigation."

"You ever hear of the First Amendment?"

I handed the phone to Ray. "You talk to him."

Ray gave Oshiro the statement he wanted, though it lacked much detail, and in turn Greg provided the number. Greg promised if he came up with anything in his profile that might be relevant to our investigation, he'd let us know. I wish I believed him. The only way I'd get anything from him was via the newspaper.

"I always admire your people skills," Ray said, hanging up the phone.

"Greg Oshiro's not a person, he's a reptile."

"Or a valued member of the fourth estate. Depends on how you look at it."

I growled at him, and he laughed, turning to his computer to check out the agency where Maile worked, the Department of Agriculture Quality Assurance, whose offices were not far from police headquarters.

"You want to get some coffee?" I asked Ray. "How about we pay a visit to Dexter Trale at the Kope Bean, then go see Maile?"

"Somehow I don't see this guy as a barista."

We hopped in the Jeep and took the H1 to the airport exit, navigating the local streets to find the address Karen had given us. It was a long, single-story building in an industrial park. A small sign over the front door read "Kope Bean Receiving."

"Guess you were right. Dex is not a barista."

There was no one in the reception area, and though the desk was cluttered with papers, it didn't look like anyone regularly sat there. I pushed the door open into the warehouse, and the pungent aroma of roasted coffee beans swept out over us.

"Should have stopped for coffee before we got here," Ray sighed.

The ceiling was about ten feet high, and all the ventilation ducts were exposed below the flat roof. Pendant light fixtures hung every twenty feet or so. The walls were lined with wooden pallets, stacked with boxes of coffee cups, napkins, sugar and so on. There was some classic Hawaiian music playing softly in the background, the kind of stuff my parents used to listen to when I was a kid. I thought it might be Sonny Chillingworth, but I wasn't sure.

Along the right-hand wall, a middle-aged Thai woman sat at a computer terminal, with a phone headset, talking and typing.

"Let me repeat the order back to you," she said. "One carton of stirrers, four cartons of napkins, two bottles of macadamia nut syrup and your regular order of beans. You know we're having a promotion on the logo mugs? Can I send you a box of them for display? Great. Talk to you tomorrow."

She pulled the headset off and turned to us. "Can I help you?"

"We're looking for Dexter Trale."

"He's the skinny haole over there by the loading dock." Her phone rang, and she popped the headset back on. "Thank you for calling the Kope Bean central distribution center."

We looked in the direction she had pointed, where a tough, wiry haole was arguing with a big Samoan guy. "Mr. Trale?" I interrupted. "Honolulu police detectives. Can we have a word with you?"

The Samoan slapped his hands together, said, "Your problem now, brah," and walked away, toward an open loading dock door. As we showed Dex our IDs, the Samoan slammed the back of his truck closed, got in and drove away.

"Thanks a fucking lot," Dex said. "Now I've got to explain why that delivery was short."

"Sorry, brah. Bad timing. But we've got some questions for

you."

"I didn't do anything."

I doubted that was true. But he shrugged, and said, "I need a smoke. You want, you can follow me."

A guy on a pallet jack zoomed past us, carrying a load of boxes. He stopped under a sign that read "Store #3" and began offloading as we walked past him.

"You the boss here?" I asked Dex.

"You could say that. We handle the distribution for all the Kope Bean stores on O'ahu." We came to the row of open doors on the loading dock. "The store managers call their orders into Tuli over there, and she puts them into the computer. That generates tickets for the pickers and packers in the back. They put together the pallets, and the jockey brings them up here and lines them up for the trucks. Me, I just stand around and make sure nobody fucks up."

He pulled a pack of cigarettes from its place under the sleeve of his snug T-shirt. He was a guy who liked to show off his body; if that shirt had been any tighter you'd have called it another layer of skin. His faded jeans were just as snug, cupping his ass; the back pocket was artfully ripped to show a glimpse of what looked like red satin boxers.

He jumped lightly from the dock to the ground, and I pulled my attention back from Dex's ass to do the same. He took a lighter from his jeans pocket, but the wind was kicking up so it took him two tries. When he got it lit, he peered at both of us.

"We're looking into the murder of Edith Kapana," Ray said. "Want to tell us about her?"

"She was some kind of aunt or cousin of my girlfriend's. Last year, her house got knocked out on the Big Island, so she came to live with us."

"How was that working out?"

"She was a meddling old busybody, but she helped Leelee with the baby and she handed over her Social Security. And what the hell, you can't just toss an old lady out on her ass, can you?"

"You know anybody who had a grudge against her?"

Dex looked from Ray to me and back. "You think somebody killed her?"

"Body in the morgue makes that pretty clear," Ray said.

"Nah, man, I mean, like somebody killed her on purpose? Not just 'cause she happened to be marching in the wrong place?"

"Somebody wants to shoot up the crowd, they spray a lot of bullets around," Ray said. "Whoever shot Edith was aiming at her and was a damn good shot, too."

Dex fumbled his cigarette, and it fell to the ground. He crushed it out with his heel, then pulled another from his pack. "I don't know nothing about it," he said, head down, focused on lighting the cigarette.

"Where were you Friday morning?" Ray asked.

Dex looked up, his dark eyes focused on my partner. "Here. Working."

"Somebody can back you up?"

Dex shrugged, took a long drag from his cigarette. "We got a time clock. I punch in when I get here, punch out when I leave."

Ray looked at me, and I raised my eyebrows. Then he handed Dex his card. "You think of anything, you give us a call, all right?" he asked.

Dex shoved the card in the torn back pocket of his jeans, the white paper half hidden by denim, the other half stark against red satin.

"What do you think?" Ray asked, after Dex had gone back in the warehouse, and we were walking back to the Jeep.

"I don't trust him. But you see how he kept fumbling those cigarettes? I don't know that he's got the kind of steady hand you need to aim so precisely."

"They have drugs for that," Ray said.

"Yeah, I know. They have drugs for everything."

THE MAN WHO WOULD BE KING

Maile Kanuha's office was only a couple of blocks from headquarters, so rather than mess with downtown traffic and parking, we left the Jeep at the police garage and walked. We found her surrounded by piles of paperwork, with a phone in one ear, typing something on her computer. She was an older woman, with iron-gray hair in tight pin curls. When she finished the call, we showed her our ID and said we had questions about the KOH.

"I'm not supposed to talk about personal business on state time."

"I'd be happy to clear it with your supervisor. This is a murder investigation, and that takes precedence over…" I looked at the top file on her desk. "Licensing dealers in bee pollen."

She looked at the clock. "I guess I can take a coffee break. Come with me."

We went into a small kitchen with a couple of round tables and plastic chairs. "You want coffee?" she asked. "We get the best beans here, grind them ourselves."

"Can't resist an offer like that," I said, and Ray agreed. We didn't talk over the noise of the grinder, but once Maile had dumped the grounds into the filter, she sat down at the table with us to wait for the brew to finish.

"How about if you fill us in on the background of the Kingdom of Hawai'i," I asked. "We've read, but I know the media tends to distort the truth."

She smiled. "I couldn't agree with you more. The KOH begins with Ezekiel Kapuāiwa, who grew up in a small town on the Big Island, raised by his grandmother Victoria, who was a direct descendant of Kamehameha V."

"I thought Kamehameha V died a bachelor," I said.

"Yes, that's true. But you don't need to be married to father a child." A sharp tang rose up from the coffee pot and snaked through the room. It didn't smell like the kind of fresh beans Maile had promised.

"He has proof of this?" I asked.

"There are no records of the birth of Ezekiel's great-great-grandfather," she said. "But the family lore is that Ulumaheihei Kapuāiwa was the *manuahi* of Kamehameha V."

"A manuahi is an illegitimate son," I said to Ray.

"Kamehameha studied at the Royal School," Maile continued. "And the records show that some female students who were there at that time were expelled and married off quickly. Ezekiel was told that the family of the girl was ashamed, so they kept the secret of his parentage. Kamehameha wanted his son to succeed him, but his advisors refused to let him make the boy his heir, because the girl had claimed publicly that her husband was the boy's father, and it would have caused a great rift. That's why he declined to name a successor."

"And the son did nothing when Kamehameha died?" I asked. "Never stepped up, never made a claim?"

She shook her head. "When his father died, Ulumaheihei was seventeen. His mother was dead, and his maternal grandfather insisted that he was not qualified to lead the people. The Legislature took over then, electing our kings and queens, right up to Lili'uokalani. When she was deposed, Ulumaheihei was already dead, and his son Moses was only twelve years old. The family kept hiding him, afraid for his safety."

"We learned a bunch of those old folk tales when I was in Hawaiian school," I said. "Pele and Lono and the other gods and goddesses. What makes Ezekiel's story more believable than any of those?"

The coffee finished brewing, and Maile got up and poured for each of us. The paper cup was thin and burned my fingers as I picked it up.

Maile's mouth was set in a firm line. "I believe Ezekiel Kapuāiwa because I believe the Hawaiian people need a leader to bring them to freedom. I don't think it's a coincidence that his great-grandfather's name was Moses."

But Moses came from the Old Testament, the very Bible that the missionaries, including my own grandmother, used to subjugate the Hawaiian people, to wipe out their old gods and to replace them with Jesus and his disciples. I didn't see any point in arguing about gods and history with her, so I just asked, "How does Ezekiel connect to Moses?"

"Moses had a daughter, Victoria, who was Ezekiel's grandmother. She raised him after his parents died, and she always told him it was his burden and responsibility to bring the people of Hawai'i out of their indentured servitude." Maile smiled. "About five years ago, he accepted his legacy and began to work on behalf of his people to restore their historic rights and privileges."

Ray must have sensed my growing frustration, because he put a hand on my arm and stepped in. "There are other groups with similar claims to the throne," he said. "You think any of them could have tried to disrupt the rally on Friday?"

"I'm sure of it," Maile said. "You have to understand, there's a lot at stake here. In 1893, the US took over an independent nation, and our people have lived under a prolonged military occupation ever since. If things work out the way we hope, we could gain reparations in the millions of dollars, as well as the return of crown lands to the people of Hawai'i."

"The *indigenous* people of Hawai'i," Ray said. "Newcomers need not apply."

I sat back against the plastic chair, sipped my cooling coffee and watched the two of them spar.

"The traditional definition of a Hawaiian is someone who is descended, at least in part, from the aboriginal people inhabiting the islands at the time of first contact with the Western world," Maile said. "I'm not going to debate the position of those who have profited from this illegal occupation."

Ray made a few notes, then looked up. "We're not interested

in a debate, either. Do you know of anyone in particular who might want to sabotage your efforts? Get any threatening notes? People who have disagreed with you?"

Maile laughed. "There are at least ten different organizations competing for the right to rule the kingdom of Hawai'i. When you consider the entrenched interests—the corporations, the attorneys, the landowners who would have their properties taken from them and returned to the people—the list is endless."

She didn't know anything about the rumors the police department had heard and couldn't name any names. And the coffee wasn't that great, either.

Walking back to headquarters after our meeting, I was lost in thought. How could the simple killing of an old woman have so many suspects and so many complications? Would we ever be able to find anything?

"What did she mean by returning crown lands to the people?" Ray asked, bringing me back to the present.

I sighed. "It's complicated." I motioned around us. "To the ancient Hawaiians, owning a piece of the land was as foreign as owning the sky or the ocean."

We stopped to wait for a light. The sun beat down, and sweat dripped down my back. I looked around at the crowd of tourists on their way to the Iolani Palace and at the broken coconuts on the ground beneath a palm tree.

Ray was waiting for an answer, so as the light changed, I said, "The *ali'i*, the ancient chiefs, were the stewards of the land, and they granted the people the right to live on the land and cultivate it. In 1848 Kamehameha III set up the Great *Mahele*, which changed everything and created three categories of land ownership: the crown, the government and the people."

The tourists in front of us stopped for a photo opportunity beneath a palm tree tilted at a forty-five degree angle. Ray and I dodged around them. "When Queen Lili'uokalani was overthrown in 1893, the crown lands didn't belong to her but to her position. Like Maile said, she and Kamehameha V were elected."

"Didn't know that," Ray said. "We didn't get much Hawaiian history in the Pennsylvania schools."

"Anyway, the new government of the Republic of Hawai'i took all the crown lands and lumped them in with government land. All that land then shifted to the US government in 1898 and then to the state of Hawai'i in 1959."

"How much land are we talking about?" Ray asked, as we climbed the steps into headquarters.

"Anywhere from one to three million acres. Depending on who you listen to and how you define the term. Pearl Harbor, all the Halawa valley, the land where the state capitol building stands... it could be a big deal."

"That's a whole lot of motive to disrupt anybody who's trying to be in charge."

I swung up to Papakolea on my way home, looking for the drug dealers Aunty Edith had been making trouble for. The narrow streets clustered around the slopes of Pu'owaina Crater, overgrown with banana, bougainvillea and hibiscus. There were lots of places for illicit entrepreneurs to hide from da kine police.

For the most part we call the area Punchbowl, the name of the national military cemetery built in 1948 to commemorate the soldiers and sailors who died at Pearl Harbor. There are now over 33,000 graves there. Papakolea, for many years, was a kind of living grave for Hawaiian people, the way reservations on the mainland were for Native Americans. Though things had improved, it was the right kind of place to foment support for Hawaiian nationalism.

As I circled the neighborhood a fine mist accumulated on my windshield, turning quickly to a steady light rain. Within a few minutes it was pouring, torrents of water cascading down road and ravines, and even the street-side entrepreneurs had run for shelter. I was glad to make it back to Aiea and Mike as thunder boomed and lightning crackled. It was nice cuddling with him to the sound of rain pinging off the metal roof.

Tuesday morning, I got in a few minutes before Ray and sat at my desk reading Greg Oshiro's latest article on Edith Kapana's death. He highlighted that the police had no suspects and no leads. I couldn't argue with that.

I'd just finished reading the article when the guard downstairs buzzed. "You in charge of the shooting at the rally?"

"Looks like it."

"Got a letter down here for you. Little kid dropped it off."

Ray came in, and I went down for the note while he got settled, carrying a pair of rubber gloves with me, just in case. "This Hawaiian kid ran in, T-shirt, board shorts, rubbah slippahs," the duty guard said. "He gave me the envelope and then ran away when I tried to ask him who he was or where he was from."

"Age?"

"Maybe six or seven. Dirty." He shook his head. "Can't say anything more than that. We had a tour group coming through, and he slipped out."

About the lady shot at the rally was printed in block letters on the outside of the envelope. Back at my desk I slit the flap with a letter opener with a miniature surfboard at the end. Ray leaned over as I unfolded the paper inside.

It was a flyer for a group called Ka Leo Hawai'i, the Voice of Hawai'i. The tag line was "The Voice of the Hawaiian People, Silent Since 1893." I'd seen similar flyers on display at the Papakolea community center the day before, though someone had scrawled "Killers!" on this one in red marker.

"Be nice if they'd given us some more detail," Ray said.

"Informants. Can't control 'em." I turned to the computer and Googled the group. The leader was a guy named Bunchy Parker. "Bunchy's in the news a lot," I said to Ray, pointing at the search results.

I'd known about Bunchy since I was a kid. He protested against everything from the Navy's use of Kahoolawe for target practice to genetically modified taro plants to the Superferry. I had a tendency to think of him as an unreformed hippie time had forgotten.

But there was danger in writing Bunchy off, I realized, as I watched a YouTube video of Bunchy standing on a makeshift platform next to the Wizard Stones, four basalt boulders on the beach at Waikīkī. They are said to contain the *mana*, or spiritual healing power, of four mysterious and powerful ancient healers, and as such are sacred to the Hawaiian people. Though there isn't much room for a big demonstration, the boulders made a meaningful backdrop for a rally based on Hawaiian national identity.

Bunchy was in his sixties, straight black hair cut short and graying at the temples. He was a big tough-looking guy, like my brother Haoa, the kind who would have made a great villain on *Hawaii Five-O.*

"We are the only true representatives of the people of Hawai'i," he said in the video, shaking his fist.

The crowd cheered.

"We're here to set our people free from the oppression of the state of Hawai'i. It's time for our young people to stand up and fight for their inheritance. We ask all our *kanaka* and non-kanaka supporters to fight for what is truth and what is justice."

Kanaka was the traditional word for a Hawaiian of native or Polynesian descent. It was certainly polite of Bunchy to use the term non-kanaka rather than the more pejorative haole for Caucasian, *pake* for Chinese, *katonk* for Japanese and so on.

When Bunchy finished, the crowd cheered and waved flags and chanted, "Fight, fight!" in Hawaiian. I found a lot of similar videos related to the sovereignty movement and the various events at the Iolani Palace. Seeing them all in sequence made me take the movement a lot more seriously than I had in the past.

Running Bunchy through the police department computer, I pulled up quite a record, from malicious mischief to trespassing to tax evasion to assault. The last charge had landed him in the Halawa Correctional Facility. He was still on parole after serving part of his sentence for that offense. "What do you think of this?" I asked Ray, turning my computer screen to face him.

I called Bunchy's parole officer, a young woman named Kalia Rogers. She said we could come over and talk about him if we wanted, so we walked to her office at the Hawai'i Paroling Authority on Alakea Street.

Kalia means beautiful in Hawaiian, which was an unfortunate name for her, considering she had a lumpy figure and a port-wine stain on her right cheek. "He's not in trouble again, is he?" She led us into a small conference room. "He swore to me the last time I saw him that he was going to stay clean."

"What's his problem?"

"He's a sweetheart. And he's very charismatic, so he gets all these people to follow him."

"I saw him on YouTube," I said, as we sat down at a small round table. There wasn't much in the room besides the table, four chairs and a couple of posters tacked to the walls from the Honolulu Festival, which happens every March and celebrates our connection to the various cultures of Asia. "A demonstration at the Wizard Stones. He didn't look like a sweetheart there."

"I admit, when he gets going he says some things he shouldn't," she said. "He doesn't have much impulse control."

"Jails are full of people like that," Ray said. "How's he doing on parole?"

"He comes in like clockwork. Shows me pictures of his grandkids. He cares about the legacy he's leaving for them."

All that was sweet, but the Bunchy I'd seen on YouTube could have masterminded the death of an old woman in service to his cause. "You hear about the shooting at the rally on Friday?" I asked.

"You aren't looking at Bunchy for that, are you?" she asked, her mouth opening in horror. "Because it's not like him at all."

"What about the assault charges?" Ray asked. "He sounds like a loose cannon."

"I've worked his case for the last four years." Kalia pushed a few strands of dark hair over her ear. "I know his record inside out. Every time he got in trouble, it was always impulsive. Pushing a guard away, punching somebody trying to drag protesters, that kind of thing. Bunchy isn't the kind of guy who'd shoot an old woman."

"But what about the people who follow him?" I asked, leaning forward. "You said he's charismatic. What if somebody in his group showed some initiative?"

She sighed. "I guess it's possible." She gave us Bunchy's address, which not surprisingly was back in Papakolea. As we stood up, she said, "In this job, you see a lot of people who still ought to be in jail. Some of them, you can almost hold your breath until they do something stupid, something that violates their parole or gets them in trouble all over again."

She opened the door to the conference room, then turned back to us. "Bunchy, he always seemed like one of the good guys, you know? Like you might have a problem with some of the things he did, but his heart was in the right place." She looked like she might cry. "I saw the news about that woman who was killed. I hate to think Bunchy could be behind it."

It was Ray's turn to drive, so we climbed into his Highlander and drove *mauka*. In Hawai'i, we don't use north, south, east and west; our directions are all rooted in our island geography. *Makai* means toward the ocean, while *mauka* means the other direction, toward the mountains. Going Diamond Head means toward the extinct volcano which looms over part of the island, while *Ewa* means in the other direction, toward the city of the same name.

Bunchy lived in a small ranch house off Tantalus Drive, and when we parked in front of it, he appeared in the doorway. He hadn't shaved for a couple of days, and he was barefoot, wearing a plain white T-shirt, with reading glasses perched on his nose. "That da kine police car you guys use these days?" he asked.

I didn't ask how he knew we were police. We'd been at the community center the day before, and I was sure the coconut wireless had spread the word throughout the neighborhood.

"Howzit, Uncle." I walked up to the door and showed him my ID. "Can we ask you a couple questions?"

He looked us up and down. I was in my standard work clothes: aloha shirt and khaki pants, deck shoes without socks. Ray was about the same, though the print on his shirt was louder than mine, and he wore reflective sunglasses that reminded me of the highway patrol on *CHiPs*.

Bunchy shrugged and stepped back, inviting us into the house. He motioned us to the sofa, and as I sat down I scanned the room. The walls and surfaces were decorated with Hawaiian artifacts—an old quilt, tattered at the edges; an anthurium flower made of koa wood with a blossom of whalebone; a collection of stone and ivory fishhooks.

Bunchy's collection was valuable. Had it come down to him from his ancestors? Or was somebody with big bucks funding him?

"Talk to us about this group you run. Ka Leo. Been getting into any trouble lately?"

"What, you think I go round killing old ladies now?"

I held my hands out, palms up. "Did I ask you that, Bunchy? I grew up watching you on TV. The stuff you did for Kahoolawe, Uncle, that's history."

"But you asking around about Aunty Edith," Bunchy said.

"You know her?" Ray asked.

"Shoot, everybody in Papakolea know Aunty Edith. She real kahiko lady, she know everything about these islands, about the history of our people. She talk story lots, about old days, Big Island. She like the record keeper for her town. She have all kine stuff in her room. She say one day she make a book out of it."

I remembered the piles of papers and photos we had seen in Edith's room. They had seemed like ordinary memorabilia, but maybe we should have looked closer at them.

"I heard she was a nosy old lady, sticking her two cents in all over the place," I said. "Somebody told me she was hanai tūtū to Ezekiel Kapuāiwa. If she could prove what he says about his family background, that could make KOH come out on top, and Ka Leo the loser. That would piss you off, wouldn't it?"

"What you trying to say?" Bunchy frowned and clenched one fist. "You want make beef with me?"

The harmless old *fut* had fallen away, and I saw a man who could lead a movement by the force of his personality. Behind him, I noticed a group of photographs, Bunchy with young people at various rallies.

"She talking stink about Ka Leo?" I asked. "Trying to get people to support her hanai grandson instead?"

I guessed Bunchy was composing his thoughts, trying to rein in those impulses Kalia Rogers had talked about, the undercurrent of violence I'd seen in his behavior at the Wizard Stones rally.

"Aunty Edith, she not the type to talk stink. These groups, they just names. Everybody want same thing. Hawai'i for Hawaiian people."

I didn't believe him for a minute. The Bunchy I grew up watching on TV and reading about in the paper wasn't the kind to give up so easily. He didn't claim, like Ezekiel did, to be a direct descendant of the Hawaiian royal family, which put Ka Leo at a disadvantage when it came to who might rule an independent Hawai'i. Discrediting Ezekiel and destroying his movement could position Ka Leo to gain a lot of power, money and land. That was a good motive for murder.

Bunchy wouldn't say much more, though we tried asking the same questions in different ways. Aunty Edith was a talkative old woman, there wasn't any harm in her and he couldn't see anybody wanting to kill her. There was some rivalry between groups, but nothing worth killing over.

"I kill anybody, it be some haole *okole*," he said. "Not a kupuna."

We were back in the Highlander when Ray asked, "What's an okole? You think that was some kind of jab at me?"

"Okole means butt. And no, I don't think he meant you. More like some haole who wants to stand in the way of his goals."

"And the police don't?"

"Not if he stays within the law," I said.

"Long as we're out here," Ray said. "Suppose we stop by Aunty Edith's house again, make sure Leelee's doing OK? I'm worried about her and that kid."

"You have a soft heart," I said. "But you're driving. Go to town."

Leelee answered the door and said, "I was just gone call you. You must be psychic or something, like on the TV."

"Yeah?" Ray asked. "What's up?"

"Somebody buss up Aunty Edith's room."

Leelee was once again balancing that dirty little boy on her hip. "I went into Aunty Edith's room this morning, 'cause she had some toys for baby. It all buss up. I couldn't call you till Dex left for work, though. He don't like no pilikia, 'specially not with police."

"Can we take a look?"

She shrugged. As we walked alongside the house to Aunty Edith's door, we established that the break-in had to have occurred sometime between Saturday afternoon, when we'd looked at the room, and six that morning, when the baby began crying.

Leelee pulled a faded plastic card from her pocket and slid it between the door and the jamb. "We lost the key long time ago," she said, as the door popped open. "Old credit card work just as well. Ain't got no credit anyway."

Edith's mattress had been taken off the bed and sliced open; the same for her pillows. Her clothes were strewn on the floor, along with cheap paper fans, plastic leis and stuffed animals she must have used to amuse the baby.

Her small desk had been loaded with papers on Saturday, but most of them were gone. All the pictures had been taken down from the walls, and the photo albums were gone, too.

"Dat ice," Leelee said. "Da kine ice head always breaking in places. Somebody knew Aunt Edith *wen maki*, they come steal anything she left." The baby started crying again, and she jiggled him on her hip as she headed back to her own door.

"You think it was ice?" Ray asked when she was gone. We saw lots of crimes committed by people hooked on ice, the smokable form of crystal meth, but it didn't look like an addict had broken into Aunty Edith's. I shook my head.

"Me neither," Ray said. "The burglar was looking for something."

"Something we should have found when we were here Saturday." I remembered the piles of papers and photos. What had been valuable there? What would someone be willing to kill for?

"Maybe, maybe not." Ray pulled out a pair of rubber gloves. "Let's see if there's anything left."

The folders Edith had kept next to the desk were gone, along with all the newspaper clippings and copies of official documents. The only papers left were a scattering of grocery coupons and some pages from a child's story book.

"Let's analyze this," Ray said. "The thief took all her pictures, all that paperwork she had saved. And then went looking for something more. What do you think it was?"

"No idea."

"Why take all those photographs?" Ray asked. "You know this place, this culture. You remember any of them?"

I closed my eyes and concentrated. "I thought they were family pictures. Some were those square, sepia-toned ones like we have of my parents as kids."

"So somebody wanted those pictures," Ray said. "Why?"

"Because of who's in them?"

"Any way those old pictures could be valuable?"

"I suppose you could take them out to the Aloha Bowl flea market and sell them for a nickel or a dime apiece," I said. "Somebody decorating a restaurant or looking for instant ancestors. Not really a motive for robbery, much less murder."

I walked over and looked at the wall. Most of the thumbtacks were still there, along with torn bits that showed the pictures hadn't been removed carefully.

"Whoever took these was either angry or in a hurry. Maybe she had some newer pictures of those drug dealers she was making trouble for."

"How about the documents? You remember what they were?"

I shook my head. "I didn't look that closely. I think a lot of them were from the Big Island. I remember there were photocopies of some property deeds. But they weren't originals, so it's not like you could use them to transfer ownership."

We gave up thinking and went back to searching. Under a pile of Edith's clothes I found three large koa wood bowls, and I only recognized that they might be valuable because my mother collected them. I had a feeling they were worth a few thousand bucks apiece.

Stuck in a corner of the desk, where it might have been overlooked, was a business card for Adam O'Malley, an attorney from the law firm of Fields and Yamato in downtown Honolulu.

Why did Aunty Edith have his business card? Was she a defendant in a law suit, or a plaintiff? Perhaps O'Malley had written her will or was handling some property transfer. I slid the card into my pocket.

Ray called for a crime scene tech. With luck, the burglar had left behind a fingerprint that might give us a lead on Aunty Edith's killer. Leelee came by to check on us while we waited, the baby still crying. Ray said, "You need a hand changing him?"

Leelee looked at him like he was crazy. Ray put his fingers up and squeezed his nose, and Leelee said, "Oh."

"I did a lot of babysitting as a kid," he said. "Come on, show me the diapers."

"Better you than me, brah," I said under my breath, as Leelee led Ray back to her part of the house. Ryan Kainoa, a vampire-pale crime scene tech with long black hair pulled into a ponytail and shoved under a baseball cap, showed up while they were gone, and I explained what we were looking for.

Ray returned as Ryan was dusting for fingerprints. "That girl needs help," Ray said. "She had the wrong kind of diapers, and she didn't even know how to change them right."

I didn't know what to say. As a cop, I can do a lot of things, but changing diapers is outside my realm of expertise.

Ryan found a lot of fingerprints, but most of them looked the same, probably Aunty Edith's or Leelee's. Before we left, Leelee came back into Aunty Edith's room, this time without the baby, and asked if there was any kind of victims' fund that might compensate the family for Edith's loss.

"She give us her Social Security every month for food and diapers," Leelee said. "Now we got none."

"You talk to the Department of Human Services?" I asked. "They have programs to help people with kids."

"They say Dex make too much money. But he don't give me hardly anything for the house or the baby, playing *pai gow*. That where most of the money goes."

Pai gow is a Chinese gambling game played with dice, popular in unsanctioned casinos in Chinese communities. I was surprised that a haole like Dex played pai gow but figured his money was good as anyone's.

I looked around the room, thinking. If Dex didn't give Leelee enough money to live on, that was between them. It wasn't something the police could get involved with unless she wanted to sue him for child support. I spotted the three koa bowls on the desk and got an idea.

From what we could tell, Edith had no family beyond Leelee, which meant that the bowls now belonged to her. If I could get her some cash directly, she wouldn't have to tell Dex, and she'd be able to buy what she needed.

"You willing to sell these bowls?" I asked, holding one up.

"Just buss up old bowls," she said. "Nobody pay for dem."

"I might have somebody who would. You going to be around this afternoon?"

"Where I go?" From the house, we heard the baby cry again.

I went outside and called my mother. "You know anybody who wants some big koa bowls?" I told her about Leelee and Aunty Edith.

"I can't say without looking at them. Would you like me to come down there?"

"That would be nice. If you want them, it would help Leelee get through the month if you could give her some cash for them." I paused. "You remember how to change a diaper?"

My mother laughed. "Who do you think taught Liliha and Tatiana? What, this girl has a baby?"

"Yeah, and she seems overwhelmed."

She said she'd drive right over, and I hung up feeling I had done a good deed for both of them. My father's declining health had meant that my mother had to curtail a lot of her activities, including volunteering as a docent at the Bishop Museum, and helping Leelee would be a nice project for her. It could also keep her from going to any more rallies where she might get shot.

I made a couple of notes, told Leelee my mom was on her way over and promised we would be back in touch. "Let's go back to what we were talking about before," Ray said, as we walked away from the house. "What do you think the burglar was looking for?"

"She had a lot of old newspaper articles," I said. "Now, I wish we'd taken all that stuff into evidence, but at the time it just looked like junk."

"You remember anything about what she had? Was it about

Kingdom of Hawai'i?"

"No, it was all older stuff," I said. "Genealogy. Some birth and marriage announcements. Like from her family. And there was some stuff about volcanoes, places destroyed by the lava flows."

"Didn't the old folks say she came from some place that had been wiped out?"

"Yup. So those could just be personal stuff, mementoes."

Ray thumped the steering wheel. "Maybe the burglar didn't find what he was looking for—that's why he ripped everything up and that's why he took all those albums and folders."

"We should go back and see if Edith owned any property, had any bank accounts, that kind of thing."

We stopped at a Zippy's for lunch on our way back to headquarters, and over teriyaki burgers Ray asked, "What do we know about Edith, anyway? People say she came from some little town on the Big Island, destroyed by lava. Convenient, isn't it? You think that's the truth?"

"We can check it out. Leelee seemed to think all Edith had was her Social Security. If she still owned some property on the Big Island, the killer could be looking for deeds or bankbooks."

I made a couple of notes, and then we relaxed and ate. They were playing an album I recognized as Hapa's *Surf Madness* from the late 90s, and I tapped my foot along to their '50s hipster version of the *Hawaii Five-O* theme.

After lunch, we went back to headquarters, and I looked online for whatever the state had on Edith Kapana. The database of birth records indicated she had been born at home in 1935 in a small town called Opihi. I searched map sites but couldn't find it, eventually discovering, from an *Star-Advertiser* article in the online archive, that the town had been wiped out a year ago by an eruption of Kilauea.

According to the article, Opihi was a tiny hamlet populated by a handful of Native Hawaiian families. They led a hardscrabble life, farming and fishing. When their homes were destroyed their way of life went with it. They relocated or moved in with distant relations, like Aunty Edith did. In a much later article, a reporter who interviewed Ezekiel Kapuāiwa, the leader of Kingdom of Hawai'i, pointed out that he had been born there, though he had moved to O'ahu before the destruction.

Edith didn't have any bank accounts that we could find, and she only owned a small piece of land in Opihi which once had a small house on it. The record indicated the property had been condemned after the lava destroyed it. She had one brother, who died years before. I tracked his life, discovering that he had moved to Honolulu in 1958, married and bought the house in Papakolea. He and his wife had two children: Elizabeth, born in 1959, and Amos, born in 1960.

Elizabeth Kapana died in 2007; I found an obituary for her online, which listed her brother and daughter, Leelee as survivors. There was no birth certificate for Leelee in Hawai'i, so I did a national search, discovering she had been born in Las Vegas in 1992. No father was listed. But that did make her eighteen, despite her younger looks.

Amos Kapana was the legal owner of the house where Edith, Dex, Leelee and the baby lived. But where was he? Leelee said he didn't live there anymore. I put in a request for his work records from Karen Gold at Social Security and kept hunting. There was no death certificate on file for him, but he had not renewed his driver's license when it expired in January.

Karen faxed over Amos Kapana's sketchy work record a little later. His last job had been over a year ago, with a temp agency that farmed out manual laborers. The woman there told me he had never picked up his last paycheck.

"He was a drunk," she said. "Very unreliable."

While I was working on Edith, Ray did more research on Bunchy. "Listen to this," he said, as I made a note to tell Leelee about the paycheck. "Bunchy has three sons. The youngest one, Brian, served a tour in Iraq, and he's living with his dad."

"What did he do in Iraq?" I asked. "You think he's qualified on rifles?"

"I've got a friend who works in Army intelligence," Ray said. "I'll give him a call, see if the name Brian Parker means anything to him."

I was intrigued by the links between Ezekiel Kapuāiwa and Aunty Edith. She may have been more influential in KOH than we had thought.

"I think it's time we talked to Ezekiel," I said, when Ray finished his call. "Maybe he knows something."

I phoned Maile Kanuha and asked how I could get hold of Ezekiel. "He's not strong," she said. "The appearance at the rally took a lot of out of him. He'd rather be left alone."

Her evasiveness was suspicious. "Whether he wants to or not, we still need to talk to him."

"I'll have to get in touch with him and see what he says."

"Maile, we're the police. When we want to speak to somebody, they don't have much choice."

"I know, Detective. I'll still have to get back to you, though."

Next, I called Adam O'Malley, the attorney whose card we'd found in Edith's desk. His secretary said he was in court on the mainland, and took a message.

By the end of shift, I was frustrated. We had no leads, and it felt like we were sitting on our hands waiting for information or new developments. I didn't like that and knew that if I went straight home I'd fuss around, get even more agitated and then probably pick a fight with Mike just to let off steam.

So instead I made a detour up to my parents' house in St. Louis Heights, a steep, mountainous suburb of twisting streets and houses more expensive than any Mike or I could ever afford.

"Howzit, Mom?" I asked when my mother answered the door. I kissed her cheek. "You go see Leelee?"

"That girl needs help," she said. "I don't see why her neighbors aren't doing anything for her. She even had the wrong kind of diapers."

"Yeah, I heard that from Ray." I followed her to the den, where my father was watching a nature special on sharks. I leaned down and kissed the top of his head, then sat across from him. "You buy the bowls from her?"

"Those bowls," she said, sitting across from my father. "Kimo, you have no idea."

"What? They looked valuable to me."

"Those are beyond value. You know how rare it is to have koa wood bowls that large?"

The three big bowls sat on the armoire beyond the TV. My mother picked one up and brought it over to show me. "Ones this size were restricted to the royal family," she said. "See how it hasn't been turned, but scooped out instead?"

"I'll take your word for it."

She turned the bowl upside down. "And see these repairs?"

"Yeah. Don't they make the bowl less valuable?"

She shook her head. "I took a class at the Bishop Museum. They stopped doing this kind of repair before 1900. That means these are very old, in addition to being very large."

"So how much did you give her?" I asked. "For the three of them."

"I didn't buy them. I said I would take the bowls to the museum, then come back and tell her what they're worth. She's just a child. And she said that boyfriend of hers spends every penny, drinking and playing pai gow."

"We took her shopping," my father said. "To Costco."

"I'm confused."

"We bought her diapers, formula. Some clothes. Food. I showed her how to change the baby. Apparently that poor woman who died took care of the child."

"Wow. That was so nice of you. I didn't expect you to do so

much."

My father grumbled.

"You have to help where you can," my mother said. "It's ohana."

Although the strict definition of ohana is family, in Hawai'i it means more—things like the way that a community comes together to take care of those in need. I wondered why the people of Papakolea had not been taking care of Leelee when she was one of their own. I asked my mother that.

My father grumbled again.

My mother sighed. "It sounds like the boyfriend treats her badly, and he's rude to the neighbors. And the girl, well, you saw her. She doesn't seem to care about anything." She stood up. "I'm going to take the bowls to the museum tomorrow. If they're as valuable as I think, they'll want to talk to her."

She asked if I wanted to stay for dinner. I called Mike, who was on his way home. "Want to detour up here?"

My parents have liked Mike since the first time I brought him home, and even when we were broken up, they never said a word against him.

"What's for dinner?"

"Like you care. As long as somebody else cooks it."

Mike laughed. "You're right. I'll be there in about twenty minutes."

The Book of Ezekiel

The next morning, I called Maile Kanuha again. "You never called me back yesterday, Maile. We really need to speak to Ezekiel. If he won't come in we'll come out and get him."

"I can bring him over to you around noon. It's my lunch hour," she said, like that was supposed to make me feel bad.

While we waited, I checked with my friend Ricky Koele, who works at the Division of Business Licensing. Even non-profit groups were required to register, and I asked him to pull up any records he had on Kingdom of Hawai'i.

Ricky was two years behind me at Punahou, and I did him a favor a couple of years ago when his brother was murdered. Since then, he's been happy to help when I need something from his department. After leaving me on hold, he returned to the line and said, "I'm printing the records. I'll fax them to you."

"Thanks, brah. I owe you."

"No, Kimo," he said. "I'm always going to owe you."

The pages came through the fax a couple of minutes later. Kingdom of Hawai'i was registered as a 501(c)(4) organization, a charitable non-profit, able to collect tax-deductible contributions but also allowed to lobby for legislative change. One of the main distinguishing factors between it and the more common 501(c)(3) was a restricted membership—in their case, limited to those people who could trace at least partial ancestry to the original inhabitants of the islands. The Hawaiian term is *kanaka maoli*, and I'd seen that on posters in the background of the video of Bunchy's demonstration at the Wizard Stones. It was often used among Hawaiian sovereignty groups.

The incorporation documents didn't list anyone with the organization; the contact of record was the Honolulu law firm which had filed the paperwork in 2005 with the Hawai'i Secretary of State's office, Fields and Yamato.

I sat back in my chair. Adam O'Malley, whose business card I found on Edith's desk, worked for that firm. Had she come in contact with him through her volunteer work for the organization? I called his office again and left another message for him. "Please tell him it's regarding an ongoing police investigation."

"I will, Detective," his secretary said. "But it's a very important case, and with the time difference between here and Washington, DC he probably just hasn't had a chance to get back to you."

"Does this case involve Kingdom of Hawai'i?" I asked.

"You'd have to talk to Mr. O'Malley. It's our firm's policy not to discuss clients or ongoing litigation."

I did a quick Google search on Adam O'Malley and Fields and Yamato, trying to figure out what sort of case might have taken him to Washington. The firm specialized in land use issues, but I couldn't pull up anything on a specific case that was going on in DC at the moment.

When I saw Ezekiel up close I was surprised to see that he was older than I'd expected, or maybe it was that life had treated him harshly. Although he was only in his forties, his hair was graying, there were bags under his eyes and his left eye twitched. He wore a faded blue polo shirt and cheap jeans, the kind that always look too shiny no matter how much you wash them.

"Thanks for coming in," I said.

"I don't have much time," Maile said. She treated Ezekiel as if she were his mother, though I doubted she was much older than he was. Maybe I just got a motherly impression from her dowdy clothes and old-fashioned pin curls. "My boss is coming down on me for the time I've been spending on KOH."

"You can wait out here," I told her. "We'll try and get Mr. Kapuāiwa in and out as fast as we can."

"I'd rather stay with Ezekiel."

"Sorry, that's not the way we do things here." I put my hand on Ezekiel's shoulder and turned him toward an interview room. We sat down across the table from him, after he'd declined our offers of coffee or soda.

"We'll make this quick," I said. "Mr. Kapuāiwa, did you know Edith Kapana?"

He nodded. "Growing up, on the Big Island. Aunty Edith lived in our village."

"That would be Opihi?"

"Yes. Madame Pele was not kind to us, and our houses were destroyed by Kilauea." From the casual way he talked about the goddess of fire, whom ancient Hawaiians thought controlled volcanoes, you'd think she was a neighbor back in Opihi just like Edith Kapana.

He spoke in an oddly stilted way, as if he were reading a script and didn't understand the words himself. "Did you and Edith both move here to O'ahu at the same time?"

He shook his head. "I had already left Opihi some time before."

"But you had been in touch with her recently?"

He looked down at the table. "Aunty Edith was a volunteer for Kingdom of Hawai'i," he said, in his strange monotone. "She was very kahiko, a great reservoir of information about the Hawaiian people."

"This information. Was it written down? Records of some kind?"

He looked back up. "Not that I know of. It was more like history and lore than actual records." His eye twitched rapidly, and he clutched the edge of the table. His fingernails were ragged, and his knuckles were scarred.

"Do you know any reason why someone might want to kill her?"

He pursed his lips together and blinked his eyes rapidly. "No, not at all."

"How about why someone might break into her room and tear it apart?"

His hands started to shake. "No, no," he said.

I looked at Ray. I was afraid Ezekiel would have some kind of nervous breakdown or epileptic fit if we kept going. Ray nodded, and we both stood.

"We may have some more questions for you later, Mr. Kapuāiwa. Thank you for coming in." We led him back to the reception area, where Maile glared at us and took charge of him, hustling him out.

"The guy's a little squirrely, isn't he?" Ray asked after they'd left. "And what's she, like his keeper?"

"Don't know. There is something strange going on, though." I remembered that Israel at the community center had said sometimes he thought Ezekiel was babooze, stupid, and sometimes lolo, crazy. I wondered which it was. I was surprised that someone so odd could be the leader of an organization and a public figure, but perhaps he looked better on TV or behind a podium.

"Ezekiel couldn't have shot her, because he was in the parade. But she did know him, and he seems nutty enough that he could have taken a dislike to her and gotten somebody from his group to kill her."

"I don't see him having that kind of power. I mean, all you have to do is talk to the guy for a few minutes to see that he's off his rocker. Maybe he's some kind of figurehead. They just trot him out to wave at the crowd."

"Possible. He has the lineage, but there could be someone else behind him pulling the strings."

"Maile Kanuha?"

I shook my head. "I think she's just a volunteer. We should request the tax records for KOH, see who's funding the operation."

"You're going to need a subpoena for that," Ray said. "You have anything to show a judge?"

"You're a real party pooper, you know that?" I sighed.

"Well, then, let's see what we can find out about Ezekiel. Maybe something in his background will lead us to whoever is pulling his strings."

We got some takeout for lunch and did a full search on Ezekiel Kapuāiwa. He had no criminal record, and the only information we could find about him online was either in news articles or at the KOH website. He didn't appear in any databases not even in the division of driver's licenses.

"How can he live without driving?" Ray asked.

"Maile Kanuha."

"Nice to have that kind of service."

"Hey, I drove you around for months before you and Julie got a second car."

"If Edith knew his family, she might have known something shady in his background that could be embarrassing for people to find out," Ray said. "Maybe there's something he was hiding."

It was like a light bulb went on over my head. "All those clippings and records Edith kept. Maybe there was something about Ezekiel there, something he wouldn't want public."

"You think Greg Oshiro could tell us anything more?" Ray asked. "He's been writing about KOH for a while."

"Maybe you. He wouldn't piss on me if I was on fire."

"Ah, but that's your stellar interpersonal skills."

Ray called Greg, and I listened in from another phone. "Maybe we can share some information," Ray said. "You know, a real give and take with the fourth estate."

"You're full of shit, Detective," Greg said. "But my job is to cover the police beat, so if you want to talk, I'm happy to listen."

"That's what I like about you, Greg," Ray said. "That cooperative spirit."

He arranged to meet Greg at the Kope Bean near the *Star-Advertiser* office in twenty minutes. "Have fun," I said.

Ray shook his head. "I'm not going alone. You're my partner."

I started to protest, but Ray interrupted, "Besides, you're buying the coffee."

Thunder boomed as we drove out of the headquarters parking garage, and a lightning strike lit up the gray sky over the Aloha Tower. The palms on South Beretania flapped as a steady rain beat down. By the time we reached the Kope Bean, the shower had passed, though the parking lot was flooded, and a trash can had tipped over, spilling paper cups, napkins and stirrers onto the pavement.

Greg Oshiro's attitude turned cold as soon as he realized I was behind Ray. "Detectives," he said, nodding. I took his order and Ray's and went up to the counter, while the two of them settled in comfy chairs in the corner. Slack key guitar played through the speakers, and though I couldn't identify the artists, I got into the groove of the music.

I ordered us all the chain's signature drink, the Macadamia Latte, in the Longboard size, their largest. By the time I brought the coffees over, Ray and Greg were laughing like old friends, but that dried up as I pulled up a wooden chair and sat down.

"What have you got for me?" Greg asked, turning all business.

I resisted the urge to open my mouth and let Ray do the talking.

"You know that somebody broke into the house of the woman who was killed at the rally?"

Greg pulled out a notebook and flipped it open to a clean page. "When?"

Ray gave him the details.

"You think it was related to her death?"

"We're looking into her background," Ray said. "On the surface, it looks like she was an innocent victim. But we'll see."

He sipped his coffee as Greg took notes. When the reporter looked up, he saw both of us watching him. His body language eased, and I had the feeling he was ready to give us something.

"What can I tell you?" Greg asked. "You must have read my

profile in the paper. She came up clean. Just an old woman who was dedicated to helping Hawaiian people."

"How about the group?" Ray said. "Kingdom of Hawai'i. You know who's behind it? Can't just be Ezekiel Kapuiawa."

"They're a lot like many of the groups. Although Ezekiel is the front man, volunteers set up the events, generate the publicity, raise the money. You've met Maile Kanuha, right?" We both nodded.

"She's dedicated, and there are a few more like her."

"How about the money?" I asked. "Just small contributions? Or anything bigger?"

"There's something shaky about the foundation of the group. I looked up all their contributors, and a lot of the money comes from a bunch of businesses. The Kope Bean is one of them." He motioned with his cup toward the café's logo, a coffee bean on a surfboard. "But figuring out who's behind those corporate donors is another story."

"What do you mean?" Ray asked.

"The Kope Bean is owned by a corporation, Mahalo Coffee, LLC. But who owns Mahalo Coffee? Another corporation, out of Japan. The other big corporate donors are the same—owned by another corporation, which is in turn owned by another. I haven't been able to track them back to real people."

Ray made some notes, getting Greg to spell out all the corporations he hadn't been able to track. "Anything else?" I asked. "Anything that hasn't made it into the paper yet?"

Greg chewed on his bottom lip for a minute. "You know they advocate genetic testing?"

We both shook our heads. "They haven't gone public with it yet—I have a source who told me about this program they're going to start. They want to identify people who have as close to 100% Native Hawaiian genes, and then encourage those people to marry others with the same genetic profile."

"Sounds like the Nazis and racial purity," Ray said.

"They say they're trying to protect the native people. But Ezekiel's own background is cloudy. There are these big gaps in his history. Was he out of the country? In hiding? Everybody's got records these days. Job history, driver's license, bank records. Kapuāiwa doesn't have a lot of that. Maybe it's that Ezekiel himself is kind of weird. I have a feeling he's hiding something."

"I had that feeling, too, when we talked to him." I remembered how nutty Ezekiel had appeared and wondered again if there was something between him and Aunty Edith, something that had caused her death.

"Ezekiel says the birth records from his little town were destroyed when Kilauea erupted, so he can't prove that he's 100% Hawaiian himself," Greg continued. "And he doesn't have a wife or kids to keep his line going—so it sounds like a case of do as I say, not as I do." He eyed us both. "Cops can get into places reporters can't. You might find something I haven't been able to."

"Thanks. We'll take a closer look at him," Ray said, making a note.

"And let me know what you find?"

"Within limits," I said. "The guy's got a right to privacy, after all. If what he's hiding isn't germane to his cause or our investigation, we can't just hand it out."

"I understand." He stood up. "Thanks for the coffee." Without offering to shake hands or even give us a goodbye salute, he turned and walked out.

"I wish I knew why he's so cold to me," I said, as Ray and I stood up. "And before you say anything, I already know about my winning personality."

"He's jealous," Ray said, opening the door to the street. "You get to be out and proud, and he's stuck in the closet."

I looked at him. "You think he's gay?"

Ray laughed. "Dude, where's your gaydar? How come I can spot gay guys better than you can?"

"That's something you should take up with your wife."

He knocked into me with his hip as we walked down the sidewalk. "I told you about my cousin Joey," he said.

"The gay one you grew up with?"

"That's the one. I spent a lot of time with him. I got to know the signs." He looked over at me. "Seriously? You don't get that vibe?"

I thought about it. What did I know about Greg Oshiro, after all? I'd never seen him at the Rod and Reel Club, my favorite gay bar on Waikīkī. I had run into him at a couple of police functions, but he never had a date of either sex. And I'd never heard Gunter, the biggest gossip queen on the island, say a word about him. But that didn't mean he wasn't gay.

I'd known Greg for a few years before I came out of the closet, and we'd gotten along fine. I'd even thought we were friends, of a sort. Then after I came out, he gave me the cold shoulder. I'd figured him for a homophobe, especially when he covered any of my cases that had a gay context.

But what if he was gay, and closeted? That put a whole new light on things. I didn't think it had anything to do with the case, but if I could figure Greg Oshiro out, I could make him into a useful source again.

When we got back to the station, Sampson wanted to talk to us. "Tell me how you're doing," he said, when Ray and I walked in to his office. He was wearing a navy blue polo shirt, and his hair was getting shaggy. I wondered if I should suggest a haircut, but decided against it. You *can* be too gay on the job, after all.

"We're looking into Ezekiel Kapuāiwa," I said. "He's the guy in charge of KOH. There's something that doesn't add up about him."

"Yeah, but he's just too squirrelly," Ray said. "Even with Greg Oshiro's suspicions. I can't see Ezekiel convincing somebody to do the job for him."

"So you say. But he grew up in the same little town where she lived, and he was in charge of the organization that ran the rally where she was killed."

"But why kill her at the rally?" Ray asked. "It doesn't make sense. Her death could cause big problems for his group."

"Unless she knew something that could cause even bigger problems. I want to know more about him."

"Play nice, boys," Sampson said. "Any other leads?"

Ray said, "I've got my eye on a guy. Bunchy Parker."

Sampson looked interested. I was sure he knew who Bunchy was.

"If Edith's death was a means to discredit KOH, then Ka Leo, the group Bunchy runs, could become the most prominent of the sovereignty groups. That means Bunchy could someday be the elected King of Hawai'i."

"I want a suspect, and I want one soon. Put in some overtime this afternoon if you need to."

As we went back to our desks, Ray said, "I didn't mean to sabotage you."

"Hey, a little creative dissent shows Sampson we're actually working."

"We'll follow your hunch," he said. "What do we know about Ezekiel Kapuāiwa? Did he ever hold a job?"

I called Karen Gold, who verified that Ezekiel Kapuāiwa had a Social Security card and a work record. "I'll pull up what we have and fax it to you," she said.

"How come none of your friends ever asks you for a subpoena?" Ray asked, after I hung up. "That guy at the division of business licensing. This girl at Social Security."

"I've known Karen Gold since kindergarten. And Ricky Koele since high school. They're part of my ohana."

"You and *Lilo and Stitch*," he said. "Ohana means nobody gets left behind."

"Yeah, and all the dogs on the island are actually aliens," I said. "Seriously, they trust me. And when we need something that has to hold up in court, we get a subpoena."

By then, the fax had kicked in, and I retrieved the pages from Karen. "We couldn't find a birth certificate for Ezekiel. How could he get a job without some proof of who he is? These days you have to hand over your Social Security card and photo ID. Soon they'll even be asking for vaccination records."

"Maybe he has a birth certificate, it just never got filed with the state," Ray said. "I had a great-uncle who was born at home, and nobody registered the birth. Got him out of serving in the Army."

"I suppose. And they probably had a little community school back then. If the teacher knew his parents, nobody would ever ask for a birth certificate."

He leaned over the page and pointed at a line. "It's like he didn't exist before 1990, when his Social Security card was issued, and he started working at the Kope Bean and started paying taxes."

"You know what this sounds like?" I asked. "Somebody with

a new identity. I can't see Ezekiel in some kind of protected witness program, though. Not to mention that Edith knew him on the Big Island."

"We know which store he worked at?" Ray asked. "There are a dozen locations, not to mention that warehouse where Dexter Trale works. You have a friend who works in their corporate office?"

"Nope. But they ought to be able to verify employment without a subpoena."

Ray called the Kope Bean's human resources department, while I thought about Ezekiel and wondered if he knew Dex and Leelee. It made sense that he would; Aunty Edith connected them both.

Ray hung up the phone. "He worked at the Kaneohe store from 1990 to 2005."

We looked back at his records, which showed that starting in 2005, he began drawing a small salary from Kingdom of Hawai'i. "You up for a second trip to the Kope Bean in one day?" he said. "At least we're going to a different branch."

"Reading my mind, partner." We drove up the Pali Highway and over the mountain to Kaneohe. We found the Kope Bean at the end of a strip shopping center, the kind my father used to build and own. The room was decorated with murals of coffee, which was appropriate since 'kope' means coffee in Hawaiian.

A heavyset haole woman sat in the front window, knitting what looked like a very long scarf with bright red yarn. She kept looking around, furtively, as if a cat might appear from under one of the armchairs and steal her ball of yarn.

"Madame Defarge over there looks like a long-time customer," I whispered to Ray. "I'll get the coffee if you talk to her. See if maybe Ezekiel still comes in here, for old times' sake."

"You know her name?"

I sighed. "It's a long story."

He looked at me.

"Called *A Tale of Two Cities*, by Charles Dickens. There's a character in it named Madame Defarge, who knits."

"English major," Ray snorted, but he headed over to the woman.

I ordered our macadamia lattes from the barista, a teenager with a big bush of blond hair spilling out the back of his ball cap, and after he'd rung me up I showed him my ID and said, "Can I ask you some questions?"

There were no other customers, so he shrugged and said, "Sure." Leilani Rivera Bond was singing a love song in a Tahitian dialect through the store's speakers. Ray was sitting with the knitting lady, smiling and nodding.

I showed the clerk a picture of Ezekiel. "You ever see this guy come in here? He used to work here."

"Don't recognize him. But I've only been here six months."

"Anybody who's been here longer?" I asked.

"Mili," he called toward the back. He started making our coffees, and Ray joined me at the bar.

"Mrs. Defarge up there didn't recognize the picture," he said. "But she did offer to make me a scarf."

A short gray-haired woman came out from the back office as the barista was handing us our coffees. He said, "These guys want to know about some dude worked here years ago."

"Years ago is my specialty," she said. "How can I help you?"

Ray introduced us and asked if she knew Ezekiel Kapuāiwa. "Of course. Ezekiel worked here for quite a while."

She took us over to a leather sofa faced by two armchairs, and we sat down, Ray and I holding our coffees. "Is Ezekiel in some kind of trouble?"

"What makes you ask that?" Ray asked.

She sighed. "Ezekiel is—special. Sometimes he's not all there, you know? I worried about him when he left. He said he was going to be the King of Hawai'i." She smiled. "I thought maybe he had stopped taking his medication, but no, he said there was a whole organization, wanted to throw off the chains of oppression by the United States and make him the new king of the islands."

"Kingdom of Hawai'i," I said.

"That's it. I have trouble keeping track of all those groups. There are so many, and each one thinks they should be in charge."

I remembered the big koa bowls we had found in Edith Kapana's room and how my mother believed those bowls had been restricted to members of the royal family. Maybe there was some credence to Ezekiel's claim—what if those bowls had been part of his claim to royal descent, held for him by someone he trusted?

I realized Ray was still asking Mili questions and put aside the bowls to focus on what she was saying.

"You mentioned some medication," Ray said, making notes. "Do you know what that was for?"

"He had his good days and his bad days." Mili had very pale skin, as if she never went out in the tropical sun, and her bony hands were stained with liver spots. "I never asked what was wrong with him, but when he started working here he was living at the Ohana Ola Kino, so there had to be something wrong."

"What is that?" I asked. "The Ohana Ola Kino?" Ohana means family, and *ola kino* means healthy. So it could be anything from a nursing home to a rehab center to who knows what.

"Sort of a group home," Mili said. "I never asked him why he was there or what was wrong with him. It's just down down the street, and a lot of their residents, like that lady there, come in here." She nodded toward the knitting woman. "We just give them ice water and let them sit, as long as they don't make trouble."

"He ever show a tendency to violence?" Ray asked.

Mili looked horrified. "Oh, no, Ezekiel was always very sweet. When he got moody he'd go all quiet. That's when I put him to work in the storeroom. Other times, he was the friendliest guy, making conversation with the customers. When he left, I can't tell you how many people asked after him."

We thanked Mili, finished our coffee and walked back out to Ray's Highlander. "You want to try the group home, see if anyone would talk to us?" Ray asked.

I shook my head. "Places like that, you need a subpoena for anything. And we have nothing to base a subpoena on. We're fishing, at this point. Judges tend to frown on that."

"If you don't go fishing, you never catch anything."

We got back to our desks around four. The evening shift was already there, taking calls, and we tried to stay out of their way. Ray started looking at everyone who belonged to Bunchy's group to see if any of them had sharpshooting skills and a criminal record.

The website for the Ohana Ola Kino wasn't very helpful; it only listed the facility's name and address. There was a link at the bottom of the page, though, to its board of directors, and that's where I found my friend Terri's name.

Terri Clark Gonsalves has been my best female friend since we were in high school together at Punahou. Her family is one of the oldest haole ones in the islands, descended from the original missionaries. Her father was the chairman of Clark's, the biggest independent department store chain in Hawai'i after Liberty House. When he retired, the chain was sold, dropping a big wad of cash into the family charity, the Sandwich Islands Trust.

Terri, a widow with a young son, had taken over running the trust from her great-aunt. I wasn't surprised to find her on the board of Ohana Ola Kino. She was a dynamo, determined to use the money in the Trust to help people wherever she could. I called her cell and asked if we could get together.

"I'm swamped right now," she said. "I have a federal filing deadline for the Trust coming up, and I'm about to go into a meeting with our attorneys. My mom is watching Danny for me so I can go directly from here to dinner with Levi. Why don't you and Mike join us? Seven o'clock at the Golden Dragon."

Levi was her boyfriend, a successful mainland entrepreneur who'd come to the islands to restart his life after a difficult divorce. I liked him and thought he was good for Terri. We made plans to meet at the Golden Dragon, a Chinatown favorite, and I called Mike to make sure it was okay with him.

"It would have been nice if you'd asked me first, instead of committing us."

"I can cancel. I wanted to ask her some questions, and she said she was busy—she suggested dinner."

"Last night we had dinner at your folks. Tonight with Terri and Levi. Are we going to spend any time together?"

"That's why I moved in with you, isn't it? So we could be together?"

"Fine. Whatever you want."

"Mike."

"I'm busy now. I'll be home around five thirty." He hung up.

"Asshole," I said, to the dial tone.

"Ain't love grand?" Ray said.

I looked over at him. "How do you do it? You're always picking up special duty, Julie's always studying. Don't either of you ever get fed up?"

He pushed the papers on his desk away in what looked like surrender. "We're both Italian, you know. So we don't hold back. I'd say we have at least one big fight a month, but it clears the air and we go back to business as usual."

"Really? I don't remember my parents fighting more than a few times my whole childhood."

He shrugged. "Different strokes for different folks. We don't let stuff build up. Last week, Julie was going on and on about this other grad student, this guy. He was so smart; he was so charming; he was so handsome. I told her that if he was so great, she was welcome to go marry him."

I laughed. "You didn't say that."

"Sure I did. Then she threw a book at me. Hit me right in the chest." He rubbed what I figured was the sore spot. "Big fucking book, too. The point is, I didn't let it fester, start to go crazy over it. She loves me, I love her. We both know that. Everything else is just domestic drama."

"Speaking of which," I said. "Are we giving up on this case? I'll find out what I can tonight about the Ohana, but I doubt that will get us much. I'm assuming you didn't come up with anything on Ka Leo."

"Nope. But you never know what will come up tomorrow."

We called it quits. I hated a stalled investigation, but I didn't know anything else we could do. I went out to my Jeep, where I pawed through the debris on the front seat to find the new Kalei Gamiao ukulele CD. As the music kicked in, I thought about Mike.

I had believed that by moving in together, we could short-circuit a lot of our problems—neither of us ever being at home when we were together, missing each other when we weren't, the sense that we couldn't be committed to each other until we shared the same bed, night after night. Some of those problems had indeed gone away, only to be replaced with new ones.

I was a slob, but there was a method to my messiness. Mike couldn't see that. He obsessed over tiny spots on the kitchen counter but left his clean laundry piled on the dining room table until I put it away for him. Once we'd moved in together, he'd relegated me to the role of chauffeur, complaining that he had to drive all over the island in his investigations.

We had a long way to go before our lives were fully integrated, before I could anticipate how he'd react to something as simple as dinner with friends. I could only hope we'd make it to that point without breaking up or killing each other.

DINNER IN CHINATOWN

Mike was taking a nap when I got home, so I padded around the kitchen and the living room, cleaning up and then reading. He woke around 6:30 and came out of the bedroom in his underwear.

Even after all the time that has passed between us, a sight like that still makes me hard. I love the way his white briefs contrasted with his tanned skin and black hair, the way I can see the muscles in his abdomen ripple as he walked. He yawned and scratched his balls. "What time do we have to leave for dinner?"

"You don't have to go if you don't want to."

"What time?"

"Soon. You going to get dressed?"

"No, I thought I'd go in my shorts." He stroked his crotch a couple of times. "You like that?"

I got up from the couch and walked over to him. Then I dropped to my knees, grabbed his ass and started licking his dick through his briefs.

He groaned. "We're going to be late for dinner if you keep that up."

I stopped licking for a minute to say, "You're the one who has to keep it up." He laughed and grabbed my head. The shorts came down, and his dick went into my mouth. An appetizer before dinner.

As we drove down to Chinatown in my Jeep, I told him how frustrated I was that the investigation into Edith's death was stalled.

"I know, it happens. But that doesn't make it any easier."

"It'll come together when it's time," Mike said. "You know that. You just keep your head down, keep following your leads and something will break."

"I hope so. How was your day?"

"Fire out in Waipahu last night. Mother, father, six kids living in this wood-framed bungalow must have been built fifty years ago. Place went up like tinder. They've been overloading the wiring, and last night the dryer shorted out while everybody was asleep."

"Anybody make it out?"

"They all did. The dog woke them up, you believe it? Golden retriever saved the whole family. Started barking like crazy, ran around the house grabbing them and tugging."

"That's sweet. My brother's station will get a lot of mileage out of a story like that." My oldest brother, Lui, was the manager of KVOL, "Your Volcano Alert Station, Erupting News All The Time," the scrabbling independent in Honolulu. KVOL concentrated on the most inflammatory stories, but I knew they'd love a heroic dog.

"So I was talking to the dad today, as I'm poking through the ashes. He's trying to save anything he can, a picture, a kid's toy, because they've got nothing. And he's totally bummed because he and his wife had a fight before they went to bed, and he feels like it was that bad karma that brought the fire down on them."

He looked over at me. "When we argue, you think you can make everything better by sucking my dick."

"It's worked so far. Seriously, it's better than fighting, isn't it?"

He had a devilish grin on his face. "Sometimes fighting can be fun."

I pulled into a parking spot a block from the restaurant. "Hold that thought, tiger," I said. "We'll get back to it later."

We ran into Terri and Levi on the street in front of the restaurant, and we all went in together. They made a nice couple. Terri was tall, slim and tanned, wearing a floral print dress with a strand of pearls—you might take her for a pampered wife, if you didn't know that she'd been trained since birth for a life of public service.

Levi was about ten years older, a couple of inches taller, with the bearing of a corporate executive. His face was deeply tanned from hours spent on his sailboat, and he'd given up suits in favor of striped shirts and khakis.

The Golden Dragon's plate glass windows were cluttered with menus and posters of local events. The inside wasn't much, either, just a big aquarium with tropical fish, a bunch of rundown booths and rice paper calendars and pictures of China on the walls. But the food was terrific; my friends and I had been going there since high school. Some of the elderly waiters and waitresses had been there that long, and sometimes I thought they'd still be there long after we had passed on.

After we'd been seated, made some conversation and had our orders taken, Terri asked, "So, what did you want to know?"

"You're on the board of the Ohana Ola Kino, right? What kind of place is it?"

"It's a halfway house for men and women transitioning back to the community after treatment in a residential mental health facility," Terri said. "Mostly the Hawai'i State Hospital. Patients who don't have a support system go to the Ohana for a place to live, job training and so on. They have residential space for thirty clients and serve another hundred or so with counseling and programs."

"What's your interest?" Levi asked.

"Do you know a man named Ezekiel Kapuāiwa? He lived at the Ohana for a while a couple of years ago?"

The waitress brought out a platter of crab rangoon and bowls of won ton soup, and we dug in. Terri said, "I joined the board of the Ohana about five or six years ago. I spent a lot of time there at first, getting to know the staff and some of the clients. I met Ezekiel then."

She speared a piece of crab with her chopsticks and lifted it to her mouth. When she finished chewing, she said, "You have to understand, the clients at the Ohana all have problems. So Ezekiel didn't stand out. But then one day, we were having a benefit lunch, and I happened to sit at a table with him and a man named Jun Tanaka, who we were cultivating to join the board."

"I don't trust Tanaka," Levi said. "There's something shady about him."

"Levi is determined that Jun Tanaka has some devious interest in the Ohana," Terri said.

I finished my soup and pushed the bowl away. "If you think he's involved in something criminal, I want to hear about it. But first, I need to focus on my case."

Terri continued. "At this lunch, with Jun Tanaka, Ezekiel started bragging about being descended from King Kamehameha, and honestly, I wasn't paying him any mind. Delusions of grandeur, you know. I figured it was part of whatever was wrong with him. But Jun was fascinated. He kept Ezekiel talking, and then a week later Jun agreed to join the board. I didn't make the connection until I heard that Ezekiel had started the Kingdom of Hawai'i, and Jun was one of his backers."

The busboy took away the empty dishes, and on his heels the waitress brought platters of honey garlic chicken, pepper steak, sizzling shrimp, and big metal bowls of white rice. When we'd finished serving ourselves, Terri picked up the story.

"Jun Tanaka is a Japanese businessman. His grandfather came here before the Second World War and then was interned at Honouliuli."

"There were internment camps in Hawai'i?" Mike asked, between bites of chicken. "I thought the camps were all on the mainland."

"Most of them were," I said. "They couldn't intern all the Japanese-Americans in the islands because there were too many of them, and the economy would have fallen apart. I think they only locked up the people they thought were dangerous."

"My point exactly," Levi said.

"You can't blame Jun for something his grandfather may or may not have done," Terri said. "Look at all the things people accused my grandfather of."

Terri's grandfather had built Clark's from a single store in Honolulu to a chain throughout the islands. I knew there were stories about other merchants he forced out of business, landowners he bought from cheaply. But I also knew that he had fought against statehood because he wanted the islands to retain their independence, started the Sandwich Islands Trust and challenged his family to do good works.

"Jun's father was born in Honouliuli, and then the family was deported to Japan after the war," she said. "His father became a successful businessman in Japan, but he held onto his US citizenship. He arranged for Jun to be born in Honolulu, and then he sent Jun here to expand the family's business interests."

"I think the man's a crook," Levi said.

"How do you know him? And why do you think he's a crook?" I asked.

"Terri asked me to help out," he said. "I'm not on the board officially, but I go to meetings and look over the financial statements. And I get a bad feeling from Tanaka. He's shady about where his money comes from. Maybe it's that Ezekiel is so patently crazy that I think there's got to be something behind Jun's backing him."

Levi didn't have any evidence to support his accusations, but I promised I'd look into Tanaka, and we moved on to coffee and dessert. "Do you know why Ezekiel left the Ohana?" I asked Terri.

"It's not supposed to be a lifelong residence," she said. "He had a job, at a coffeehouse, and eventually he found an apartment. There are always new clients ready to take any places that come open."

The conversation shifted to more social topics, and the evening became a fun dinner with friends. I was glad to see that Terri and I had been able to integrate Levi and Mike into our friendship without anything changing between us.

I insisted on paying for dinner, even though Terri and Levi could have bought and sold Mike and me a dozen times over.

They'd taken us out many times, at more expensive restaurants.

"Get what you needed?" Mike asked, as we drove home.

"You know the drill. You don't know what's important until you put all the pieces together."

"I've seen this Ezekiel guy on TV a couple of times. Now I understand why he sounds nuts. I mean, come on. Hawai'i secede from the US?"

"Just because he's crazy doesn't mean he doesn't make some good points. The US took down a sovereign government so that some American businessmen could make money."

"And the US hasn't been good to Hawai'i?"

"You ever go out to Papakolea?" I asked. "To the Hawaiian homestead land? You think those people are benefiting from the way the land was stolen from their ancestors?"

"Don't tell me you believe that crap."

"It's not crap. My people were here for centuries before the missionaries got here and everything started."

"Your people? Wasn't your dad's mother a haole teacher from Montana?"

"That's not the point."

"Yeah, it is the point. You're full of shit."

I pulled the Jeep into the driveway. "Yeah. Thanks for your opinion." I slammed the door and stalked in the house.

MORNING STONERS

There was a well-defined space between Mike and me in bed that night. In the morning, we kissed and wished each other a good day, but I felt the residue of our arguments simmering under the surface.

At headquarters later, I told Ray what I'd learned from Terri. "Yeah, it's all interesting," he said. "But how does it relate to Edith Kapana's death?"

"I just have a feeling. Levi thinks there's something illicit going on with Jun Tanaka. And I keep thinking that there's some correlation between the Ohana and Edith's death."

We pulled out the case files and started thumbing through the pages. "Remember that woman at the community center who told us Edith was making trouble for pakalolo dealers?" I asked. "You want to go downstairs with me? Maybe Vice can tell us something."

We took the elevator down to the B1 level, the first of two levels below ground. The photo lab, narcotics and the special investigations section, where they do research on evidence, are down there, along with Vice.

Lieutenant Kee's secretary, Juanita Lum, is a heavyset, no-nonsense Filipina, with lustrous black hair and skin so smooth she could do soap ads. From her wedding picture, which sat in a heart-shaped frame on her desk, you could see she'd been a real looker when she was younger.

"Howzit, Kimo?" she asked. "Morning, Ray."

I explained what we were looking for.

"Let me see what I can dig up for you." She turned to her computer, and her fingers, with their long pink nails, flew across the keyboard. Pages started spewing out of the printer next to her desk. "I pulled up everybody with intent to sell in that area." She grabbed a half-dozen pages from the printer and handed them to me.

Juanita had provided us with eight guys who had a history of dealing on Hawaiian homestead land. Back at our desks, we spent an hour looking into them. Two of the guys on the list were dead, and another three had been penal guests of the state of Hawai'i since well before Aunty Edith's murder. With a few phone calls, we knocked one more out—he was a student at U.H. who'd been buying some Maui Wowie to distribute to friends back at the dorm.

That left us with two brothers who lived in Papakolea. It was barely ten a.m., an hour when all serious potheads are tucked up in bed. We drove up to their address in the Jeep, with the side flaps rolled up, the fresh morning air cooling as we climbed uphill through the curving streets.

"I thought you knew your way around this whole island," Ray said, as another street turned out to be a cul-de-sac that didn't go through where I wanted it to.

I made a U-turn and said, "You like this neighborhood? Because I can drop you anywhere around here you want."

"I'm just saying."

Two more U-turns later, I found the narrow street off Tantalus Drive where Leroy and Larry Campbell lived in a beat-up shack. Weeds grew around the foundation of the shack; it had once been white, but the tropical sun had faded it to the color of dried spit. One of the windows was broken and covered over with cardboard.

Ray rapped on the door and called out, "Mr. Campbell. Police. Open up."

We waited, and Ray was about to knock again when the door opened. A fat Hawaiian guy with dark dreadlocks stuck his head out. "Help you?"

"Mr. Campbell?" Ray showed him his ID. "Honolulu Police. Can you step outside?"

We heard someone call out from inside the shack, and the fat guy turned to answer. "It's da kine police."

"That your brother in there?" Ray asked. "We'd like to talk to him, too."

I saw curtains flicking across the street, some nosy old kupuna keeping tabs on the brothers. After another minute or two, both of them came outside. They were both big guys, though Leroy was bald, and Larry was the one with the dreadlocks.

They were typical stoners, slow to wake up and even slower to process our questions. They knew Aunty Edith, because of the trouble she'd been causing for them, but when Ray asked if they knew who had killed her, they laughed.

"Yeah, man, we climb up on da roof and shoot her," Leroy said, making a gun with his thumb and index finger. "Bang, bang!"

He and his brother laughed like Santa Claus, their big bellies shaking. They pretend shot each other, each grabbing his chest and staggering around as if dying. "Yo, dude, a lady's dead," Ray said. "Have some respect."

They sobered for a minute, then started giggling again. I looked at Ray. I couldn't imagine either of these idiots getting it together enough to come up with a plan to shoot Edith Kapana—no less carry it out. But I had to ask. "Where were you last Friday morning?"

Leroy opened his hands like he had a pretend datebook in them and flipped the pages. "Last Friday. Dat da day we was knocking back beers wid da mayor?" he asked his brother. "Or wuz we climbing Diamond Head fo' admire the view?"

"Nah, bruddah, dat the day we wuz practicing da hula," Larry said, waving his hands and swaying his hips.

Both of them dissolved into laughter again.

"Listen, jerkwads, you don't have a good alibi, we take you downtown," Ray said.

Leroy sobered up. "What you want us tell you?" he asked. "We no wake up until noon any day. Only alibi I got is my bruddah.

Plus, we ain't got no car. You think we take guns on da Bus?"

Ray and I looked at each other. "We may have more questions for you," I said. "Don't leave town."

Leroy pulled his shorts up on his thigh, kicked his leg and stuck his thumb out as if he was hitching a ride. He and his brother collapsed into laughter once more, and they were pretend shooting each other again as we walked away.

We went across the street, and the nosy neighbor confirmed that the Campbell brothers rarely, if ever, woke before noon. They were lazy, no-account pakalolo dealers, she said, and she thought we should lock them up just on general principles.

"I wish we could," Ray said. We thanked her for her help and went back to the Highlander. By then Leroy and Larry had gone back in the shack, and I could sniff the pungent aroma of Maui Wowie wafting out of the front window.

"I think you had the right idea yesterday," I said, as I backed down the driveway. "Going over to the Ohana Ola Kino. Even without a subpoena for medical records, we could nose around the facility, see what we can find out."

"Can't work out any less useful than this was."

We took a couple of winding roads over the mountains and into Kaneohe. The Ohana was a one-story building that hugged a hillside a few blocks from the Windward Mall, just down the street from the Kope Bean branch we'd visited the day before. It looked like a nursing home—a central foyer with a reception desk and an office, and two wings of client rooms on either side. A couple of strip shopping centers and an empty lot were its closest neighbors.

The receptionist was an elderly Japanese woman. Ray and I showed our IDs and asked if we could talk to someone about the facility.

That flustered her. She muddled and dithered for a while, then called a tall, slim haole from the office behind her. "I'm David Currie," he said. "I'm the administrator here. How can I help you?"

He led us into his office, which was cluttered with books and papers and photos and certificates on the walls. "We're here about Ezekiel Kapuāiwa," I said. "I understand he was a client here?"

"I can't give you any information about our clients without a warrant. All our records are confidential."

"We don't have a reason to get a warrant," Ray said. "We want to learn about Ezekiel. Whatever you feel you can tell us without compromising his privacy."

Currie pursed his lips and thought for a while. Then he said, "Ezekiel is one of our success stories. He reintegrated with the mainstream very well, and indeed, he's become a community leader. I'd like to think that whatever is in his past should stay in the past."

"I'd like that, too. But sometimes the past has a way of catching up to us."

He couldn't, or wouldn't, tell us anything about Ezekiel's diagnosis or hospitalization. "I can tell you, though, that you're not the first person to come up here asking about Ezekiel's mental health."

"Really?"

He nodded. "An elderly woman was here last week. She said they came from the same town on the Big Island. She was worried about him."

"You get a name for her?" Ray asked.

He looked around on his desk. "I told her I couldn't say anything, but she insisted on leaving me her phone number in case I changed my mind." He pulled a piece of paper out and handed it to me. "I recognized the name when I saw it on the news the other day."

The name was Edith Kapana.

I showed it to Ray, trying not to give away anything in front of Currie.

I picked up the questioning then, following up on Levi's suspicions the night before. If Tanaka was a backer of KOH, he could be connected to the case. "How about Jun Tanaka?" I asked. "What can you tell us about him?"

"Mr. Tanaka is one of our board members."

"How about his relationship with Mr. Kapuāiwa? Would you call them friends? Business associates? I understand Mr. Tanaka is one of the backers of Kingdom of Hawai'i."

"I don't know anything about that," Currie said. "It's not uncommon for a board member to take a special interest in the rehabilitation of a client. Many of our board members provide jobs, housing or other assistance to clients. That's why they get involved with us in the first place. So they can help people."

"But you don't know what kind of help Mr. Tanaka has provided?"

"We have twenty-five to thirty clients living here at any one time," Currie said. "The average stay is anywhere from six months to two years. We also provide outpatient services to another hundred clients. That's a lot of people for me to keep track of."

Because of all the laws about privacy, health care and education are the hardest places to get information from without a subpoena, so we knew that there wasn't much else we could get from David Currie. We gave him our cards and asked him to call if he recalled anything we should know.

"Well, that was a useful visit," Ray said, as we walked out. "Too bad we can't subpoena his ass and look at the records ourselves."

"But we did find a connection to Edith Kapana. Why do you think she was interested in Ezekiel's mental health?"

"She was volunteering for the KOH," Ray said. "Maybe she saw Ezekiel acting crazy, and she wanted to know what was wrong with him. People said she was a nosy old woman."

We stopped in front of the Jeep, in the small parking lot in front of the Ohana. Flat cirrus clouds hung over the horizon, and there wasn't even a hint of a breeze.

"She knew him back on the Big Island. Suppose he was crazy back then, and she knew it. If she started telling people that he was nuts, that he'd been hospitalized, it could destroy KOH's chances to run Hawai'i."

"You keep assuming that this is a real possibility," Ray said, leaning against the back of the Jeep. "You think any of these groups have a chance at seceding from the US?"

"I don't think Hawai'i will ever secede. But I do think there will be a financial settlement someday. Reparations. Whoever's on top has the chance to control that money."

"How about those papers that were stolen from her room?" Ray asked. "You think any of them could have been from the Hawai'i State Hospital? His records?"

"I wish I had looked closer. I suppose. Edith was his hanai grandmother, after all; she might have been the person who had him committed."

"Maybe she didn't have the paperwork herself," Ray suggested, and I turned back to look at him. "So she came up here to get some proof, but Currie wouldn't give it to her."

"We should call the hospital. See if they can confirm Ezekiel was a patient there without a subpoena."

"Good luck with that."

Across the street, I saw a middle-aged haole waiting for the bus. He was wearing a faded blue baseball cap and a cheap windbreaker, smoking a cigarette. "See that guy over there," I said to Ray. "You think maybe he's a client here?"

The guy was nodding his head to an unseen beat, and his right leg shook. "Looks crazy to me. But I think that about half the population of Honolulu."

"I'll meet you back here. I want to see what I can find out." I waited until there was a break in traffic, and then walked over to the bus stop. The bus route sign had been painted over with graffiti, so I asked the guy, "Bus go into Honolulu from here?"

"Yeah, the bus goes from here," he said. "But the bus doesn't go that often. When the bus goes, it goes. But it doesn't always go when you want it to."

Okay, so the guy probably was a client at the Ohana Ola Kino. I watched as he lit another cigarette with the butt of the first one, and said, "They want me to go live across the street. So I gotta know that I can get the bus here."

"I live there," he said. "And I take the bus every day. Every day, I wait here for the bus. The bus goes to my job."

"Really? What kind of job?"

"I sit with the coffee," he said. "At night. In case anybody comes for it. I take the bus every day, to sit with the coffee."

"You know a guy at the Ohana named Ezekiel?"

He shook his head violently. "They're all crazy there," he said. "I don't talk to nobody if I can help it."

"How about this woman?" I asked, pulling out a picture of Edith. "You ever see her around?"

"You ask a lot of questions." He rocked back and forth, puffing on his cigarette. "Is this some kind of test? I don't like it when they make me take tests. I never know the answers."

I went back to pretending I was going to live at the Ohana and wanted to know about it. We talked for a couple of more minutes, but it was all variations on the same theme. He sat around with coffee, babysitting it somehow, and he took the bus to get to work.

"I guess I have to get a job," I said. "They fix you up with this coffee job back there?" I nodded toward the Ohana.

He nodded. "Lotta people work with the coffee. But not like me."

Then the bus pulled up. "Mahalo," he said, even though there wasn't anything to thank me for, other than for keeping him company while he waited. I stayed on the bench, and as the bus drove away, he pushed his face against the window and watched me.

I admired people who devoted themselves to taking care of others. People like David Currie, who protected the clients at the Ohana. And Terri, who used her position and her family's money to better the community. Sometimes, as a cop, you get the sense that you are doing good—protecting the people, putting away the bad guys. Most of the time, though, you feel like you're butting your head against a wall, that nothing you do will ever lead to change. I was having one of those kind of days.

I looked across the street and saw Ray leaning against the side of the Jeep. "You waiting for a ride?" he called. "Or you just going to sit there?"

Riding back to headquarters, I told Ray what the crazy guy had said. "Coffee?" he asked. "You ask him where?"

"What do you mean?"

"Where he babysits the coffee," Ray said, real slow, like I was a child or a client at the Ohana. "You think he works at the Kope Bean?"

"Shit. I was so focused on asking about Ezekiel and Edith and the Ohana I guess I wasn't paying attention."

"Just seems like there's a lot of coffee floating around in this case," Ray said. "And it all circles back to the Kope Bean."

"He said a lot of people from the Ohana work with the coffee. Edith knew both Dex and Ezekiel. And both of them worked for the Kope Bean. But Ezekiel was a barista, and Dex works in the warehouse." I flipped through our notes. "But look here. Ezekiel stopped working at the Kope Bean in 2005." I turned to a different page. "According to Leelee, Dex didn't move in with her and her uncle and Edith until 2007."

"So it's not like Ezekiel got Dex the job," Ray said. "And Currie said the clients move in and out, so it's not even likely that the crazy guy and Ezekiel lived in the Ohana at the same time or worked at the Kope Bean at the same time. It's probably just some kind of placement deal. The Kope Bean has a bunch of minimum wage jobs, and they hire clients from the Ohana. May even get tax credits for it, you know, hiring the disabled. I know a place in Philly used to work that way."

When we got back to our desks, Ray called the Hawai'i State Hospital to ask about Ezekiel. I went back to our notes looking for loose threads and found that we hadn't followed up on Bunchy Parker's son Brian, the Iraq veteran who might have some sharpshooting skills.

I called Bunchy, who said Brian was out. "I'm not his secretary, brah," Bunchy said. "He don't tell me where he go."

"Has he been home at all since we talked to you two days ago?"

"No."

"He usually stay away from home that long?"

"He's a grown man," Bunchy grumbled. "He don't care about his father no more."

"Tell him to call us when you do see him." I hung up, wondering what Brian Parker was hiding from or running away from.

Ray had about as much luck with the hospital. They wouldn't confirm or deny anything about a patient without a subpoena for records. Though we felt there had to be a tie to Edith's death, because of their history together and her death at the rally, I didn't see a judge considering our argument strong enough to violate Ezekiel's right to privacy. And we didn't know for sure that his mental health was connected to her death, at least not yet.

Jun Tanaka's name was on the incorporation papers for the non-profit and in an annual report we found filed with the state. But he was never quoted in any of the newspaper articles on KOH, and doing an online search for "Kingdom of Hawai" and "Tanaka" together gave us no results.

There were a couple of Jun Tanakas in the system, but none of them matched the few details we had. Since that exhausted my computer skills, I called my best friend since high school, Harry Ho.

At Punahou, Terri Clark, Harry and I were an invincible trio. Terri provided emotional insights that escaped testosterone-based life forms like Harry and me, and Harry was able to use his computer skills to find information that would defeat lesser brains. I was never quite sure what I brought to the equation, other than determination and loyalty.

"Howzit, brah?" I asked. "Think you could pull yourself away for a few minutes to do some searching for me?"

Harry and his girlfriend, Arleen, had gotten married a couple of months before. Terri was the maid of honor, and I was the best man. After a long honeymoon in Japan and China, they had settled into a cute little house in Aiea, a couple of blocks from Mike and me.

"I could use a break," he said. "What do you need?"

I told him about Jun Tanaka and Ezekiel Kapuāiwa, about their connection to KOH and our suspicions. "Can you see what you can find about them both?"

"With pleasure." Harry and I grew up on reruns of the original *Hawaii Five-O*, and he's always fancied himself a slim version of Chin Ho. I had a crush on Danny, but I don't think that's what led me to the police academy. Well, maybe that was one of the things. I used to have a thing for men in uniform, until I had to wear one myself.

"See if you can connect either of them to a woman named Edith Kapana," I added.

"That the woman who was killed at the rally? Think one of them killed her?"

"Don't know," I said. "We're chasing our tails right now."

It was frustrating to have so many dead ends and loose ends in a case. Most of the time, homicides are committed by people with clear motives, means and opportunity. Investigating the crime is a matter of putting the pieces together in a way that will hold up in court and convince a judge or a jury.

This case, though, was anything but ordinary. We still hadn't figured out why anyone would kill Edith, though we had some ideas. And until we knew that, it was going to be tough to identify the means—the particular rifle that had been used—and the opportunity—putting our suspect on that rooftop at the time Edith was shot.

Sampson passed by our desks just before the end of our shift. "I've got a meeting at the substation in Wahiawa," he said. "We'll talk about your case tomorrow."

"You got it," I said.

I looked at Ray as Sampson walked away, and he grinned. "Anything else we can do today?" Ray asked me.

"We have no suspects," I said. "Nobody left to interview. We're still waiting for your friend to come up with some information on Brian Parker and for Harry to see what he can find that connects Jun Tanaka and Ezekiel Kapuāiwa to Edith. I say we call it quits and hope tomorrow's a better day."

I couldn't stop thinking about Edith as I drove home. How she had been dressed like my mother at the rally; how only a block or so had separated them; how devastated my whole family would have been if anything had happened to her.

My eyes were moistening a little as I dialed my parents' house. "Howzit, mom? You guys doing okay?"

"I'm glad you called, Kimo," she said. "I was right about those bowls. The curator at the Bishop Museum is very excited. She wants to talk to Leelee and find out how long they've been in the family."

"Leelee won't know anything. Remember, those bowls belonged to Edith, and Leelee had no idea they were anything special."

"That's right. That poor woman. Have you found out who killed her yet?"

"Working on it." We talked for a couple of minutes, about my father's new pills, a cute card one of my nephews had sent. By the time I hung up I had made a resolution to make sure I talked to both my parents as often as I could, while I still had the chance to.

Mike's truck was in the driveway when I got home. I opened the door of the house, ready to call out to him, when a big golden dog barreled into me, barking like crazy. For a minute I thought I was under attack, until the dog stood up on his back paws, resting the front ones on my groin, and sniffed me.

I stepped back into the yard as Mike rushed forward and

grabbed the dog by the collar. "Roby! Down, boy!"

Roby hopped to the ground and started dancing around us. Mike couldn't hang on to him, and I couldn't help but laugh. I said, "Roby. Sit," in my most commanding cop voice, and the dog obediently plopped his butt on the grass and looked up at us, his long pink tongue lolling out of the right side of his mouth.

"Damn. I've been trying to get that dog to sit since I brought him home."

"And what's he doing here?"

Mike looked sheepish as he snapped a leash on and led the dog back inside. In the kitchen, I saw a wooden stand with two metal bowls in it on the floor and a big bag of dog chow on the counter. Mike unhooked Roby and handed him a rawhide bone. The dog dropped to the floor, gnawing happily, one end of the bone in his mouth, the other immobilized by a big golden paw.

"We talked about getting a dog," Mike said. "You said we could someday."

"Someday." I leaned up against the kitchen counter and folded my arms across my chest.

"You remember the fire I told you about yesterday? In Waipahu?"

"This is the dog that saved the family?"

He nodded. "The only place they found to live won't let them keep the dog. He was going to have to go to the pound."

"Where people go when they want to adopt dogs."

"He's such a good boy," Mike said, reaching down to scratch behind the dog's ears. "I mean, what a great dog for a fireman, right? A dog that saved his family from a fire."

"I thought firemen liked Dalmatians."

"Come on, Kimo. Give him a chance. He's a sweetheart."

A line of drool had dripped from Roby's mouth and stretched across his jaw and down the side of his mouth. He stopped chewing the rawhide for a moment and looked up at me.

We had a dog for a while when I was a kid, but he bonded with my mother, who fed and walked him. When he ran away I didn't miss him. Most of the dogs I had run across on the job were either small and angry or big and sloppy. This one looked like the latter.

"Who's going to walk him and pick up after him?"

"We could both do it," Mike said. "Think about it. The three of us out in the morning, walking together, enjoying nature and each other's company."

"Yeah. Do we know if he's housebroken?"

"Mr. Gresham swears he is. He's had all his shots. He's a little wild sometimes, I admit, but between the two of us we can tame him."

I laughed. "We haven't been able to tame each other yet. What makes you think the dog will be any different?"

Mike grilled a couple of steaks for us in the backyard, Roby sitting at attention next to the barbecue. Then he followed Mike inside with the meat, resting on his haunches next to the table.

"No people food," I said to Mike, as I saw him cutting a piece of steak I was sure was intended for the dog. "He's got his chow. Otherwise he'll always be pestering us."

I glared at the dog, and he sunk down on all four paws, his head resting mournfully on the floor. As we were cleaning up, Mike said, "I've got to go see my dad. You want to come with me? My mom might have dessert."

"I'd better stay here with the dog. Make sure he doesn't get into any mischief."

"You can't keep avoiding them. I know you think my dad hates you, but he doesn't. He's just trying to protect me."

"Don't eat too much dessert," I said.

Mike scratched the dog's ears and then walked out the back door.

Despite his outward acceptance of Mike's sexuality, I worried that Dr. Riccardi really wanted his son to be straight—and that I was a reminder of how many ways Mike hadn't lived up to his father's ambitions for him. He hadn't married a sweet girl and provided grandchildren. He hadn't gone to medical school or picked what his father thought of as a grown-up profession.

Mike was a terrific guy, the kind of son any parent should be proud of. He was handsome, sweet, smart and caring. He had moved up in the fire department hierarchy, and he was respected by his peers. But his father treated him like some kind of teenaged fuckup, and I resented that, on Mike's behalf, and on my own.

Mike came back an hour later, as I was reading a gay mystery by Joseph Hansen, and we didn't talk about his parents at all. When we went to bed, the dog turned around a couple of times and then settled on the floor next to my side.

In the morning, I woke before Mike, and as soon as I was stirring in bed, the dog popped up and stuck his big furry head in my face. "Get away from me, you big moose," I said, pushing him aside.

I went into the bathroom, and when I finished, the dog was sitting by the bedroom door looking expectant. Mike was snoring, so I shrugged into a T-shirt and shorts, found the dog's leash on the counter and grabbed a plastic Foodland bag in case the dog had any business to do.

He did. Lots of business. I picked it up like a good citizen, sealed the bag and stashed it in the trash can by the garage. "I suppose you want to eat now," I said to the dog, as we walked inside. "Now that you've pooped."

I figured out how much of the dog chow to give him, and he ate noisily as I sat down at the kitchen table with the morning *Star-Advertiser* and a bowl of cereal. Though I wasn't yet sold on the idea of dog ownership, I have to admit it was nice and domestic. Mike and I had been a couple for a while, and now we were expanding to become a family. It wasn't what I'd envisioned for myself, growing up, but it was turning out just fine.

The A Team

Sampson was in a meeting Friday morning when Ray and I got to headquarters. The fingerprint report from the break-in at Edith Kapana's room was waiting for us. There were three sets of matches: to Edith herself, to Leelee and to Dexter Trale. A bunch of tiny smudges probably belonged to the baby. There were no unidentified prints.

"Remember the woman at the community center who said Edith was making trouble for some pakalolo dealers?" I asked Ray. "Suppose one of those dealers was her niece's boyfriend?"

"And Dex broke into her room to take any evidence she had against him," Ray said.

"That's one explanation."

While I looked over the report one more time, Ray checked his e-mail and found a message from his friend. He couldn't send us Brian Parker's records without a subpoena, but he did point us toward an article in an old base newsletter online, which indicated that Brian had been his squad's designated marksman.

"I think this moves Brian up on our list of suspects in Edith's murder," Ray said. "He can shoot a rifle, and he might have killed Edith as a way to sabotage KOH."

"KOH competes with his father's group," I said. "If Ka Leo eventually gets chosen for a leadership role in a sovereign Hawai'i or if Ka Leo ends up in control of reparations money, Brian could really make out."

"Where can we look for him?" Ray asked. "He doesn't have a job, at least not one Social Security knows about."

"We have to go back and see Bunchy." It was a gorgeous day, temperatures in the low seventies and mauka trade winds. We wound our way along Tantalus Drive, where arching kukui trees framed the occasional view of downtown and Waikīkī. A mottled brown cat streaked past the Highlander as we climbed, and we surprised a flock of monk parakeets into flight. It was a different world up on the mountain.

Bunchy met us on his doorstep. "I told you, brah, Brian left couple days ago. I don't know where he go. He come back *bumbye*."

Bumbye was pidgin for later on, like saying "whenever." The Dodge pickup registered to Brian wasn't in the driveway, but we asked to take a look in the house. "*Hele on*, brah," Bunchy said, stepping out of the doorway and encouraging us to get moving.

He showed us Brian's room, which looked untouched from his time as a Kamehameha High football star. I saw a Nintendo Wii with a stack of games and a closet full of jeans and T-shirts. Wherever he'd gone, he hadn't gone for long.

The walls were hung with photos of him at his graduation, draped in leis, and of him as a soldier, his rifle casually slung over his shoulder. "He still shoot?" I asked Bunchy.

"He go down to the range in Waikīkī sometimes," Bunchy said. "Why you care? You trying to lock him up for killing Aunty Edith?"

"Not trying to lock anybody up unless they're guilty," I said. "Right now we just want to talk to Brian."

"My boy's a good boy." Bunchy glared at me, his hands on his hips.

"Loves his father?" I asked. "Wants to protect him, make sure his group gets a share of the reparation money?"

He shook his index finger at me. "You got no cause to go accusing my boy."

"You know any place we can look for Brian?" I asked. "Friends? Other family he might be staying with?"

"You talk to my attorney." Bunchy walked to the front door and stood aside as we walked out. He remained in his doorway, watching to make sure we drove away.

"That went well," Ray said.

"Let's go down to that gun range. You have a picture of Brian Parker on you?" I couldn't remember if we'd ever found one.

"Think so." He handed me the binder we had been carrying around which had the records of this investigation, and I found a photo we'd downloaded from a veterans' website. We had a good mug shot of Dexter Trale, too, so I suggested we show both pictures around.

The range was on the second floor of a building on Kalākaua, a few blocks from Fort DeRussy. They catered to tourists, locals and the occasional member of the military; I'd been there a few times, though for the most part I did my shooting at the police range. The guy on duty was busy fitting out a group of British tourists with protective headgear, ammunition and rental guns.

"This is awesome, mate," one of them said, in a broad accent. "Can't do nothing like this back home."

I thought about pointing out the lower rate of homicides involving guns in his country but held back. When they were gone, Ray introduced us.

"Can we show you a couple of pictures, brah?" he asked, sounding almost like a local.

"These guys criminals?" the clerk asked.

"Right now we're just doing some preliminary checking," Ray said. "Want to see if any of these guys are qualified with rifles."

He showed Brian Parker's picture, and the clerk recognized him right away. "He's ex-military. Brings his own weapons. Nice guy."

"Rifles?" Ray asked.

"Rifles, handguns. He's got a really awesome Colt Python." I knew that was a pretty high-end collectible gun, which pegged Brian Parker as someone who knew his weapons.

Ray showed the clerk Dex's picture next. "Not sure," the clerk said. "Maybe. But he looks like a lot of guys, you know?"

We couldn't get anything more definite from him. Ray needed some gun oil, so while he picked some up, I browsed. There was a sweet leather holster for my Glock that I might like to find under the Christmas tree. I made a note to tell Mike. That was a nice feeling, knowing I had someone special to shop for come the holidays, someone who'd be shopping for me, too.

We picked up some takeout for lunch and went back to headquarters, where I put out a BOLO—be on the lookout—for Brian's pickup. I felt comfortable doing that based on his record as a sharpshooter and the fact that he seemed to have gone to ground. Why was he hiding, if he wasn't responsible for Edith's death?

"We need to find this guy," Ray said. "Ideas?"

I thought back to Brian's room. "Maybe he's in touch with his old teammates," I said. "Or people he used to work with. I'll find the Kamehameha High team roster and start calling those guys. You start with the last place he worked then go backwards."

We spent a couple of fruitless hours tracking down men and women who had lost touch with Brian Parker. The most information came from the Kamehameha quarterback, whom I managed to get hold of by phone via a friend who had gone to U.H. with him. "He changed when he come back from Iraq," the guy said. "Used to be one fun guy. Now he stay on his own."

I hung up and said, "This is useless. Suppose we go talk to Dex again, ask him about his fingerprints in Aunty Edith's room?"

Even though we thought we had a good suspect for Edith's death in Brian Parker, we both felt obliged to follow any leads. Until you have a suspect in custody and an iron-clad case against him, you can't let any loose threads go uninvestigated.

We drove down to the Kope Bean warehouse. When we walked inside and smelled the pungent aroma of the bags of coffee beans, I remembered the crazy guy from the Ohana who babysat coffee. I wondered if he worked at the warehouse.

But I didn't see how that could connect to Edith's murder, so I pushed the thought aside and focused on Dexter Trale. "Tell us about Tuesday morning," I said, when we had him outside again. "What were you looking for in Edith's room?"

"Shit, you guys still messing around with Aunty Edith?"

"Yeah, Dex, that's what we do. We found your fingerprints in Edith's room."

He looked at us. "I live in the fucking house. You gonna find my prints all over the fucking place."

"So you didn't go in and toss her room?" Ray asked.

Dex laughed. "You think dat old kupuna had any money? All she had was the Social Security, and she gave Leelee that check every month, exchange for room and board."

He lit a cigarette, and I noticed that his hands weren't shaking the way they had the last time we spoke to him. "That all you smoke, Dex? How about a little pakalolo?"

He looked at us suspiciously. "I don't do nothing to violate my parole."

Dex was on parole for something. Interesting. That's probably why he liked to avoid pilikia with the cops, as Leelee had said. "But you'd know where to buy some stuff, wouldn't you?" I asked. "You know the Campbell brothers?"

He laughed. "Man, Aunty Edith had a bug up her ass about them. You think maybe they broke into her room?" He laughed so hard he started to choke. "Leroy and Larry couldn't break into their own house if they lost the key."

I noticed again how fit Dex was and wondered if he knew how to shoot a rifle. He might have had a beef with Edith over dope or money or some domestic drama and used the cover of the rally to get her out of the way.

That made me start thinking about Leelee's uncle Amos. He'd been missing for a year, and they hadn't reported he was gone because they were afraid of getting kicked off homestead land. Or so Leelee said. What if Dex was systematically wiping out her family?

We had never searched the part of the house where Dex and Leelee lived. I wondered if we'd find a gun if we did. But we still didn't have enough for a search warrant, and even if Leelee gave us permission to search when Dex wasn't home, I wasn't sure the results would stand up in court without probable cause.

Dex didn't know or wouldn't say, anything more about Aunty Edith, so we gave up. "You think he was telling the truth?" I asked as we walked to the Highlander.

"I don't think Dexter Trale would know the truth if it bit him in the ass," Ray said.

"And we'd certainly see the bite through those tight jeans."

"Speak for yourself, pal." We walked out the front door, and he said, "Hey, look, over there. It's your buddy."

It was the crazy guy I'd met the day before at the bus stop by the Ohana. So he did work at the warehouse after all. He walked up toward me, head down, muttering, then looked up and spotted me. "Hey, it's you. The guy from the bus. I take the bus to work."

"Yeah," I said. "I remember you."

Though he lived at the Ohana, he looked like he was homeless—not just the strange look in his eye, but the layers of clothes—a white T-shirt, a plaid shirt, and then a sweater and a scarf over it, as if he carried his whole wardrobe with him wherever he went.

"I'm Kimo," I said, reaching out my hand. "This is my buddy Ray."

"I'm Stuey." At first I thought he said he was screwy, which would have made sense. He made no attempt to shake my hand, though, so I pulled it back.

"You work here?" I asked.

He nodded. "I have to be there on time, or Mr. T, he gets mad. I work with Mr. T. Mr. T, he's the boss."

Dexter Trale. Mr. T. "What do you do?" I asked.

"I check the lists, the lists have got to be right," Stuey said. "The stores have to get what they need. They need the stuff every day." He tugged at the scarf around his neck, and I wondered that he could wear so much clothing when it was so hot outside. It was going on three o'clock, and the morning trade winds had disappeared, leaving us to broil under the sun.

"You wouldn't believe how much coffee they go through," Stuey continued. "Ground coffee. Coffee beans. Boy, it smells here, you know. It smells like coffee." He sniffed the air. "Even out here, you smell it. The coffee."

I nodded. Stuey was on a roll. "I don't touch the money, though. Mr. T always says, 'Stuey, you don't touch the money.' So I don't."

"What kind of money?" Ray asked.

"The money," Stuey said. "Mr. T brings it in a big satchel bag, and he runs it through the machine. The machine counts the money."

I was trying to figure out how to get Stuey back on track, when he said, "Mr. T wraps the money up and takes it to the bank." That threw me. Who would give a guy like Dexter Trale, a man with a gambling problem and a criminal record, access to piles of cash? There had to be something wrong.

Oh, yeah, Stuey was crazy.

"I gotta go," he said, suddenly changing track. "I gotta get to work. Mr. T don't like it if I'm late. Even if the bus is late, I'm supposed to be on time."

"What time you work?" Ray asked.

"Three to twelve," Stuey said, over his shoulder, as he rushed away from us.

I looked back and saw Dexter Trale standing at the door of the warehouse. Stuey climbed the steps two at a time and disappeared inside, his scarf flapping behind him.

"Mr. T," Ray said. "Guess that makes us *The A Team*."

"What do you think Stuey meant when he was talking about the money?" Ray asked, as we walked back to the Highlander.

"They must bring the receipts from the stores in to the warehouse, count it all up before they take it to the bank."

Ray shook his head. "That doesn't sound right. I worked at this pizza place when I was in college, and the manager took the cash to the night deposit as soon as we closed."

"Was the pizza place a chain?"

"Nah, just a local shop."

"Well, maybe they need to make one big deposit." I'd never worked retail; I'd always done construction for my dad or taught surfing, until I went to the police academy.

Sampson was still at Honolulu Hale, so we clocked out for the weekend. With luck, something would break by Monday, and we'd be able to stay on Edith's murder. If not, the case would get shelved, and we'd move on. I didn't like that, but it was the way of the world. You do your best with each case, and the ones you can't solve stay with you.

I wore myself out on the drive home trying to find an angle we hadn't explored, a lead we hadn't followed. By the time I got home, all I wanted was to get a beer and collapse on the sofa. But Mike wasn't home yet, and the dog went crazy when he saw me, jumping up and down like I was his best friend, and he hadn't seen me for years.

I sighed, grabbed the leash and a bag, and we went for a walk. Down the hill, around the corner, back up another street, eventually making a big circle. Roby was fascinated by every tree and bush and street sign, stopping to sniff, sometimes even licking the grass.

"Stop that," I said, jerking on his chain. "That's gross."

He peed copiously. By the time we got home I wondered that he had any fluid left in him at all. And of course, Mike was home by then, sitting on the sofa as I'd wanted to be, his shirt off, a Kona Fire Rock Ale in his hand. As soon as I let him off the leash, Roby deserted me and rushed over to Mike, jumping up on the sofa and licking Mike's face.

"I thought he was supposed to be your dog," I said, dropping the leash on the kitchen counter with a clank.

"He is," Mike said, rubbing the golden dog behind his ears.

"Then why am I the only one who does anything to take care of him? I fed and walked him this morning, and I walked him now."

"Don't whine." Mike got up from the sofa. "You want some bowl food?" he asked Roby. "Come on, Daddy will feed you."

"Daddy? Give me a fucking break."

"You know what? Fuck you," he said. "I'm getting tired of this spoiled baby act. The world doesn't revolve around you, you know."

"Fuck you, too." I grabbed a beer and stalked into the bedroom. I heard Mike's truck start up a few minutes later, and when he pulled back into the driveway I saw him carrying a takeout bag from the Zippy's down the hill. "Asshole," I muttered.

I sat down at the computer and surfed for a while, ending up at a gay chat room. I logged in, but I didn't type anything; I just sat there and watched other guys communicate. It was Friday night, and guys were comparing plans for clubbing.

I kept running over in my head how stupid I had been to give up everything I had in Waikīkī to move in with a selfish, self-involved jerk like Mike. By the time he came in, I was in bed pretending to be asleep.

No tossing and turning for him, though. Within a few minutes he was snoring gently, his lips flapping. The dog came in and settled on the floor next to me again, and soon he was snoring too.

I must have dozed off, because I woke up to the sound of Mike's beeper going off. As the fire investigator for his district, he's on call 24/7 for any fires of suspicious origin. Fortunately, he didn't get beeped much in his off hours.

He got out of bed and stumbled over to the bureau, where the beeper was vibrating, stubbing his toe on one of Roby's rawhide bones on his way and swearing. I snickered into my pillow.

His side of the conversation was quick and simple. He got the location of the fire and said that he was on his way. I sat up and yawned as he was getting dressed.

"Sorry I woke you," he said. "I've gotta go out to a fire."

I believe in karma, and I was damned if I was going to let him go off to some dangerous situation with things bad between us.

"Be careful," I said, stifling another yawn. "I love you."

"Love you, too." He kissed my forehead, and I drifted back to sleep.

He didn't get back until Saturday morning, when I'd already gotten up and walked and fed the dog. He handed me a macadamia latte in a Kope Bean cup, kissed my cheek, and then went back to bed.

"Guess it's just you and me," I said to Roby. He looked up, his ears perking.

My brother Haoa has four kids and a beagle mix, so I took Roby over there for a play date while Mike slept. Somehow my fourteen-year-old niece, Ashley, roped me into taking her out to Makapu'u Point for some surfing, and before I knew it her brother Alec and her cousins Jeffrey and Keoni were piled into my Jeep, a gaggle of surfboards sticking out the back.

By the time we got back, the kids were jumping off the walls, I was beat and Roby was asleep in the back yard with the beagle's head resting on his stomach. My sister-in-law Tatiana wanted us to stick around for a barbecue, but I figured I had to get back to Mike, who'd already complained about not enough "us time."

I'd left my cell phone at Haoa's house when we went surfing, and I didn't look at the display until I was already heading home. There were five missed calls, all from Mike, and one very angry message. "If you took my dog to the pound, don't even think about coming back here."

He came to the front door as I pulled up in the driveway, and Roby jumped over me in his excitement to get to Mike. "Hey, boy," Mike said, ruffling the dog's ears and scratching his belly, as he rolled around on the ground in ecstasy. Then he looked up at me. "Where the fuck have you been? And why weren't you answering your cell?"

"I took Roby over to Haoa's to play, and then I went surfing with the kids. I thought you'd appreciate the chance to sleep."

"Yeah, you thought," Mike said. "You thought you'd do just as you pleased."

"You want to argue out here in the front yard?" I asked. "Because we can. Maybe get your parents in on it, too. They can tell us both what a big fucking mistake this was."

Suddenly, it was like someone had let the air out of the argument. Mike said, "I'm sorry. Come on in."

"I'm sorry, too," I said, following him inside.

Liability and Protection

Mike sat down on the sofa, his back against one arm, and I sat next to him, turned sideways so we could face each other. "It scares me when we fight because it makes me think we're not getting along," he said. "I love you, and I want to make this work."

Roby paced nervously around the sofa, finally sprawling on the tile floor between us. "Ray said he and Julie fight all the time, because they're letting their feelings out and clearing the air."

"That's not the way I grew up. You've seen my dad. He's the master of control, and my mom has that whole Asian inscrutable thing going on. The two of them never raise their voices, never use a curse word."

"We're never going to be like that," I said. "When I was a kid, my dad was always yelling and blustering, and my mom would just let him run out of steam. I know I inherited his temper, and I have to work harder not to let little things irritate me."

"We're both Type A personalities," Mike said, smiling. "And we've both been living on our own for a while, and we're both accustomed to getting our own way."

I wanted a beer, but I didn't get up from the sofa. "We need to communicate more. I should have asked you before I committed us to dinner with Terri and Levi, and you should have asked me before you brought the dog home."

"We'll make a schedule. Some days I walk and feed him, some days you do."

"We don't have to be that rigid. Some days I'll be out late, some days you will be. As long as we work together we can figure things out as we go."

He took the dog out while I showered and rinsed off the ocean salt, and then we went to dinner at an Italian place, Frank Sinatra singing about *amore*. Over antipasto, Mike told me about the case he'd been called on when he left so early in the morning.

"Arson homicide," he said, as we ate garlic rolls and drank red wine. "Somebody torched this poor homeless guy out in a warehouse district near the airport."

"Wow." I shook my head. "What do you think it was? Kids?" There had been a rash of incidents where teens and young men had beaten up homeless people, though this was the first time someone had been set on fire.

"Don't know. Steve Hart caught the case."

Steve was another homicide detective in my district. He and I had a complicated history; I'd taken away one of his first big cases, and he'd had a chip on his shoulder about me ever since.

"Any evidence?" I asked.

"Looks like they used a Molotov cocktail. Glass bottle, with a rag soaked in gasoline in the neck. Poor guy didn't have a chance. I talked with the guys from ATF; none of them know anyone using that MO."

By the time we stumbled home, stuffed with pasta and tiramisu, it was as if our argument had never happened. We started kissing in the living room and left a trail of clothes from the front door to the bedroom. Roby tried to get in on the fun, but we pushed him away. He settled into a corner of the floor and went to sleep.

The next morning, we slept late, then took Roby out into the mountains with a Frisbee, and we tired him out running and catching it, then bringing it back for more. When we got home, Mike said, "I told my dad I'd help him clean out his garage this afternoon. You want to help?"

"I think I'll pass," I said, even though I knew I ought to make more of an effort to get along with Mike's dad. I went out and ran some errands. By the time I got home, Mike was back, and we went out to dinner together.

Monday morning, Ray was at his desk when I arrived. "Bad news," he said. "You see what happened over the weekend?"

"Brah, I just walked in."

He showed me a report for the arson homicide Mike had been called to on Friday night. "Take a look at the victim's ID." Like Edith Kapana, the homeless man had a Hawai'i state identification certificate, which had survived the fire.

Only he wasn't homeless; he lived in Kaneohe. "It's the address of the Ohana Ola Kino," Ray said. "I checked."

"Wow."

"Look at the name." It was Stuart McKinney. "I called up there, too. There was only one client named Stuart. So that makes him that guy you talked to, Screwy Stuey."

We looked at each other. "Holy fuck," I said.

"You can say that again, brah."

We went in to see Lieutenant Sampson and laid out our idea that Stuey's death was connected somehow to Aunty Edith's.

"This McKinney knew your victim?" Sampson asked, pushing aside a pile of department paperwork.

"We don't know that. But there are a lot of links between them. He lived at the Ohana, where Edith visited just before she died, asking for information. He works with Dexter Trale, who lived with Edith."

"And we spoke to him Friday afternoon, just a few hours before he died," Ray added. "He was crazy, for sure, but he was talking about money moving through the Kope Bean warehouse."

"Edith might have known about whatever is going on there through Dex," I said.

"All right, all right," Sampson said. "You've convinced me. I'll transfer the case to you from Hart and Kawika. But I expect you to go full out on this, even if you find it doesn't connect to your other case."

Back at my desk, I called over to the medical examiner's office and asked to have the autopsy results sent to me.

"Mike found residue from a Molotov cocktail," I said to Ray.

"So it's possible that some kids or other idiots were out looking for trouble, they saw Stuey and they lit him up."

The fax machine began spitting out the pages of the autopsy report. "Look at this," Ray said, pointing. "Someone cracked Stuart McKinney's sternum before they set him on fire." The report indicated the weapon was a blunt object similar to a baseball bat.

"This doesn't look like a random attack. Look where it happened. That's a couple of blocks from the Kope Bean warehouse."

"And it was called in right after midnight," Ray said. "The poor guy must have just gotten off work."

I sat down at the computer and pulled up the schedule for TheBus. There was a stop a block farther from the warehouse; Stuey had probably been on his way there when he'd been assaulted and then set on fire.

"Somebody is seriously sick," Ray said. "I mean, why set the poor guy on fire, when they'd already bashed his chest in?"

"Insurance?" I asked. "Send a message to somebody?"

"But who?"

"Hey, that's why we're the cops. We figure this stuff out. My gut tells me this is connected to our case. He lived where Ezekiel used to, he worked at the Kope Bean."

"But he didn't know Edith. He didn't live at the Ohana at the same time Ezekiel did. The only connection is that he worked with Dex, and Dex lived with Edith. That's a pretty slim coincidence."

"There's no such thing as coincidence when it comes to homicide," I said.

"The next logical place to get information about Stuey is the Ohana," Ray said. So we drove up to Kaneohe, and the same Japanese woman was at the Ohana's front desk, her eyes red and her cheeks damp. We asked for David Currie. She said he was out at the funeral home, making the arrangements for Stuey, but he'd be back soon.

"Did you know Mr. McKinney?" I asked.

She nodded and pulled a tissue out of the pocket of her pink knitted sweater. As she dabbed her eye, I asked, "Know any reason why someone might want to kill him?"

"He was such a sweet man." She lowered her voice. "A little crazy, but then who isn't? Especially here."

Ray and I stood in front of her cheap metal desk. There were no personal touches—no family pictures, candy dish or decorative paperweights. "Tell us about this place. People come here directly from the hospital?"

She nodded. "That's how I did. After my husband died, I was very sad. We never had any children, and we kept to ourselves so we didn't have a lot of friends." She held out her hands, palms up, and I could see the scars on her wrists. "After my neighbor found me, they took me to the hospital. I lost my apartment and my job, and I didn't have anywhere else to go. The Ohana took me in."

The industrial look of the receptionist's desk was repeated in the rest of the lobby. There were two hard plastic chairs along one side of the room and a couple of amateur landscapes, most likely painted by Ohana clients.

"This is a good place, Detective. Mr. Currie, he's the kindest person you could ever want to meet."

"Good to know," I said. "But Mr. McKinney?"

"He came here about six months ago." She twisted the tissue in her hand. "We have a job placement program, you know, but you have to wait a month for a complete evaluation before you can be placed. He talks a lot, so he didn't work out at the first place. But this job at the Kope Bean warehouse was perfect for him. He was the only one there, so he could talk all he wanted. And he's an obsessive compulsive, so he's very meticulous about his job."

She started to cry again.

"Who knew about his work schedule?" I asked, when she'd dried her eyes.

"There's a roster in the community room with all the client names and their work and therapy hours. Anybody here could have known." Her mouth dropped open in horror. "You're not suggesting…" she said. "I thought it was just some horrible random accident."

"We don't know anything yet," I said. "It could have been."

David Currie came in then, somber in a dark suit, seeming even thinner than he had the last time we were there. He looked unhappy that the receptionist had been talking to us. He led us into his office, once again. "I assume this is a formality."

"Too early to assume anything," I said. "I understand from your receptionist that anyone here in the Ohana could have known about Mr. McKinney's schedule?"

"She shouldn't have told you that."

"And why not?" Ray asked. "Is there a reason why you would want to hinder our investigation? Something shady going on up here you don't want the police to know about?"

"I resent that, Detective." Currie crossed his arms in front of him and sat back in his chair.

"You have to admit, it looks pretty suspicious. This is the second time we've come up here for a homicide investigation, and you've been reluctant to cooperate. We're beginning to wonder what you're hiding."

"I'm not hiding anything. I'm protecting the privacy of our clients."

I shook my head. "You can't do that, sir. Not when one of your clients could be guilty of murder. If you want, we'll get a subpoena for the records on every client here. Any of them have problems with anger management? Any arsonists? Firebugs? We'll dig through all your secrets until we find what we need."

It was as if we'd stuck a pin in him, and he deflated. "Let me get Mr. McKinney's file." He swiveled around to the file cabinet and pulled out a hanging folder. Then he turned back and pulled out three others.

"I have to ask you to read this material here," he said. "Just showing you these files without the appropriate court order could be enough to get my license to run this place revoked. But I'm trusting you and trying to balance my own liability with protecting my clients."

"Works for us," I said.

Ray and I read McKinney's file together. He was born in Nebraska and had a degree in accounting. He worked in Nevada and California, and then, according to the case worker's report, he came to Hawai'i on vacation and had some kind of psychotic break. He was kicked out of his hotel for non-payment and became a street person.

After an incident with a bus driver (there was that bus motif again) he was hospitalized, with a diagnosis of obsessive-compulsive disorder. He had been discharged from the Hawai'i State Hospital six months before and had been living at the Ohana since then.

He argued with some of the other residents, but the case manager indicated that he always submitted to dispute resolution. She hoped that within another six months he would be able to live independently, as long as he continued with therapy and maintained his job at the Kope Bean warehouse.

The other three folders were about Ohana clients with a history of violence. When we'd finished reading them, Currie said, "We have a key card reader on the front door. At eight o'clock we lock the door, and the only way in or out is to swipe a card." He turned his computer monitor around to us.

"This is the record for Friday night. You can see that all our residents were checked in by the time Mr. McKinney was killed."

"Except him."

Currie nodded. "We instituted the key card system because some of our clients had night jobs. We couldn't just lock the door or do a bed check."

I looked at the display on the screen. It listed every resident at the Ohana, along with the record of his or her card transactions from midnight Thursday to midnight Friday. Every listed resident had clocked in by 10:00 p.m. except Stuart McKinney.

"What about staff?" Ray asked. "You all have to clock in and out as well?"

He shook his head. "The staff goes home at five. One of our residents acts as the night guard from five to eight, and locks the door at the end of his shift. If there's an emergency, I have a key card for the front door, but because I'm not a client, there's no record kept of my coming and going. Before you ask, I was at an orientation program for incoming freshmen at Farrington High on Friday night with my wife and daughter. The program ended around nine, and then we all went home together. My daughter went to bed at ten, and my wife and I watched David Letterman, then went to sleep."

He introduced us to the two counselors and the nurse. None of them had much to say about Stuey, and none of them knew any reason why someone would want to kill him. One counselor had a second job as a security guard at a condo complex, and he'd been at work when Stuey was killed. The other had been out to dinner with his wife, then back home by nine. The nurse, who lived on the premises, had gone to the movies with a girlfriend and been back by ten.

When we were finished we stopped at Currie's office. "Thank you," I said. "We appreciate your help. We'll be back in touch if we have any other questions."

He stood in the door of his office as we left, perhaps to make sure that the receptionist didn't tell us anything else. Or maybe he was just being polite.

PAI GOW

We spent some time sitting in the Ohana parking lot, making calls to confirm the alibis of Currie and his staff, even though we didn't consider any of them suspects. Then we headed over to the Kope Bean warehouse. Maybe one of Stuey's co-workers got tired of his endless chatter and decided to torch him. It could be that simple; you never know.

I parked at the front of the building, and we went back over our conversation with Stuey on Friday afternoon. Thinking out loud, I said, "Why would somebody bring a lot of cash to the warehouse and trust Dexter Trale with it?"

"Why not take it directly from the store to the bank?" Ray asked.

It was like a light bulb went on over my head. "Maybe it's making a detour on the way," I said. "Remember how Leelee said that Dex played pai gow?"

Ray nodded. "A game like that takes in a lot of cash," I went on. "What can whoever's running the game do with it? You can't go directly to the bank, because they track big deposits."

"But the Kope Bean takes in cash every day," Ray said. "Dexter could mix the cash from the game with the day's receipts from each store. The bank would notice a separate deposit of ten grand or so, but they wouldn't notice a grand extra from each store."

"That assumes that whoever runs the game also owns the Kope Bean."

"And who does own the Kope Bean, anyway?" Ray asked.

"What an excellent question. I see why you're a detective." I looked through our notes and found that Greg Oshiro had only been able to trace the ownership of the chain back to a Japanese corporation. But Greg didn't know Ricky Koele.

Unfortunately, the Division of Business Licensing was

suffering from the same economic problems as the rest of state government, and the office was closed that day, the employees on unpaid furlough.

"You can get your buddy to track the corporation's ownership tomorrow." Ray paused. "When we were talking to Stuey on Friday, Dex was watching him from the door of the warehouse. Was he just waiting for Stuey to show up? Or did he overhear Stuey talking to us?"

"Only one way to find out," I said. We walked around to the loading dock, where we found Dex watching the pallet jockey unload a truck.

"Afternoon, Dex," I said. "We talk to you?"

He frowned, but he waved at the pallet jockey and then jumped down into the parking lot with us.

"This has gotta be quick," he said. "The night guy bailed on me so I've got to check every goddamn pallet before I can leave."

"Yeah, it's about the night guy. You know him?"

"Screwy Stuey? Just to turn things over to him. The guy's a flake. I'm not surprised he quit. Tuli got a call this morning from the nut house where he lived, said he's not coming back any more. No explanation. " He shook his head.

"So you didn't know he was dead?"

Dex stopped in the middle of lighting his cigarette, and I noticed his hand wasn't shaking. "What do you mean, dead?"

"Dead means dead. Somebody set him on fire on his way home from work. You know anything about that?"

"Jesus," Dex said, and I noticed his hand start shaking again. He had to cup the flame in his hands in order to light the cigarette. He took a deep drag. "You're not shitting me? Somebody lit him up? Why?"

"That's what we're trying to figure out."

"I don't know anything about it," Dex said. "He showed up here on Friday right before three. I went over the manifests with him, then clocked out. You can check my time card."

"So what goes on here in the evening?" Ray asked. "Stuey run the shift like you do?"

Dex shook his head. "Everybody but Tuli leaves at three. She stays 'till five to take orders. Stuey's just like a caretaker, see, a warm body. He used to be some kind of accountant, I guess, so he checks the manifests against the pallets and signs them out to the drivers. Then, I don't know, he sits around and plays with himself until midnight."

"We saw you looking out the front door Friday afternoon as we were talking to Stuey," I said. "He was talking about money. You counting money and bundling it up. What's that all about?"

"What the fuck? I don't touch any cash. Everything's on the manifest, they charge the stores directly."

"That's not what Stuey said."

"Stuey's nuts. You know that."

That was true. But it didn't mean he was making up his story. I changed direction, hoping I could trip Dex up. "So where do you go when you leave here?" I asked. "Chinatown? Pai gow?"

He took one last drag and stubbed his cigarette out. I could see he'd been smoking a lot out there. "What's it to you? What I do on my off hours?"

"I'm thinking you go play some pai gow," I said. "And then you bring the cash from the game back here. Who do you work for, Dex? Who would want to keep Stuey quiet about that money?"

"Shit, I don't know what the fuck you guys are talking about," Dex said. "The only pai gow money I win goes right back into the game. And sure as shit, nobody gives me any cash to bring back here."

"Where were you Friday night?" I asked. "After midnight?"

"Home. With Leelee. I went out for a while after dinner, had a couple of drinks. But by midnight I was tucked up in bed. You ask Leelee. She'll tell you."

Leelee would tell us whatever Dex told her to, but I wrote the alibi down. I didn't know why Dex would kill Stuey, but I was sure there could be a reason.

Dex jumped back up onto the loading dock. He was a wiry guy, with strong arms that could have wielded whatever bashed Stuart McKinney's chest in. "I gotta get back to work," he said and disappeared into the dark warehouse.

"He sure freaked when he heard Stuey was dead," Ray said.

"Yeah. That doesn't mean he didn't kill him, though. You look at those arms?"

"First the guy's ass, now his arms," Ray said.

"He has the upper body strength to cave in Stuey's chest. And I'm sure he knows more about that pai gow game than he's letting on."

We followed Dex into the warehouse, where we interviewed a couple of pallet jockeys and Tuli, the Thai woman who worked the switchboard. The warehouse workers left at three, just as Stuey was arriving; none of them even knew his name.

Tuli was with Stuey until five, but she said she was on the switchboard most of the time, and when he started to talk she just tuned him out. None of them seemed to have a motive, and they all had alibis which needed to be verified.

"Considering I'm fresh off the boat from Philadelphia," Ray said, as we drove back to headquarters. "You want to tell me what this pai gow thing is?"

"Chinese domino game. I don't know all the rules, but you start out with four tiles, and the goal is to group them into two pairs. If you bet on the game, you can win big or lose big. I've heard about games where ten or fifteen grand changes hands over the course of the evening. My godfather used to play, and I watched him sometimes."

"That the old tong guy?" Ray asked.

I nodded. My father's best friend, and my godfather, was a man I knew as a child as Uncle Chin. It was only when I became a cop that I discovered Uncle Chin was also a leader of one of the Honolulu tongs, or Chinese gangs. He was retired by that point, so I was never forced to investigate or arrest him, but by the time he passed away I had learned more than I wanted to about his criminal past.

We speculated for a while. "My mother told me that Leelee complained about Dex playing pai gow," I said. "Maybe we've been looking at Edith's death all wrong. Suppose she knew something about the game from living with Dex, and he killed her because of it."

"And then when Stuey started to talk about the money to us, Dex had to kill him, too," Ray said.

"We need to know more about this pai gow game. If it really is at the center of the case."

We got back to headquarters, where Steve Hart wasn't happy to learn that Ray and I had taken over Stuart McKinney's murder from him and his partner. The chip on his shoulder seemed so heavy he was listing to one side. If he wasn't so damn tall he would have tipped over.

"We think it's related to the old lady shot at the rally," I said, trying to be patient. "We interviewed McKinney the afternoon before he was killed."

"It's a loser case." He looked at me like he was trying to figure out what my angle was, why once again I was trying to shoulder him out of an investigation. "You think you know who did it?"

His eyes opened wider. "Hey, that fire investigator," he said. "Riccardi. He's a buddy of yours, isn't he? Wasn't he like, your boyfriend or something? That why you want this case? He giving you some information he wouldn't give to me?"

"Not at all," I said. "He agrees with you, thinks it was just a random thing."

"That's what you're going to find. That it was just kids preying on a homeless guy."

"He wasn't homeless," I said. But it was useless to argue with

Steve. He handed over the notes he had, and I took them back to my desk to go over with Ray.

Despite the fact that I thought Steve Hart was a jerk, he was a competent investigator, and his notes were thorough. He had sketched the area where McKinney's body had been found and recorded his interview with Mike, whose last name he had misspelled.

He and Kawika had attempted a canvass, but it was an industrial neighborhood, and the offices and warehouses had all been closed. Ray and I split up the alibis for the Kope Bean warehouse workers and started making calls. It didn't take long to discover that they all checked out. Leelee said Dex had been with her all night, which didn't match his story, but did place him in Papakolea at the time of Stuey's murder.

When I hung up with Leelee, I called my old partner from Waikīkī, Akoni Hapa'ele, who had transferred to Vice after both of us moved downtown. "We're looking for information on a pai gow game in Chinatown. You know anything about it?"

He yawned. "I know a little. You want to meet me at the Kope Bean on Hotel Street? I've got a serious caffeine jones going. The *keiki* kept us up all night."

Akoni and his wife, Mealoha, had a baby boy, and after years of protesting that he didn't want to bring a kid into this lousy world, he'd become the most devoted father I'd ever seen.

We were drowning in coffee in this case, and it all seemed to revolve around the Kope Bean. Ray and I drove into the heart of Chinatown, parking in a garage on Pauahi Street, named for one of the royal families of Hawai'i.

Chinatown used to be an exotic location, a place where GIs on R&R from Vietnam found comfort in the arms of prostitutes. But now the streets are dirty, with old soda cans, shriveled dog turds and shreds of newspaper rustling in the wind. Most of the storefronts are shuttered, and many are scrawled with graffiti; the prostitutes only come out at night, along with the ice dealers, and there's nothing much Chinese about it.

There are still a bunch of lei stores on South Beretania and Maunakea Streets, but they're tiny rooms with folding shutters or rolling grills, and most of the leis are behind glass refrigerator cases. You can walk past and only smell car exhaust and fried oil, just a light scent from the flowers the old ladies are stringing. North King is the only street with any life on it—groceries with tubs spilling out to the street, stacked with garlic, ginger, hard-boiled eggs and packages of dried mushrooms, noodles and soy sauce.

There was tinny Chinese music playing somewhere as we walked over to Hotel Street, past a stand with row upon row of leis made of orchids, velvety orange 'ilima flowers and fragrant maile leaves intertwined with tiny white pikake blossoms. Behind the counter, an elderly grandmother sat stringing even more. Chattering teenagers and haole tourists crowded around the booth, debating the merits of different leis and bargaining for better prices.

Akoni was waiting for us with a longboard-sized macadamia latte in his hand. He's the kind of oversized Hawaiian you see working the surfboard concessions at Kuhio Beach Park, wearing a XXL aloha shirt, board shorts and rubber slippers. Tack a badge on his shirt and a gun on his hip, and you've got my ex-partner.

The room was pungent with the smell of fresh-ground coffee, decorated like the others in the chain with sepia-tinted photos of coffee pickers and plantations. A group of Japanese tourists sat in the corner comparing pictures on their digital cameras, and a bald old man with a spotted skull stood by the bar telling stories to the barista.

After Ray and I got our own caffeine bursts, we sat down with Akoni. After seeing pictures of the baby and hearing about how big his lungs were, I asked, "You said you knew about a pai gow game?"

"There are a few games that float around. You know anything specific?"

I told him about Dexter Trale and our suspicion that he was laundering money from a Chinatown game through the Kope

Bean stores.

"You're talking a high stakes game," Akoni said. "To generate that much cash. There's only one game for high rollers. We think it runs out of a back room behind the Wing Wah restaurant, but we haven't been able to get in."

"Tell us about how you play. I told Ray all that I knew, which wasn't much."

"There are seven players. Your four tiles are divided into a front hand and a back hand, two tiles each. You twist them around, trying to match up the dots so you end up with two pair."

He took a sip of his coffee and sighed happily. "If you lose both hands, you lose whatever you bet. If you win one hand and lose the other, it's a push, and you get your bet back."

"Are you playing against all the other players?" I asked.

He shook his head. "It's like blackjack, in that you play against the bank—although the bank can move from person to person. That's how you win big, but it's also how you can lose a ton, if you're the bank and you have to pay off the winners."

"You know when the next game is?" Ray asked.

"Rumor on the street is that there's one going on tonight," Akoni said. "But it's a closed game—you'll never get in the front door."

"We don't need to get in the game—we just need to follow Dexter Trale. He's going to have to stay at the Kope Bean warehouse past his usual shift, because the night guy got killed. We figure he won't bother going home when he finishes—that he'll just go direct to this game. You want to help out with a surveillance?"

Akoni yawned. "Tonight?"

"If you can stay awake that long."

"It'll take a lot more caffeine than this," Akoni said, holding up his paper cup.

We worked out the details and left Akoni calling his partner to set up his end. Back at headquarters, I called Bunchy Parker again. We still needed to talk to his son Brian about his ability to shoot a rifle and his whereabouts when Edith was killed. But Bunchy swore his son wasn't there, and he hadn't seen or spoken to him since the boy left.

"Who knows, maybe he'll show up in Chinatown tonight," Ray said. "If Edith's death and Stuey's are connected to each other and to this game."

I put a request in to see if Brian had left the island by plane, but that was going to take a while. We pitched the stakeout to Lieutenant Sampson, who complained about his budget but eventually authorized the overtime.

By three o'clock, Ray and I were positioned across from the Kope Bean warehouse in my Jeep, in a parking lot for a shipping company where there was enough traffic that we wouldn't be noticed.

We watched as the pallet jockeys left. Dexter remained inside, as we expected, and a beat-up white pickup that matched his registration stayed in the parking lot, sporting a peeling bumper sticker that read "Welcome to Hawai'i. Now go home." A truck arrived from a restaurant supply company, and from our vantage point we could see the driver unload pallets and Dex check them off on a clipboard.

A Kope Bean truck pulled in after the supply truck left, and Dex and the driver loaded it up. After that, nothing more happened until five, when Tuli left.

I called Mike and left a message on his cell that I'd be out late. Akoni and his partner Tony Lee had gone home to take a nap, and around seven they showed up to relieve us. Ray and I went off to dinner, and as we were finishing, Akoni called and said that Dex was on the move.

Trading the lead back and forth, we tracked Dex to Chinatown, where he parked on a side street off North Hotel Street, around the corner from the Wing Wah restaurant. I pulled around to the front of the restaurant and parked down the block, where

Ray and I had a good view of people going in and out. Akoni and Tony parked by the side door, facing the alley behind the restaurant.

It was about nine o'clock by then, and the restaurant was busy. We hunkered down for a long wait. But no more than a few minutes had passed before I saw a familiar figure approach the restaurant and knock on the side door. The sight was so unexpected, though, that it took me until the door had opened, and he'd been ushered in to realize that it was my oldest brother, Lui.

"What's up?" Ray asked. "You recognize somebody?"

I looked over at him. You have to trust your partner; if you hold back information on one case, then you start to get into a pattern, and that's the kind of thing that can get you killed.

"My brother. Lui."

"That's the one from the TV station? You think he's going in there to eat?"

"I wish I knew. We don't even know for certain there's a pai gow game going on in there."

"He ever gamble that you know of?"

I couldn't remember. "My other brother, Haoa, he puts a few bets down on ball games. But Lui, he's always been the straight arrow."

My cell rang. "Hey, brah, isn't that your brother?" Akoni asked. We'd been friends since the academy and partners in Waikīkī for a couple of years, so he'd had the chance to meet my family a bunch of times.

"Yeah."

"Well, get him the fuck out of there. You don't want him falling in the middle of our case."

I couldn't walk up to that side door myself, because ever since I'd come out of the closet and had my picture splashed on the front page of the *Honolulu Advertiser* and the *Star-Bulletin* and become part of the nightly news on Lui's station, KVOL, I was recognized all over town. Usually it was a gay or lesbian person, but I had no way of knowing who would be in that restaurant. And if I saw Dex he'd know we were on to him.

Ray wouldn't be any good, either; Dex knew him, too. And scratch Akoni and his partner; as soon as vice cops walk in some place, everything closes down.

"All right. Give me a few minutes to work something out." I hung up on Akoni, then punched in Haoa's number.

After I exchanged some pleasantries with my sister-in-law, she put my brother on the phone.

"Can you get down to Chinatown, brah? Right now? I need your help."

"I'm gonna miss the last half of the game," he grumbled.

"Call my cell when you're on the road. I'll fill you in."

I slapped the phone shut and looked around. Chinatown's a different place at night. It wakes up, and lights flicker behind storefronts shuttered during the day, though shades are pulled down over any big windows. Restaurant neon glows on every block, and brave tourists mingle with shadowy figures dealing in drugs or other human vices.

A couple of minutes later Haoa and I were on the phone again. I told him only that we had a pai gow game staked out, and I wanted to make sure Lui wasn't involved.

"Shit," Haoa said. "I told him that game was bad news."

"You knew he was playing?"

"He hinted, thought I might want to join in. You know how much money you can run through in a game like that? I told him no thanks."

A guy walked by carrying half a dragon costume, and couples passed us every so often, many talking in Chinese. A string of round red lanterns was suspended over the street, and across from me, a strand of tiny white lights had been wrapped around the trunk of a palm tree.

When Haoa pulled up down the block and walked over to my Jeep, I said, "We're not going to bust the game tonight. I want to know if he's in there for dinner, or if he's in some back room gambling."

"You really want to know?" Haoa said. He's as tall as I am but broader in the chest, and his skin is a shade darker. He was wearing a dark green U.H. Warriors T-shirt, ratty sweat pants and rubber Crocs. "What if he's got some girl there?"

Lui had never said anything, but both Haoa and I thought our oldest brother had stepped out on his wife a time or two. "Whatever he's doing, it's a mistake. I want to know, and you do, too."

"Yeah. I'll be back."

I watched him walk across the street and go into the restaurant. "You think this is a smart idea?" Ray asked.

"Maybe, maybe not. But it's the only one I've got."

My cell rang, with a call from Harry. I let it go to voice mail, figuring I'd get back to him when things were slow. Then Haoa stepped out onto the sidewalk and pulled his cell out of his pocket. It was weird watching him dial, then having my phone ring with his call.

"I don't see Lui anywhere," he said. "That side door must lead to a private room. Keep your mouth shut. I'm going to conference him in."

I was impressed. I didn't know how to set up a conference call on my cell; I barely knew how to turn the damn thing on and off. I held the phone out so Ray could listen, too, and we heard the sound of dialing and ringing. Then I heard Lui's voice, low. "This is a bad time, brah."

"You bet it is," Haoa said, keeping his own voice low so no one on Lui's end could overhear him. "If you're in a pai gow game at the Wing Wah restaurant, get your ass outside pronto."

"How the fuck do you know where I am?" Lui said, and I was so surprised at hearing my very proper big brother curse I nearly dropped the phone.

"Outside. Now," Haoa said. "Or you're going to be in a world of trouble."

Haoa hung up, and I did too. And then we waited.

About five minutes passed before Lui walked out of the front door of the restaurant. I saw him start to argue with Haoa, who motioned over toward my Jeep. I said, "I'll be right back," to Ray and jumped out.

"Are you fucking spying on me?" Lui said to me as I walked up. "Your own brother?"

His tie was askew, and there was alcohol on his breath. This was not the brother I knew, the one who was always so well-groomed, so much in control.

"Jesus, Lui, get a grip. You walked right in the middle of my case. You expect me to leave you in there?"

The red neon from the Wing Wah window played against his face. "For real?" he asked.

"Let's get you a cup of coffee." I turned to Haoa. "Thanks, brah. I can take it from here."

"I don't even want to know," Haoa said, and he walked off toward his truck.

I motioned to Ray to join us, and we all walked around the corner to the same Kope Bean where we'd met Akoni earlier in the day. While Ray ordered three more of the macadamia lattes and my brother sat in an overstuffed chair looking sick, I called Akoni and filled him in.

"We'll keep an eye on Dex," he said. "Let me know what your brother has to say."

"You put me in a bad situation," Lui said, when we'd sat down. "The game had just started, and I had to fold."

"You put yourself in the bad situation, brah. Start from the beginning. How long have you been playing?"

"Off and on? Since college."

It was my turn to be incredulous. "For real?" I asked, echoing him.

He shrugged.

"How long at this game?"

He pursed his lips. "Maybe six, nine months. A buddy of mine introduced me."

"Some buddy. In addition to gambling being illegal, which a solid, upstanding citizen like you ought to know, we're thinking there's something corrupt about this game, that it's connected to a couple of murders."

"It was just a little innocent gambling, like betting on ball games. Where's the harm in that?"

"Are you stupid, brah?" I asked. "Where's the harm? The harm is in violating the law. You want to get pulled in on a sting one day? See your face in the *Star-Advertiser*? Maybe even one of the camera guys from your station films you doing the perp walk? How long you think you can keep your fancy job, your big house, your Mercedes, after they arrest you?"

He opened his mouth to argue and then shut it. It looked like he was finally realizing the trouble he was in.

It was nearly ten, and I'd been on the go since six when I woke up and walked the dog. I was running out of patience, even for a guy who changed my diapers a time or two. "You know a *moke* named Dexter Trale?" I asked Lui, trying to soften my voice a little. Moke was an island term for a two-bit hood, which was a pretty good description of Dex.

"We don't use names. Everybody has a Chinese nickname."

"Skinny haole. Tattooed like crazy."

"Yeah. That's Lan Long. Blue dragon. Like his tattoo."

"I have to ask. What's yours?"

"Yuan."

I racked my brain for the little Chinese I knew. "Money?"

"It either means dollar, or first," he said.

Of course. Lui was the first of us boys and the one who cared most about money. "How much cash changes hands in a typical game?" I asked, thinking of Stuey's assertion that Dexter Trale was packing up bundles of cash in the warehouse at night.

"I don't pay that much attention," Lui said, but I knew he was lying.

I kept looking at him.

"Maybe twenty grand a night," he said, looking down at his lap.

Ray whistled. "From seven players?"

"High stakes," Lui said.

I didn't even ask if his wife Liliha knew what he was doing—because of course, she didn't. "Who walks off with the money at the end of the night?"

"Depends on who wins."

Again, I looked at him.

"I win sometimes, all right? This guy we call Tung runs the game. He always walks away with some cash."

"Not Dexter—I mean Blue Dragon?"

He shook his head. "Lan Long's the worst player. I think he works for Tung somehow, that's how he gets in the game. And plus, he's so bad, he draws money out from the rest of us."

"How often do you play?" I asked.

"Once a week. That's all, I swear. I just lose a couple of grand here and there."

"Still, if Tung walks away with ten or fifteen grand for a night, it's hardly worth a big money laundering operation," I said, frowning.

Lui looked back toward the restaurant. His profile was tense. "It's not the only game." He looked back at me. "Tung runs a couple of games. *Fan tan*, 13 card, a couple of other pai gow games with lower stakes. And he's got a room full of video poker machines in an old warehouse off River Street."

I pulled out a pad and pen. "Details, brah."

"I never played any of the other games," Lui said. "But Tung mentions them now and then. And he said any time we want to play video poker, we just let him know."

"What do you know about this guy Tung?" I asked. "Chinese?"

He shook his head. "Japanese. Scary. He was changing his shirt one day and his whole body looks like it's covered in tattoos. Like a yakuza, you know?"

The yakuza were Japan's version of the Mafia, a criminal network that had its fingers in all kinds of bad stuff, there and in the US.

"Could be he just likes tattoos," Ray said.

"You see rings on his arms?" I asked Lui.

He nodded. "Bunch of them."

"Yakuza tattoo a ring around the arm for each crime they commit," I said. "Yeah, it could be he's just an ordinary Japanese guy who happens to like tattoos. Or he could be a yakuza. Considering he's running illegal gambling, I'm tending to think he's a criminal."

Lui either didn't have more details than that, or he wasn't saying. He kept drumming his fingers on the arm of the chair and licking his lips. I realized he was scared, and that was something I'd never seen in my big brother, the one who had always seemed to have everything under control.

"Time for you to head home, brah. Don't even think about going back to that game. Not unless you want your brothers dragging you out of there on your ass."

"You won't tell Liliha, will you?"

For a minute there, I could see my brother Lui, maybe fifteen or sixteen, asking me to keep a secret from our parents. I don't even remember what it was, but I didn't tell then, and I wouldn't now.

"Go home. Your wife and kids love you."

We all stood up together, and my reserved brother, the one I almost never see without a suit and tie, hugged me. I hugged him back, my arms reaching around his broad back as if I could protect him from his own bad impulses.

I yawned as Lui walked out. We hadn't heard anything from Akoni, which meant the game was still going on.

"Big money," Ray said. "And your brother thinks Dexter works for this guy called Tung. You think maybe he's Mr. T? Tung? Not Dexter?"

"Don't know. But I think those nicknames stay in the game. I wouldn't expect an outsider like Stuey to know that name."

"But what if Dexter called him that?"

My cell rang. "Looks like the game's breaking up," Akoni said. "You out front?"

We were, in a manner of speaking. "Yup. We'll cover the front door. And tomorrow, brah, I gotta talk to you."

We saw a group of men exit, Dexter Trale among them. A couple were laughing and talking, while the others were silent. Winners and losers, I thought.

One of the guys, Japanese by the looks of him, was wearing a bright aloha shirt with a pattern of 'ilima flowers, the kind used in fragrant leis, and carrying a white canvas bag with a wooden handle.

Ray and I had a choice. We could go after Dexter Trale or the guy with the satchel. It seemed a no-brainer to follow the money. I called Akoni, and he pulled up behind us as the guy in the 'ilima shirt got into a Mercedes sedan. We traded off following him, one of us dropping back while the other stayed close, then reversing positions, until he led us to the Kope Bean warehouse.

We both parked under a kiawe tree across the street and watched as the man with the satchel walked up to the warehouse building, punched a code at the front door and stepped inside. I dialed Akoni.

"I'd love to know what's going on in there. But I don't see how we can. We don't have a warrant, and we don't have any grounds to get one, especially without some testimony by the late Stuart McKinney."

"Just adding data to the bank," he said.

I called the license plate in to the dispatcher, who put me on hold. When he came back he said the car was registered to a corporation—Mahalo Coffee, LLC.

"That doesn't tell us much," Ray said. "We're at the Kope Bean warehouse, and we know Mahalo is the name of the corporate parent."

We sat there and watched and waited. There was a constant hum of traffic from the H1, a block away. Clouds moved across the dark sky, obscuring the quarter moon and whatever stars might be shining. A few minutes after midnight, a man walked out the front door. I pulled out my binoculars and adjusted the focus. It was Ezekiel Kapuāiwa.

Akoni called. "You know who that is?"

I filled him in on Ezekiel. "He used to work at the Kope Bean. Maybe somebody called him to help out now that McKinney's dead."

Ezekiel walked over to the Mercedes and stood there. A couple of minutes later, the man in the ʻilima shirt came out. Both got into the Mercedes, which pulled out of the parking lot. I called Akoni. "You ready to follow again?"

"You take lead," he said.

We followed the Mercedes, which ducked under the H1 freeway and continued up into Papakolea. Ezekiel got out in front of a house a few blocks from where Edith Kapana had lived, and the Mercedes returned the way it had come, getting on the H1 going Diamond Head.

Akoni and I traded off position on the highway as we followed the Mercedes off the H1 and onto local roads all the way to Black Point, an exclusive neighborhood on the far side of Diamond Head. The car pulled up in front of a wrought-iron gate, which slowly swung open as we cruised past.

We noted the address, and Akoni headed back toward the highway.

"What's going on here?" Ray asked, as we drove away. "Does Edith's murder tie into the pai gow game? How could she have known about the game or the money laundering?"

"Well, she lived with Dexter Trale, and Dex worked with Stuey at the Kope Bean warehouse. Maybe she overheard Dex talking to Leelee. Everybody said she was a nosy old woman."

"I can't see Ezekiel playing pai gow; he doesn't seem to have two nickels to rub together," Ray said.

"Suppose Edith knew money from the game was going to support KOH. She believed in the kahiko ways, the old-time beliefs. So she probably didn't like gambling. Ezekiel told Edith, and she tried to either stop the game or stop the money coming to KOH."

We kept going back to her visit to the Ohana, where she had been asking about Ezekiel. What was that about? Was she trying to get in touch with him to confirm her beliefs about the pai gow game?

By the time I dropped Ray off at his place and got back to Aiea, my brain felt like it had been disconnected. There were too many loose ends, and none of them led us back to Edith's death.

It was almost midnight, and all I wanted to do was collapse into bed. Roby was so excited to see me, though, that I had to stop and play with him for a minute. I was grateful that Mike was already asleep, so I didn't have to tell him about my day or what I'd learned about Stuart McKinney's murder. I stripped down, slid beside him and was asleep in minutes, lulled by the even rhythm of his breathing.

Unknown Number

The next morning, Roby stopped to sniff a trash can with a broken surfboard sticking up out of it. That reminded me that besides the outing with my nieces and nephews, I hadn't been surfing much since I'd moved up to Mike's house. I couldn't just grab my board and walk down the street. And now that we had a dog who needed to be walked every morning, I had that much less time. I wondered if that was part of growing up—or if I was sacrificing something I loved in order to make life with Mike work.

By the time Roby and I got back to the house, Mike was up, in the kitchen pouring cereal into a bowl. "What time did you get home last night?" he asked.

I tried not to hear accusation in his voice. "After midnight." I told him about the pai gow game and the results of our surveillance.

"Your brother?" He stopped eating to look at me.

"We've all got secrets. Look at the big one I kept for so long."

Mike didn't say anything. His parents know he's gay and so do at least a few of the guys he works with. But he believed that his sexual orientation was his own business. So it wasn't actually a secret he was keeping, but close enough.

I hurried on. "We got the coroner's report on Stuart McKinney. He was knocked out with a blunt instrument before he was set on fire. And by the way, he wasn't homeless—he was on his way back to the Ohana after work."

"Why are you on that case? I thought it was Hart and Kawika."

"Ray and I took it over." I told him about our conversation with McKinney, about all the connections between victims, the Ohana and the Kope Bean.

"I still think this was random. The guy was wearing three layers of clothes, he had shaggy hair and dirty fingernails. He looked homeless." He stood up, rinsed his cereal bowl and put it in the dishwasher. Then he turned to walk out of the kitchen.

"Hey," I said. "Kiss."

I was still sitting at the kitchen table, so he leaned down and kissed the top of my head, which wasn't what I was hoping for. A minute later I heard the shower running, and I had a perverse desire to get up and run hot water in the sink, forcing cold into the shower and getting back at him for walking out in the middle our argument about Stuey's death. All that rampant testosterone in the house, I guess. We both felt like we had to win any battle.

On his way out, Mike said, "Harry called last night. Said you weren't answering your cell, but he had some information for you."

"Thanks." I waved goodbye to Mike, then showered and dressed. On my way out the door, I called Harry. "Hey, brah, not too early to call?" It was about a quarter to eight.

"Nope, Brandon started school yesterday. This household is officially on morning time. You want to stop by, see what I found on your guys?"

"Be there in a minute."

It was only a couple of blocks downhill to their house, and I pulled up by the sidewalk. I saw Harry look out the front window and waved. Arlene had cleaned him up since the wedding; his hair no longer looked like someone had put a bowl over his head and snipped, and his ordinary black-framed glasses had been replaced with a funky pair that made him look like a '50s hipster.

Arleen had left to take Brandon to school and then go grocery shopping, so Harry and I had the house to ourselves. We sat at his dining room table as he showed me what he'd found. "Your Jun Tanaka is a slippery guy. Took me a while to find anything on him. But nobody hides from me for too long."

"Yeah, yeah, you're a super hero. What do you have?"

"I got interested, so I started digging," he said. "Most of this comes from legal sources, places you could go yourself if you knew where to look. So it'll hold up in court if you have to go there."

"Most?"

"I'll get to that part."

Ray would be happy with the legitimate stuff, but I knew he wouldn't want to touch anything Harry got by hacking. Ray was my conscience when it came to cutting corners. He was a by-the-book cop, always remembering that anything we did had to follow the letter of the law. I was more like a bull in a china shop, trying anything I could to get the job done and catch the bad guys. We made a good team. I'd see what Harry had before making any judgments.

Harry pushed a couple of printouts toward me. "Tanaka started making regular trips to the States years ago. There's a possibility that things got hot for him in Japan around that time; I found some documents, but Arleen can only speak the language, she can't read it that well. If it matters, you'll have to get a translator."

"OK," I said. "Next?"

"He owns a holding company called Tanaka Investments," Harry continued. "There's a complex web of interlocking companies, but I figured out that it's the corporate parent for the Kope Bean chain of coffee shops, as well as a bunch of other businesses."

"The Kope Bean."

"Yeah. Since you mentioned Kingdom of Hawai'i I did a cross-reference. The Kope Bean is the largest single donor to KOH, according to an annual report they filed with the state. A couple of other companies under Tanaka Investments are also big donors."

Threads were starting to come together. Tanaka's companies contributed heavily to Kingdom of Hawai'i, and Edith Kapana was murdered at a KOH rally. Stuart McKinney and Dexter Trale worked for the Kope Bean, which meant there might a link between Stuey's death and the pai gow game in Chinatown. But those were tenuous associations; we had no smoking gun, no motive for either death. Just cop intuition.

I told Harry about McKinney's murder and all the connections between the Kope Bean and the Ohana.

"Makes sense," he said. "If he's on the board of this Ohana place, then he'd want to help out, right? He'd be willing to hire some of their clients."

"I hope that's all it is." He handed me a few pages of corporate mumbo jumbo, and I put it aside to look at more carefully later. "Anything about him personally? Other than his involvement with the Ohana?"

"He has a wife and a son back in Tokyo, but he hasn't been to Japan in at least five years, which makes me think he might not be welcome there anymore. Now here's where it gets interesting. His father is a guy named Hisoshi Tanaka, and from what I can tell he's a big time criminal."

I struggled to remember my conversation with Terri about Tanaka's background. "Was his father born in an internment camp?" I asked.

"That's him. Hisoshi was born in the Honouliuli camp, up near Schofield Barracks, then sent back to Japan with his family when he was a kid. He was arrested for gambling and prostitution in Japan, when he was young, but then it looks like he got smart. The papers call him a crime boss, but he hasn't been in jail in years."

"And Jun Tanaka is his son."

"Yup. The old man started buying property in the US in the '70s. He was connected to a toxic waste dump near Waianae and a sweatshop in Chinatown. Jun sold those businesses and reinvested in legitimate stuff, under the radar. But he still sounds shady to me—I never trust somebody who tries so hard to hide his identity and his interests."

"Good stuff. I appreciate all the work, brah." I hesitated. "So what part of this isn't quite kosher?"

"The printouts in Japanese," he said. "They might come from a computer that's connected to the Japanese national police. So you'd have to make an official request to them for criminal records on both Tanakas if you need them."

Might come, I thought, as I packed up the records. At least I knew what I could and couldn't use.

I felt that we'd wandered far away from Aunty Edith's murder, and as I drove downtown and listened to Paula Fuga's smoky voice streaming from the Jeep's CD player, I tried to figure out how we'd gotten to this point—tracking Jun Tanaka and a mysterious pai gow game—when we'd started with a single shooting.

Ray was on the phone at his desk when I walked in. "The house in Black Point where the man in the aloha shirt went last night belongs to Mahalo Coffee," he said. "And I got the plates of the Mercedes tracked to that same address, same corporate ownership."

I showed him the material I collected from Harry. "And this is all legit, by the way, in case you were worrying. Except for the stuff in Japanese, which we can't read anyway."

He tidied the corners of the Japanese printouts and put them aside without saying anything. Then he pulled out a pen and a piece of paper and we started to draw lines between people and organizations.

"At least we don't need to call your buddy at the Division of Business Licensing to figure out who owns the Kope Bean," Ray said, when we had it all laid out. "It's Mahalo Coffee, which means that guy we saw leave the game was probably Tanaka."

"And Tanaka is connected to every person and every organization in this case," I sad. My cell phone rang, the display reading "unknown number."

"This is Kimo," I said.

"The detective?" a woman asked.

"Yes, it is. Who's this?"

"I know who killed Stuey," she said, her voice rushing so fast she was stumbling over the words. "And I'm scared."

There was something odd about her accent, or perhaps it was just the speed or the whistling way she spoke. "OK, calm down. Tell me your name." I turned the phone so Ray could hear, too.

"I need to see you. I live at the Ohana. Can you come up here right away?"

"We can. But who do we ask for?"

"I'll find you. Just come now. Please." She hung up.

"What do you think?" I asked Ray.

"She sounds either frightened or crazy," he said. "Because she lives at the Ohana, I'm going with crazy. But that doesn't mean we don't have to go up there."

It took us close to forty-five minutes to make it up the Pali Highway, over the mountains and down into Kaneohe. As I pulled the Jeep into the Ohana parking lot we both looked around, hoping that there would be a frantic woman waiting for us at the front door.

Nothing.

There were a couple of cars in the lot—I assumed they belonged to staff—but no one out on the front lawn or by the glass door that led inside. We both got out of the Jeep and walked together toward the door. I was holding my keys in my hand, and I fumbled them, trying to get them in my pocket. They fell to the ground, and both Ray and I went down to retrieve them, nearly bumping heads as we did.

I guess that's how the shots missed us.

We both sensed the bullets whizzing above us before we heard the sound of the shots, and we tumbled to the blacktop, scrambling around to the far side of the Jeep. Both of us drew our guns, caught our breath and waited.

Traffic whizzed past on the street in front of us. No one came running out of the Ohana, and none of the shoppers going in and out of the neighboring strip centers seemed to have heard the sound of the gunshots.

"I counted four shots," Ray said, panting a little. He'd scraped his cheek on the rough pavement, and there was a trickle of blood curving around his jawbone.

"Me, too." I grabbed my phone and dialed dispatch, reporting the shots and requesting backup. As I did, Ray pulled himself up and peered over the hood of the Jeep.

"I figure the shooter was up on the hill there," he said, pointing, as I joined him. The Ohana and its neighbors all butted up against a hillside. A few trees and some low bushes stood just behind and above the strip shopping center next door, on a small outcropping.

We heard a siren in the distance and assumed that was our backup. "Think he's gone by now?" I asked.

"Only one way to tell," Ray said, and stood up, walking around the front of the Jeep. He had his gun drawn, though it wasn't going to be much good against a rifleman under cover at least a few hundred yards away.

There were no more shots. I joined Ray, and we looked around. One of the bullets had lodged in a tree just beyond us, the second and third in the stucco exterior wall of the Ohana. The fourth had embedded itself in my bumper.

"Son of a bitch," I said.

Once the patrol car arrived, Ray and I went up to the wooded spot above the shopping center while the officers waited for crime scene techs. We found the place where the shooter had lain flat on the ground, some ferns and a couple of small branches broken under his or her weight. We scoured the area for shell casings but couldn't find any.

We finally went inside and asked about our caller, though by that point we were pretty sure she hadn't been at the Ohana at all. The receptionist assured us that no one had spoken to her about expecting the police, and none of the female clients or staff we spoke to matched the accent I had heard on the phone.

On the way back to headquarters, Ray and I hashed out what we could learn from the incident. "We know for sure now that the Ohana is connected. Otherwise whoever it was that wanted to shoot us wouldn't have known to call us up there."

"The woman had your cell number," he said. "How'd she get it? Must have been off the back of your card." He opened his notebook. "Let's start with who you gave a card to."

"Too many, brah. All the old ladies marching with Aunty Edith, the tenants in the building the shooter used, the old people at the community center. And that's just for starters."

"Let's focus on the people connected to the case," he said. "Dexter Trale, Leelee, Bunchy Parker, Maile Kanuha and Ezekiel Kapuāiwa."

"David Currie at the Ohana. The receptionist and the counselors."

We worked on the list all the way back to headquarters, but none of the women on the list matched that voice I heard, and it didn't bring us any closer to finding out who had made the call.

At our desks, we went back to the pages Harry had given me and our diagram connecting people. When we finished, I said, "We've still got those pages Harry printed out in Japanese. My mother is half-Japanese, but I'm almost certain she doesn't understand written *kanji*. One of her sisters might know more, though, or one of my cousins. I'm going to call her and see if she knows anyone to translate."

"Your family's already in this case up to their butts," Ray said. He'd gotten his cheek patched up, but we were both pretty shaky after getting shot at, both of us spoiling for the fight we hadn't had a chance at with our unknown shooter. "Your mom helping Leelee, your brother gambling. Let's try and avoid drawing any more of them in, okay?" I was surprised that he didn't knock out the idea of using the pages completely. I guess I'm having an influence on him.

"You have a better idea?"

"How about we do this the right way, get a department translator?"

"Okay." I opened up my drawer and pulled out a requisition form. The department still hadn't moved far enough into the 21st century to put multi-part forms on line; this one needed signatures from our lieutenant and his boss, as well as the assistant chief in charge of support services. We had to attach copies of all the relevant documents, as well as a detailed explanation of what we needed and how it related to an ongoing investigation.

"You get to fill out the form," I said, handing it to him. "Last I heard there's a three-week backlog for translators. Be sure to indicate that we don't know where the pages came from. Call it an anonymous source. And maybe by the time we get a translator assigned, we'll have enough evidence to make the connection between Tanaka and the murders."

Ray took the paper from me and looked it up and down. He frowned, then said, "There's a Japanese guy in Julie's program. I can get her to ask him."

"Make sure you get his name and social security number, so we can run a background check on him before we give him access to sensitive materials," I said.

"You're an asshole, you know that?"

"You want to run everything by the book. Just covering your back, brah."

He slid the translator request in his desk drawer. "Call your mother."

I asked how she was doing, and she told me she was in the living room, pruning a bonsai my grandfather had created. I knew it; that stunted pine that was older than any of our living relatives. I explained what I needed. In the background, I could hear the TV going, most likely KVOL, Lui's station. That made me think about my big brother. It was one thing to pull him out of a pai gow game, but if he had a serious gambling habit that was a much bigger problem.

"Your cousin Ben," my mother said, and it took me a minute to remember what I'd asked her.

"Surfer Ben?" The last time I'd seen Ben, I was working undercover on the North Shore, and he was a competitive surfer following the waves.

"He majored in business at U.H. and minored in Japanese. Your Aunt Pua is always saying how he's going to be a big businessman when he finishes surfing. I think she's jealous that my sons are all so successful."

"Yeah, we're a bunch of princes. Any idea where Ben is these days? Surf's lousy on the North Shore."

"I'll call Pua and ask her. I owe her a call anyway."

I wondered how my mother could owe any of her sisters a call, when it seemed like she spoke to each of them every day. She was the oldest and Pua the youngest; Aunt Pua was an unreformed flower child, a hippie, far from my prim and proper mother. She was an aromatherapist at a posh resort in Hawai'i Kai and had been married and divorced three times. Ben was her youngest child.

When I hung up, Ray was pulling pages off the fax machine. It was the report we requested on Bunchy Parker's son Brian, the

Army sharpshooter who had gone missing shortly after Edith's death. "He hasn't left Oahu by plane," Ray said. "He could be on a boat, or he could be holed up somewhere."

"Or he could be dead."

"I called the morgue, but they don't have any John Does who match Brian's description."

"Doesn't mean he isn't dead. Just nobody's found the body yet."

"You're such a cheerful guy," Ray said. "I'm going to do some more checking. I still think he's a good suspect."

"While you do that, I'm going down to Vice."

I found Akoni at his desk and filled him in on what my brother had said about the other games—fan tan and 13 card, other Chinese gambling games and the video poker machines allegedly in the warehouse on River Street.

"We've been hearing rumors about those," Akoni said. "Nobody would say where they were, though. You get an address?"

"Just River Street."

"You think you could convince your brother to express an interest in them?" Akoni asked. "Get some more information?"

"I can try. He's spooked right now. You know, he's always been number one son, and nothing ever goes wrong for him. Last night was a wakeup call."

Akoni promised to keep me in the loop if he found out anything that might relate to my case, and I promised the same thing about his. When I got back upstairs, Ray and I ran the cases down for Lieutenant Sampson.

Behind him, I saw a photo of his stepdaughter Kitty, in her dark green U.H. cap and gown, holding her diploma case against her side, with a collection of leis around her neck. I wondered if her mother, who had abandoned her to Sampson's care years before, had come to her graduation, and for a moment I lost the thread of our conversation. When I snapped back I realized Ray was talking.

"What we saw last night outside the Wing Wah supports what Stuart McKinney told us—that a guy called Mr. T brought a satchel of money to the warehouse at night. At first we thought it was Dexter Trale, but now we believe it's Jun Tanaka."

Sampson leaned back in his high-backed chair. His polo shirt for the day was an olive green, which looked good with his chocolate-brown slacks.

I threw in what Levi had told us about suspecting Tanaka. "Mr. Hirsch is a savvy businessman. I believe there's something fishy going on."

"So you think someone killed McKinney because he blabbed about the money?" Sampson asked.

We both nodded.

"And how does this tie into the woman's death at the rally?"

"That's the part we're not sure about," I said. "But there are so many links."

"Sounds like you're making a lot of very tenuous assumptions." He sat back at his desk and steepled his fingers, and I felt like a kid who'd been called in to the principal's office. "Is there a single thing in your file we could take to the DA?"

I resisted the urge to open my mouth and start talking. Ray didn't, though. "We're making a lot of progress," he protested.

"How do you even know these murders are connected?" Sampson asked. "You have no direct link between the woman who was shot at the rally and the homeless man who was beaten and then set on fire."

"He wasn't homeless, just crazy." I started ticking things off on my fingers. "Stuart McKinney worked with Dexter Trale, who shared a house with Edith Kapana. Stuey lived at the Ohana, in Kaneohe, and the day before she died, Edith went up there to ask about Ezekiel Kapuāiwa. Ezekiel lived at the Ohana for a while and worked at the Kope Bean—where Stuey and Dex worked and which is owned by Jun Tanaka. Tanaka is the backer behind the Kingdom of Hawai'i, which Ezekiel leads and which sponsored the rally where Edith was killed. And somebody who knows the Ohana is involved in this case thought we were getting close enough to call us into an ambush this morning."

Ray jumped in. "Bunchy Parker runs a rival group to the Kingdom of Hawai'i. His son Brian was a sharpshooter in the Army. He could have shot Edith. And Stuey's murder could be tied into money laundering at the Kope Bean warehouse, money that could be funding KOH. Maybe Stuey told Brian or Bunchy about the money."

"That's what I mean," Sampson said. "You guys are all over the place. So essentially you've got nothing. However, you have gotten somebody scared enough to take some pot shots at you, which means you must be getting close. You have two more days to show me some progress, or I'm putting you back in the rotation."

"Two days," Ray grumbled, as we walked out of Sampson's office. "How much are we going to figure out in two days? We've had a week and a half so far, and we still don't have a strong suspect or a smoking gun."

"Then we've got work to do."

My cell rang as I reached my desk. Jimmy Chang was a beat cop I'd known for a while, who had recently been transferred downtown from Mānoa.

"Aloha, brah," he said. "We've got a visual on that Dodge pickup you were looking for. Plates match the BOLO."

It took me a few seconds to realize he meant Brian Parker's truck. "Where are you?"

"Across from a convenience store two blocks ewa from Ala Moana Mall."

"On our way." We got there about five minutes later, pulling up next to Jimmy's cruiser. He was leaning against the car, talking to an officer in uniform I recognized as Kitty Cardozo, Lieutenant Sampson's stepdaughter.

I met Kitty soon after I started working for Sampson, and she came out to me as a lesbian a few months later. The lieutenant wanted her to go to law school after she graduated from U.H., but Kitty was determined to go to the police academy. I knew from the lieutenant that she had graduated at the top of her class, but I'd never seen her on patrol before.

"Kimo!" She kissed my cheek and hugged me. "It's great to see you."

Jimmy looked at me. "You two know each other?"

I looked at Kitty. "He doesn't know?"

"I didn't want to tell anyone," she said. "I didn't want anybody to think I was riding on my dad's coattails."

Jimmy was looking confused, though I had an idea that Ray recognized her from the pictures in Sampson's office. Kitty turned to Jimmy and said, "Lieutenant Sampson in CID is my stepfather. Sorry. I guess I should have told you."

Jimmy did not look happy. "Cardozo's in the FTEP," he said

to us. FTEP stands for Field Training and Evaluation Program; newly graduated recruits were partnered with experienced officers so they could apply the theoretical knowledge they gained at the academy to hands-on field training.

I understood why Jimmy wouldn't be happy. He was young, in his late twenties, though he'd been on patrol long enough to qualify as Kitty's supervisor. If I were him, I'd worry that every screw-up, every shortcut, would end up filtering back to Sampson.

"Congratulations," I said to Kitty. "And you, too, Jimmy. You won't find a smarter, more dedicated trainee."

"And I don't tell my dad anything that happens on the job," she said.

Jimmy seemed to relax. "You see who was driving that pickup?" Ray asked, pointing to the truck we thought belonged to Brian Parker. Just as he did, though, a guy who matched Brian's description exited the convenience store and headed for the truck.

Ray and I cut him off. "Mr. Parker?" I asked, showing him my shield. "Honolulu PD. We'd like to ask you a few questions."

Brian looked around as if mapping out an escape route and saw Jimmy and Kitty behind us. "What's up?"

He had a super-sized soda in one hand and a bag of chips in the other. I wondered if he'd been smoking pakalolo, but his eyes weren't red. "We've been looking for you for a couple of days," I said. "What have you been up to?"

"Just chilling." He was a skinny guy, a couple inches under six feet, with what looked like military tattoos on his arms.

"You still pretty good with a rifle?" Ray asked. "You were some kind of marksman in the Army."

Brian shrugged and took a drink of his soda. "I get out in the country and practice sometimes. No law against that, is there?"

"How do you feel about Hawaiian nationalism?" I asked. "Your dad's pretty involved in it. How about you?"

"What's this all about? Is my dad in trouble again?"

"We'll ask the questions for a while, how's that?" Ray said. "We ask, you answer."

Brian took a long sip from his soda, then said, "The whole nationalism thing, it's my dad's gig. Me, I could care less."

I nodded. "Want to tell us where you were on Statehood Day, eleven in the morning?"

He bit his lip. "You won't tell my father, will you?"

I knew from his army records that Brian Parker was nearly thirty. Old enough that his father's opinion shouldn't matter. I wondered what he was hiding and why. "Not unless we have to," I said.

"I have a girlfriend," Brian said. "She's haole, though, and my dad don't like us to mix. So I haven't told him."

"You were with her that Friday morning?" I asked.

He nodded. "I've been working private security at night, off the books, for this rapper dude over from the mainland to work on an album. Days, I'm at her house." We got her name and address, and Ray stepped away to call her and verify the alibi.

"You know anybody involved with your dad's group, or any group for that matter, who might have had a reason to disrupt the KOH rally, kill that old lady?"

Brian relaxed and leaned back against his truck, tearing open the bag of chips. He offered it to me but I shook my head.

"My dad's got a temper, you know that," he said, grabbing a handful of chips from the bag. "But he's not the kind of guy to plan out killing someone, certainly not an old lady."

He chomped noisily and then drank some soda. I stood there in the sun, my patience wearing, as Kitty and Jimmy stood at ease in the background.

"Most of the people in my dad's group, they're the same way," Brian said, crumpling the top of the chip bag. "More interested in culture than violence. You ask me, the real nuts are the guys from KOH. You ever seen that Ezekiel dude, the one who says he's descended from Kamehameha? He's seriously crazy."

"Yeah, I got that idea myself."

Ray came back to us, and I could see from the disappointment on his face that Brian's alibi stood up. And after talking to Brian, I thought he wasn't involved, but I took his cell number, in case we needed him again.

"Doesn't mean she isn't covering for him," Ray said, as we got back in the Jeep. "Brian's girlfriend." But I could hear in his voice that he had given up.

We were frustrated. We had only two days to solve two murders, and no leads. And yet, we must be getting close, or why would someone shoot at us?

By the time we got back to headquarters it was time to clock out, and we had no reason to stick around and rack up overtime. Mike was already home by the time I got there, and he'd walked and fed the dog. They were sitting on the sofa in the living room reading the newspaper. At least Mike was; I think Roby was just looking at the pictures.

Mike suggested we go out to dinner, to the little Italian place down the hill that we'd developed a fondness for. We talked out our current cases, and some of my frustration eased just being with him and being able to share what was going on in both our lives. When we got back home we ended up in bed, and I felt pretty good about the way things were working out between us.

ROTTING BEANS

I overslept, and by the time I woke up Mike had already left for work. There was a note on the kitchen table—"I fed and walked the dog"—with no signature. Since we had no *menehunes*, little Hawaiian elves, living with us, I figured it had come from him. There was a happy face at the end of the note.

When Ray and I met up at headquarters, he said, "I've been thinking. This case keeps coming back around to the Kope Bean."

"Yeah," I said, sitting down at my desk and leaning back in my chair. We'd been to the distribution center where Dex and Stuey worked, the branch in Kaneohe where Ezekiel had been a barista, not to mention various places we'd gone just for coffee, like the Chinatown store on Hotel Street, where we'd talked with Akoni and then with my brother Lui.

"If there's money laundering going on, you'd think someone at the store level might know about it," Ray said, drumming his fingers on his desk.

"I don't know. Usually the baristas are teenagers. But there was that older woman we talked to. What was her name? Mili? We could go look her up again."

"Sounds like a good place to start."

I called the Kope Bean store and found out that Mili no longer worked there. "You know her last name?" I asked.

The girl put me on hold. I got to listen to Israel Kamakawiwo'ole while I waited, but by the third song I was ready to reach through the phone, grab his ukulele, and use it to bludgeon the clerk who'd left me on hold for so long.

When the girl came back, she said, "France."

"Excuse me? She went to France?"

"No, it's her last name," the girl said. "Mili France. Listen, I got customers. I gotta go."

She hung up on me, which didn't improve my disposition toward her. But at least we had a last name on Mili, and it wasn't Peed or Meter. I looked Mili France up in the phone book, and found an address in Kaneohe, a few blocks from the Kope Bean. I called the number, but there was no answer and no machine.

My cell rang. "I couldn't get hold of Pua until now," my mother said. "She has a new boyfriend." The ice in her voice could have chilled Kilauea.

"And?"

"Your cousin Ben is at Pua's till tomorrow."

"Thanks, Mom. Love to Dad."

I hung up and dialed my Aunt Pua's condo. Ben had just gotten in from surfing; he said he could hang around and wait for us to stop by.

"Change of plan," I told Ray. "Let's swing out to Hawai'i Kai before we look for Mili, see if my cousin can read any of the Japanese stuff Harry found."

My aunt's condo was in a two-story building on a canal with a lanai overlooking the water. I figured aromatherapy must pay well, or else she had some good alimony coming in from one or more of her previous husbands.

Ben greeted us at the door. He's good-looking, in a scrawny, surfer way, but he had a soul patch on his chin that made me want to hand him a razor. There didn't look like an ounce of fat on his six-foot something body, and he wore his black hair loose, down to his shoulders. His father was a haole Aunt Pua married and divorced in Vegas, and none of us ever met him. Like me, Ben looks a little Asian around his eyes, and his skin takes a tan well.

He offered us beers, which sadly we had to decline, though he indulged. He led us out to the lanai, where we sat down amid a forest of purple and white Vanda orchids, the music of the current in the waterway behind us.

"Can you read some Japanese stuff for us?" I asked.

"I can try."

I showed him the printouts Harry had found online.

Ben scanned them for a couple of minutes, as I leaned back in the comfortable armchair and looked at the water. A hedge of yellow hibiscus ran alongside the bank, and its blossoms were like a scattering of tiny suns. The orchids perfumed the air, and somewhere in the distance wind chimes tinkled.

Pua had owned the place for years, buying in long before prices rose to the stratosphere. If one of us won the lottery, I could see Mike and me living in a place like that someday. I wondered if the homeowner's association allowed dogs. Roby, after all, had become part of our family.

Ben looked up. "Where did you get this stuff?"

"Tell us what it is."

"As near as I can tell, it's a report about yakuza action in Yokohama," he said. "From some official agency with a long title."

"Any mention of a guy named Jun Tanaka?" Ray asked.

Ben nodded. "It looks like they knew he was involved in gambling and something else I can't understand, but they had no way to prosecute him."

He pushed the pages back to me. "I studied business Japanese. Sorry, there's a lot there I don't understand."

"Thanks, brah, I appreciate it. So where's the surf good these days?"

"I got back from the Billabong Pro in J Bay. Surf was awesome."

"Jeffreys Bay is in South Africa," I said to Ray. "Some of the most consistent waves on the planet."

"And how," Ben said. "It's a pain to get to—you've got to fly to Cape Town and then go another couple hundred miles to Eastern Cape Province."

"How'd you do?" I was already jealous; I'd never been a good enough surfer to get invited to a foreign tournament, and Jeffreys

Bay was one of those sites I'd always wanted to surf.

"I came in fifth. Kelly Slater and Mick Fanning were both on fire."

We talked surf for a while. Ben was leaving for Mundaka, on the Basque coast of Spain, for another Billabong tournament. I was glad for him, but I still wanted to knock him on the head, grab his board and take his place.

We left Ben starting to wax his board before the afternoon's surfing. As we walked back to the Jeep, I said, "I can see Tanaka putting out a hit on Stuart McKinney because he talked too much about the money at the Kope Bean warehouse. He's got the connections."

"But how can we tie him to Edith Kapana's shooting?"

"Not sure. But I feel in my bones that he's involved in it somehow."

From Hawai'i Kai I drove us up to Kaneohe to look for Mili France. We parked in front of her apartment building and rang the bell. She was home by then, and after we'd identified ourselves, she buzzed us inside.

She wore khaki shorts and a white cotton shirt with capped sleeves. She was apprehensive when she answered the door, worry etching lines in her forehead. With her close-cropped gray hair, though, she exuded a no-nonsense air.

"What can I do for you, Detectives? Are you still asking questions about Ezekiel?"

"If we could come in?" I asked.

Hesitantly, she stepped back and ushered us into the living room. The furniture was simple, but good quality, solid wood chairs and a sofa covered in a tropical floral pattern, hibiscus and bird of paradise against a green background. A galley kitchen took up the back wall.

"We'd like to ask you a few questions about the Kope Bean. You're not working there anymore?"

She shook her head. "I was let go on Friday. No notice. No

reason. Just so long, sayonara and aloha." There was a bitterness in her tone that I hadn't heard when we spoke before.

"I'll be frank with you, Mili," I said. "We're looking into some unorthodox business practices there, and we were hoping you could fill in some details."

"With pleasure. I've been around the block a few times, Detective. I know when something stinks, and it's not rotting coffee beans." She paused. "Did you ever know the Kaplans?" she asked, and we shook our heads. "Lovely people. Hyman and Sara Kaplan. They started the Kope Bean with a single store in downtown Honolulu. They had twelve locations by the time they sold to Mr. Tanaka."

I pulled out my notebook and started writing. "About five years ago, things started to change. Little things, at first. New machines that brewed with fewer beans. The coffee was weaker, but nobody noticed except some of the regulars. Then we started hiring from the Ohana."

She looked at us. "Where are my manners?" she asked. "I never even offered you something to drink. I still have a stash of good beans."

I looked at Ray. "I could use a cup of coffee," I said, and he nodded.

She stepped over to the galley kitchen and pulled a bag of the Kope Bean's signature blend of arabica beans and macadamia nut flavors from her freezer. I remembered a similar situation with Maile Kanuha at her office, when she brewed coffee for us from beans she swore by. I hoped Mili's beans were better.

We didn't talk while she ground the beans, but once the coffee was brewing she came back to us. "I have nothing against the handicapped," she said. "Some of the staff we hired were lovely people. Sometimes a little slow, to be sure, and a couple did have anger management problems and had to be let go. But…"

"But what?" Ray asked.

"Mr. Tanaka got federal funds for hiring the disabled. And I know for a fact that he fudged some of the numbers. I didn't like that."

"But you stayed," I said.

"I'm sixty-two years old, Detective. My husband dumped me ten years ago, and I hadn't held a job in twenty years. The Kaplans gave me a chance, and I felt I owed it to them to stay at the Kope Bean. I didn't want to see everything they worked for go down the drain."

She turned to the coffee pot and began to pour. "And at my age, I'm not the most employable person. You'd be surprised at what people turn a blind eye to when it means keeping a paycheck."

She brought us the coffee, and I noticed she wasn't above bringing home cups and napkins from the Kope Bean, too. "What else did you have to turn a blind eye to?" Ray asked, as she sat back down.

"We were instructed to exaggerate any shortages from suppliers, lose the occasional shipment if the driver ever got careless. Most of the staff, they're kids, they don't keep good track of their time cards. If Brittany forgot to clock in, she didn't get paid for the time. When Devin quit, his time card mysteriously disappeared, and he didn't get paid for his last week."

She stopped to drink her coffee, and so did we. It was pretty damn good, better than you could get at most coffee shops, the Kope Bean included. Without the steamed milk, the coffee and macadamia flavors were even richer.

"The Kope Bean is a chain," she said, putting her cup down on the table. "But not big enough to have much of a central office staff. Mr. Tanaka handled everything from payroll to depositing store receipts. He's a slimy snake, and I don't trust him a bit." She frowned at some memory. "As the store manager, I closed out the tills at the end of the day and bundled up the cash for the bank. With the Kaplans, I made the night deposit myself, but Mr. Tanaka started sending a runner every night to collect the cash instead."

She ran her fingers up and down along the side of her cup.

"About two years ago, I had to go to the bank to resolve a dispute, and the manager handed me a printout of deposits from our store. I was astonished to see they were sometimes three or four thousand dollars more than we took in."

"Did you do anything about it?" I asked.

She shook her head. "The manager at the Chinatown store asked me one day if I'd noticed anything funny, and that's when I figured out it was happening at his branch, too. We both knew we couldn't say anything."

She finished her coffee. The anger seemed to radiate from her. "My ex-husband handled all the finances. When we split up I didn't even know how to pay a bill. So I don't understand what was going on. But I'm sure it was something funny."

"And you never complained or told anyone?" I asked.

"Nope."

"Any idea why they fired you?"

"They had me training this young girl. A *friend* of Mr. Tanaka's. Once he saw she could do the job, it was goodbye, Mili."

We stood up. "Thanks for your time," I said. "I wish you a lot of luck in the future."

"We could subpoena the store's cash deposits and its register tapes, and compare them, documenting any discrepancies," Ray said, when we were back in the car. "But that will tip our hand. We need to nail somebody on a murder charge."

"Fraud may be all we can prove," I said, but I didn't like the idea at all.

I Told You So

From the Jeep, Ray called Greg Oshiro. "You know anything about a guy named Jun Tanaka?" He held the phone out so I could hear.

"Depends on what you want to know," Greg said. "You buy me coffee, I might spill some beans."

"Meet you in half an hour?" Ray asked.

"We just had coffee with Mili, brah," I groaned when Ray hung up. "I need food, not more caffeine."

"We'll get Mickey D's on the way."

We scarfed a couple of burgers and some fries and met Greg at the Kope Bean near the *Star-Advertiser* office on Kapiolani Boulevard. At least this time he was polite to me, and we made some chit-chat while we waited for Ray to fetch yet another round of macadamia lattes.

"You still working with that gay teen group?" Greg asked.

"Once a month. I'm going over there tomorrow night. A bunch of us rotate so the kids get a variety of voices."

"I might be willing to come over sometime, if you could use me."

Well, well. "Sure. I don't think most of them read the paper, but you could talk to them about how the media shapes our ideas about sexual orientation. That sort of thing."

He nodded, and Ray returned. "It takes a lot of cash to keep a movement going," Greg said, pulling out his notebook. "About a month ago, I started to look into where the money for KOH comes from."

He pulled out a sheet of paper. "It's a 501(c)(4) organization, a charitable non-profit," he said. "So that means individuals and corporations can make tax-deductible contributions. The last time we met I told you that the biggest donors were a bunch of corporations, including the Kope Bean. I could tell that they were interconnected, but I didn't know who was behind it all. I kept digging, and eventually I found out that it's a guy named Jun Tanaka. He has yakuza ties in Japan, and a lot of his businesses here are pretty shady-looking, too."

Interesting, I thought. He'd found out what we had—without having Harry on his team.

"What makes them shady?" Ray asked, raising his coffee to his lips.

"For example, he owns a *malasada* shop in a warehouse district near the airport," Greg said, looking back at his paper.

A malasada is a kind of Portuguese donut popular in the islands. As my dad scaled back his construction business, he'd built a few dozen of those shops around the island, because they were small and simple.

"I've been out there a couple of times," Greg continued. "It took me a while to find it because there's no sign. There's just one old lady, behind a counter with a single tray of donuts. But corporate records show it takes in nearly five grand a day in receipts. At least that's what Tanaka reports for tax purposes."

"Can you give us copies of what you've got, or should we be taking our own notes?"

He pushed some papers over to me. "Already made copies for you."

I started to get suspicious. Until we started this investigation, Greg Oshiro wouldn't have pissed on me if I was on fire. Suddenly he wanted to be my best friend, offering me documents and volunteering to meet with the gay teen group. Something was very strange.

He went over the details on the paperwork he'd given us. "How'd you put all these details about Tanaka together?" I asked.

"A friend who's an attorney pointed me in the right direction."

My suspicions got the better of me. "Why are you being so cooperative?"

For a minute it looked like he might argue, but he said, "The *Star-Advertiser's* cutting back, like papers everywhere. I'm forty, I'm fat, I've got high blood pressure and high cholesterol. I've got two kids in Kaneohe. I can't pick up and move someplace else. So I've got to do what I can to hold on to my job. I figure if I break a major exposé on KOH, or Tanaka, that gives me some job security."

Two kids in Kaneohe? I was confused. Yeah, a lot of gay guys, and couples, are having kids; it's not that unusual. But my first reaction when a guy told me that he had kids was that he was straight. Maybe, despite Ray's gaydar, Greg wasn't gay after all—just sucking up to me over the youth group so I could help him keep his job.

I looked back at the paperwork. "KOH brings in a lot of contributions in cash," I said. "You think Tanaka is washing money through them?"

He nodded. "What I don't know is where the cash comes from. I have an unverified report that he has a pakalolo operation up in the hills somewhere. I figure he's selling dope, maybe ice, and he needs a place to put that cash."

It was time for us to share with Greg. I looked at Ray, who said, "Tanaka's running at least one pai gow game. A lot of cash comes in that way."

Greg took a couple of notes. "You can't print anything about it yet," I said. "We'll let you know when it all comes together, give you an exclusive in exchange for your help."

He smiled, then slid one more piece of paper across the table. "You might want to talk to this guy. He's the attorney for KOH."

I looked down at the page. He'd scrawled Adam O'Malley's name, along with his office number. I remembered his card stuck in Aunty Edith's desk and that his firm represented KOH. "How do you know him?" I asked.

Greg blushed. "We dated a couple of times. He wanted to see somebody look into KOH, so he passed this stuff on to me."

Okay, I know I shouldn't be so focused on somebody's sexual

orientation. But I'd bounced back and forth so much about Greg during that conversation that I had to laugh. "I didn't know O'Malley was gay," I said. "Guess you and he are two of the few guys on O'ahu I didn't fool around with when I was single."

All three of us got a chuckle out of that. I thought I could detect relief in Greg's laughter, that he felt better now that he'd stuck his toe out of the closet and gotten a positive response.

I remembered the first few times I'd come out. How much relief I'd felt that I wasn't keeping secrets any more. Akoni was the first person I told, because I had to confess that I'd been at a gay bar when I found a dead body, and he hadn't taken it well. Even so, it felt like a burden had been lifted from my shoulders, and I hoped, for Greg's sake, that he felt the same way.

As we left, Ray said, "Do I say 'I told you so' now or later?"

"You have disturbingly accurate gaydar for a straight guy." We waited at a light as a dirty white pickup with a bumper sticker that read "I'd rather be pillaging" made a turn on red.

"The attorney Greg mentioned. He's the same one whose business card we found at Edith Kapana's?" Ray asked, when we started moving again.

"Yup. I called his office, and the secretary said he was on a case on the mainland. I'll call again."

O'Malley was back in Honolulu, I discovered, when I reached him later that afternoon, Ray listening in on the other phone. "Sorry I didn't get a chance to call you back, Detective," he said. "I just got back in town last night."

I said, "Greg Oshiro suggested I should talk to you about Kingdom of Hawai'i. You're their attorney?"

"Fields and Yamato handled the incorporation for Kingdom of Hawai'i. We've consulted with them on a couple of issues, but I wouldn't characterize myself as their attorney, per se."

God save me from lawyers. "Can we get together and talk?"

He didn't say anything for a minute. "There are some things you should know. But like I said, I got back from the mainland yesterday, and I'm swamped. I have depositions scheduled later today, and all day tomorrow, but I'm taking a personal day Friday. I know it's irregular, but I'd rather not have you come to my office, if you don't mind. Could you come over to my apartment around ten?"

I wondered how closeted Adam O'Malley was. Did he want me to come to his apartment because he was afraid to have a gay detective show up at his office?

Yeah, maybe I'm paranoid, but I still get crap from other officers, three years after coming out myself. And I know a lot of professional men who don't want their sexual orientation to be public knowledge. O'Malley was probably one of those.

"Maybe I should have Detective Donne meet you. He's straight."

"It's not that." O'Malley lowered his voice. "I don't parade my sex life around the office, but it's not like we're dating, Detective. It's just—I feel like there is some illegal stuff going on with Kingdom of Hawai'i, and as an officer of the court I'm obliged to report it, as long as I'm not violating any client confidences. Which I'm not, because like I said, I'm not the attorney of record. I don't want you to come to the office because there are people behind this thing that might not take kindly to my talking to the cops."

I felt dumb, projecting my own issues. So I agreed to come to his apartment on Friday, and he gave me the address, in a high rise near Ala Moana Mall.

"That was awkward," Ray said, when I hung up. "I ever tell you about this girl I interviewed, in my first case as a detective? Her name was Teresa Ambrosino, and she was a beauty. Like Julie, but with curves like the Indianapolis Speedway. The whole time I'm talking to her, I'm thinking she's coming on to me. She's leaning toward me, she's fluttering her eyebrows, pursing her lips."

"And she wasn't?"

"Nope, she was after my partner, sixty-year-old guy with

breath like dog shit. I almost asked her out, right there, but fortunately I remembered my ethics class. My partner saw me slobbering, though, and it took me months to live it down."

"Well, you'll go with me Friday. We can see which of us O'Malley makes a play for. Since you have such great gaydar and all."

"What are partners for?" he asked.

As we were packing up for the day, my cell phone rang. From the display I saw it was Lui calling. "Hey, brah, what's up?"

"I have to talk to you," he said.

"We're talking now."

"Not on the phone," Lui said. "Please, Kimo? I've got to get out of the office. Meet me at Ala Moana Mall, outside Shirokiya?"

"I'm about to head for home. Ala Moana's out of my way, but I can be there in fifteen."

He was standing in front of the store, looking in the windows like they contained treasure, when I walked up. "What was so urgent, brah?" I asked.

Lui looked around, lowered his voice. "He called me today. Tung. From the pai gow game."

"Yeah?"

"He's putting together a high-stakes game for Friday night. Big players, including a couple of Hong Kong Chinese. He wants me to be there."

"So tell him no."

"It's not that easy."

I looked at my brother. We were walking inside the mall by then. It was cool, but sweat was dripping off his forehead. His dark suit looked uncomfortably tight, the knot of his red power tie askew. His body was as tense as a guitar string waiting to be plucked.

"How much do you owe him?" I asked.

"How did you know?" Lui's whole body relaxed, as if a weight had been transferred from his shoulders.

"I'm a detective, brah. It's what I do."

"Close to a hundred grand. I was the banker a couple of

times, and I ran into some bad luck."

"So you lied to me the other day, when you said this was just penny-ante. That you won some and you lost some."

"I was embarrassed. And I thought I could deal with it. But he's pressuring me. Says he has to go back to Japan soon and he needs to collect his debts. I get one last chance to win some money before he's calling the marker. If I don't show on Friday night, he's going to go after me. He said he'll call Liliha, tell her about it. Then he'll spread the word around town, ruin me in business."

That was interesting—that Tanaka was preparing to leave town. Was it because we were closing in on him? "I'm assuming you don't have that kind of money handy," I said.

He shook his head.

"First of all, gambling's illegal. So if he starts bragging about your debt, he exposes himself as running the game." I stopped in front of the Disney Store, where a teenager in a Mickey Mouse costume waved his white gloves at shoppers. "Any threats of physical violence?"

Lui looked like he'd swallowed a sour lump of poi. "You think he might?"

"It's the standard threat. Break your kneecaps. That kind of thing."

My brother is a tough, savvy businessman. Put him across from you at a negotiating table, and you'd never have a chance. But he was way out of his league.

"I have to think about this," I said. "We think Jun Tanaka, your Tung, has ties to the yakuza back in Japan. And he's mixed up in a world of trouble here." We started walking again, and I told him that we suspected Tanaka of filtering the game's proceeds through the Kope Bean stores.

"That's money laundering," he said. "You could put him away."

"Your problems can't be solved so easily. For starters, don't get ahead of yourself. We're nowhere near bringing charges. And he wants you in that game on Friday."

I reassured my big brother that I would look out for him. I wasn't sure how I was going to do that, but I looked to my father as a role model. He'd always taken care of us, no matter what fate threw his way. I couldn't do anything less.

When I got home, Mike was out at the grill in the back yard with steaks, Roby sitting obediently next to him waiting for his chance to steal the meat. I fixed a salad and some rice, and we ate at the kitchen table, talking about movies we wanted to see, a neighbor he had spoken to, a dog Roby had befriended. Mike slipped Roby a couple of hunks of steak when he thought I wasn't looking.

We adjourned to the sofa to watch TV, a reality show about chefs living together in a house and competing to see who could cook the strangest food. Roby turned around a few times, then sprawled at the foot of the sofa. It was the kind of evening I'd hoped we would have once we lived together, and it felt really good.

The next morning, I sat down with Ray, Akoni and Tony Lee and went over what my brother had told me about the big game scheduled for Friday night.

"Why do you think they're pressuring your brother?" Akoni asked.

"Tanaka says he's going to Japan and needs to collect on his debts. He's threatening blackmail if Lui doesn't show up at the game on Friday and then pay up what he owes."

"You talked to the FBI about this?" Akoni asked. "They may already be following Tanaka. You don't want to screw up a case the Bureau is working on. Don't you know a guy over there?"

"Yeah, you're right. I need to call him." Francisco Salinas was a Fed I had worked with when an Indonesian diplomat involved in money laundering had been murdered.

When we went back upstairs I called him, and as soon as I mentioned Tanaka's name he told me we had better get over to his office pronto. That was the way it was with the FBI: give, give, give. But we were all working toward the same goal, after all, so we had to play nice.

The day was unseasonably cool for September, when we hadn't even had Labor Day, and there was a stiff breeze that made it seem almost cold outside. I wanted more heat—outside and inside our case, too, which was turning colder than the top of Haleakala at sunrise.

Just before the entrance to the FBI building, near the Ala Moana Mall, Ray swerved to avoid a tourist reading the map behind the wheel of his rented convertible and not paying attention to things like stop signs. I braced myself against the dashboard and struggled not to press my foot into the floor, the way my father had done when he was teaching me to drive.

We made it past the security checks at the entrance to the parking lot and in the building lobby and took the elevator up to the FBI regional office. Salinas was a tall, dark-haired Cuban-American haole, with a military-short hair cut and navy suit and white shirt. He came out to the reception area to meet us, and I introduced him to Ray. In his office, with a big picture window looking out at Ala Moana Beach Park, I sketched out what we knew about Jun Tanaka and the large amounts of cash he seemed to be moving around. I mentioned the yakuza tattoos and what we knew of his background.

"You found out about his record back in Japan?" Salinas leaned back in his leather chair.

I nodded. "We had a Japanese translator look over some materials." I didn't mention that my hacker friend had provided the materials or that the translator was my surfer cousin. Less is more, you know.

"We've had our eye on Mr. Tanaka for a while," he said. "And we'd love to send him back to Japan. But he was born here, and he has a US passport, and we haven't managed to pin anything on him yet that would let us send him to jail."

"What about if you catch him running a pai gow game?"

"Depends on what you mean by running. If we can tail him taking the proceeds from the game and putting it into the Kope Bean bank accounts, then we can make a case."

"What about the other guys in the game?" Ray asked. "Do they walk away? Or do they get caught in the net?"

I was glad Ray asked the question. Salinas picked up a gold Mont Blanc pen from his desk and played it back and forth between his fingers.

"You have an informant?"

We both nodded. "But we don't want Tanaka to know which of the guys ratted him out."

"I want to get Tanaka," Salinas said. "The other guys clean?"

"I don't know. I only know my informant is."

"I don't mind ignoring the other guys, if I get Tanaka. You have the details?"

I told him about the Wing Wah and the game the next night. He took notes, checking a couple of things on the computer. "I'll get a team together."

Even though Salinas said the other players didn't matter, I wanted to look out for my brother's interests. "We'll help," I said.

He shook his head. "This is a Bureau operation. We appreciate the offer, but we'll run with what you've given us."

"What about the Joint Terrorism Task Force?" I asked. "You work with HPD on that. How's this any different?"

"HPD detectives who are part of the JTTF have gone through our screening already," Salinas said. "You want to turn your case over to one of them?"

I wasn't happy, but I wasn't giving up my case, and Salinas was firm. We left, me wondering what I had dropped my brother into.

I called Lui and asked when we could talk. "I'm meeting Dad for lunch," he said. "After I told you about my trouble, I thought a long time about what I could do to get out of it. The only person I kept coming back to was Dad."

I knew how he felt. Our father had always been there for us, through our many difficulties. He was a voice of reason.

"You want to come with us?" Lui asked.

I was so accustomed to Lui being the oldest brother, the most confident, the one who always seemed to know what to do with his life, that it took me a minute to recognize the undercurrent in his voice.

"Sure," I said.

Ray and I spent the rest of the morning trying to put the pieces together. Based on what Lui had told us about the game and what Mili France had said, it sounded like there was a lot of cash moving around. "Suppose Tanaka makes cash donations to the Ohana," I said. "That gives him a tax write-off. And I'm sure he's got some creative ways of funneling the money back once it's clean."

"He could do the same with the KOH," Ray said. "Plus, he owns a couple of other businesses."

"And Edith connects to this case because she knew something about the money laundering?"

"Must be," Ray said. "She lived with Dex, she knew Ezekiel. And we know she was a nosy old woman, the kind who didn't mind stirring up trouble."

"So who killed her?"

Ray looked at me. "Dex?"

I frowned. "I saw his hand shake a couple of times when he was lighting cigarettes," I said. "You think he could make such clean shots?"

"Tanaka?"

"Could be. Tanaka knows both Dex and Ezekiel. Through either of them he could have found out about Edith."

I stood up and started pacing around. "But why shoot her at the rally?" I asked. "Tanaka's smart enough to know that a shooting at the rally could make problems for KOH."

"Yeah, but remember that flyer we got, trying to shift blame to Bunchy Parker's group," Ray said. "He could have thought shooting Edith at a KOH event would point the finger at one of the competing groups."

"And he could have hired someone." I sighed. "I hate this kind of case. Too much money, too many details—it all makes my head spin."

I was relieved when we tabled the discussion so I could head over to KVOL's headquarters in one of the gleaming high-rises downtown. Lui's position as station manager gave him access to the private club on the top floor, a white-linen place with stunning views of the airport and Honolulu Harbor.

A maitre d' in dark suit and a green tie with the U.H. logo led me to the table where my father and brother sat. Beyond them, a speedboat left a V-shaped wake as it sped past the end of Sand Island, and a Hawaiian Air jet took off, rising like an eagle into the clouds. "Haoa coming too?" my father said as I approached, quirking an eyebrow.

"He couldn't make it." I kissed the top of my father's head and slid into the third chair, knocking the table leg and rocking the water glasses. You can't take me anywhere.

Though Lui, like Haoa and me, is only part Japanese, on him those features make him look perpetually gloomy, and that morning he appeared worse for wear.

"Are you going to tell me what all this is about?" my father asked.

"After we order," Lui said. "I recommend the macadamia-crusted mahi-mahi fillet." We took his word for it and ordered three. When the waiter left, Lui sighed. "It's a long story."

He shifted uncomfortably in his plush, French-style chair. "I started gambling at Berkeley. I was pretty good, you know. I always had a head for numbers, and I could keep track of the cards."

My father shook his head. "Your mother and I, we figured you were tight with your money. That's why you never asked us for anything."

Lui smiled. "I wanted to prove I could make my own way. I gambled a little when I was single, back here in Honolulu, mostly poker. Then I married Liliha, and Jeffrey was born, and I pulled back. My luck had turned, and I figured I better focus on my family."

"Good idea," my father said.

I wanted to kick him. "Let Lui finish, Dad. I'm sure this isn't easy."

The waiter brought our salads and puffy white rolls with pats of ice-cold butter. As Lui took a roll, I noticed his hand was shaking, and that reminded me of Dexter Trale, his fellow pai gow player.

"A couple of months ago, I met this man, Jun Tanaka, at a charity fund-raiser. We talked, we joked around. Somehow we got onto the topic of pai gow. He told me he ran a game and invited me to join."

Lui started to cut into the roll with his butter knife, but his hand slipped and the roll slid off his plate. He put the knife down and took a deep breath. "Things were getting crazy at home. The kids turning into teenagers, Liliha bitching at them and me. Nothing was ever right. I had to get away sometimes."

My father looked like he smelled something bad. "How much?" he asked. "How much did you lose?"

"How do you know I lost?" Lui asked, almost belligerently. It was rare for any of us to stand up to our father, who had dominated our childhood with his height, his bulk and his often bad temper.

"Because you wouldn't have asked me here if you were winning." My father's voice was gentle, but there was steel underneath. I remembered why we all looked up to him so much.

"About a hundred grand." Lui busied himself with his salad. I already knew the figure, so I didn't stop eating, but my father put his fork down and stared at Lui. Then he shook his head.

"I don't have that much in my checking account," he said. "I'll have to sell some CDs, move some money around. It might take a couple of days."

We both gaped at him. I'd always known our parents were comfortable; my dad had his own construction business, and he and my mom had owned a couple of strip shopping centers and office buildings. But I'd never thought of them as the kind of people who had a hundred grand to throw around.

"It will come out of your inheritance," my father said. "Everything we have is divided equally between the three of you. Consider this an advance."

The waiter appeared and soundlessly slid away the salad plates and replaced them with our mahi-mahi fillets.

"I didn't," Lui said. "I mean, I couldn't."

"You did, and you could," my father said, spearing a flaky forkful of fish. "But you aren't going to gamble anymore."

"Dad, we're not kids. You can't just lock Lui up in his room."

"Lui?" My father looked at my brother, who hadn't touched his fish.

"There's a chapter of Gamblers Anonymous in Honolulu," he said quietly. "I'm going to a meeting tonight."

My father nodded and continued to eat. I sat there and looked at them. You can grow up with people, you can share blood with them and then they can still surprise you.

"I appreciate the offer, Dad," Lui said. "But like Kimo said,

I'm not a kid any more. I can't count on you to bail me out. Tanaka says he needs me at this game to help him draw out some high rollers from Hong Kong. He's going to stake me fifty grand. If I lose, it doesn't get added to what I owe, but if I win, I can use that money to pay down my debt."

"Why is he offering you such good terms?" I asked.

"Sounds like he thinks he can make a big score from these Hong Kong players. And like I told you, he's getting ready to run, so he's trying to accumulate as much cash as he can. He's betting that I can help him. I'm a good player, I swear. I've just had a run of bad luck."

My father snorted.

I explained what we knew about Jun Tanaka—the money laundering, the possible connection to two murders. "The FBI is after Tanaka, but they need to catch him red-handed, walking out of the game with cash. If Lui doesn't sit in, we won't know for sure that the game is running."

"You want to go to this game?" my father asked Lui.

He looked at me. "I have to," he said.

I hoped that somehow Salinas would pull a brace of rabbits out of his hat and haul Jun Tanaka in before the game took place. But I was pretty sure that I'd stopped believing in magic back when I was a kid.

When I got back to headquarters, Billy Kim from ballistics was in the detective bullpen, showing a piece of paper to Ray.

"What's up?" I asked.

"Billy came through," Ray said. "The same rifle was used to kill Edith and to shoot at us in front of the Ohana."

Billy showed us the striations where the shell casings matched. When he left, Ray and I started brainstorming. "This tells us for certain that whoever killed Edith shot at us two days ago at the Ohana."

"No," Ray said. "All it tells us is the same gun was used. We don't have the evidence yet to say it was the same shooter."

"Picky, picky."

"We already had the feeling that Edith's death was connected to the Ohana," Ray said. "Stuey lived there, Ezekiel used to live there and Edith went there the day before she died. Jun Tanaka is on the Ohana's board, and he's also the money man behind KOH. We've got all that. But who killed Edith? Why? How are the two deaths connected to KOH?"

We went back to the diagrams we had drawn, arrows showing the links between the cases, the people, and the organizations. "I think it all comes back to the money laundering," I said. "That's what ties everyone together. Let's say Edith knew, from either Ezekiel or Dex, that Tanaka was using KOH to legitimize his gambling profits. She was angry about it, and word got back to Tanaka."

Ray continued, "He killed her, or had her killed, to protect his operation. And Stuey talked too much so he had to die. But there are still loose ends."

"Such as?"

"What was Edith doing at the Ohana the day before she died? She wasn't looking for Ezekiel, because he hadn't lived there for years."

"Stuey?"

"We have no evidence that she knew him," Ray said. "David Currie, the administrator, said she went up there to ask about Ezekiel."

"Suppose he was lying," I said. "Maybe Ezekiel told Edith that Tanaka was making cash donations to KOH, and she wanted to see if he was still crazy or he could be trusted."

"It's a theory. Should we pull Currie in for more questions? Try and convince a judge to sign a subpoena for the Ohana's financial records?"

"There's that pesky 'j' word again," I said. "Judge. I still don't think we have enough to convince one. We don't have a single thing that actually connects Tanaka to either murder. And we don't have another strong suspect."

Ray closed the case book with a thud. "That's the sound of these murders getting shunted to the cold case files. Unless we get a major break in the next twenty-four hours."

RECRUITING

When our shift ended, I drove up to Aiea for dinner with Mike. I didn't tell him that Ray and I were going to meet Adam O'Malley at his apartment the next morning, though I should have. Mike's the jealous type and even knowing that Ray would be going with me, he would have made a big dramatic scene about me meeting some other gay guy in his apartment.

Friday morning, Sampson wanted to see us. He was wearing a black polo shirt and gray slacks, and his mood matched his clothes.

"Remember, I'm putting you back in the rotation right after Labor Day unless you convince me otherwise today."

Ray and I both shifted uncomfortably on our feet. Sampson hadn't invited us to sit, so we stood there in front of his desk like schoolboys called before the principal. "You have two open cases right now. Edith Kapana, the old woman killed at the rally. Stuart McKinney, the homeless man who got torched."

He saw me start to argue and said, "Yes, I know he wasn't technically homeless. You're trying to connect them to this pai gow game, right? And money laundering? What did the FBI have to say?"

When he's in a mood like that, best to keep it short and simple. "Francisco Salinas from the FBI has taken over the pai gow investigation, but we're following a bunch of leads which indicate that there are definite links between the sovereignty movement, the deaths of Edith Kapana and Stuart McKinney, the pai gow game and money laundering through the Kope Bean chain."

For the first time that morning, Sampson smiled. "I think that's the most concise statement I've ever heard you give, Detective. Now prove it."

"Yes, sir," we both said.

Sampson picked up his phone. "You can go."

It was barely eight o'clock, and we had two hours until our meeting with Adam O'Malley, the attorney for Kingdom of Hawai'i, at his apartment. We spent the time looking back at everything we had on KOH, preparing our questions.

"We need to know if there's an accountant for KOH," Ray said. "Or what O'Malley knows about the money trail."

"I want to know who's really in charge of that group. Is it Ezekiel, or is he just a figurehead? Is Tanaka pulling his strings? And why?"

A few minutes before ten, we headed over to O'Malley's building, a fancy tower off Ala Moana Boulevard called the Honolulu Sunset. Tourists cruised the area in top-down convertibles, and teenagers who weren't back in school yet giggled and teased each other in packs.

The concierge, a balding older black guy named Malik Jefferson, called up to O'Malley's apartment and got no answer. "We have an appointment with him," I said, showing him our ID. "You have any idea if he went out today?"

Jefferson shook his head. "I came on at seven this morning. I know Mr. O'Malley, and I know he hasn't left."

"Anyone else come to see him today?"

He shrugged. There was security in the building, he said; you were supposed to come in the front door and get buzzed through to the elevator bank. But there were a couple of loopholes. If you came in with a resident, even just tagging along behind, you could slip in without anyone noticing.

At our insistence, Jefferson led us to O'Malley's apartment on the sixteenth floor. As we rode the elevator I wondered what we would find. Had O'Malley chickened out on our meeting and left? He'd said he was frightened by someone involved with KOH.

Or had he simply gone out on an errand and run behind schedule?

At the door, Jefferson knocked and called out. And then he

stepped back, wobbling, as all three of us got a whiff of what was behind the O'Malley's door. Blood and death.

I could tell from his behavior that Jefferson recognized the smell. Without further argument, he opened the door with his master key. It was locked, but the security chain hadn't been engaged. With the door open, the odor was even stronger.

Jefferson stepped back and let Ray and me walk into the apartment ahead of him. We both drew our guns and prowled silently ahead. Ray went to the right, and I went left.

I drew the lucky straw. The master bedroom was to the left, and the body of a Caucasian male was in there, lying on his chest on the bed, naked, with an extra-large black dildo protruding from his ass. His hands and legs were secured to the corners of the four-poster bed with what looked like silk ties. His head was bent back, resting on a satin-covered pillow, and his eyes were open.

Blood soaked the sheets, and his throat had been slit.

"Bad?" Ray asked, coming up behind me.

I nodded, then went back to the living room. "I hate to do this to you, brah," I said to Malik Jefferson. "But I need you to take a look at the body and see if it's Mr. O'Malley."

Jefferson gulped and then nodded. I led him down the hall; he ducked his head in the room, took a quick look and said, "That's him," in a strangled voice. Then he hurried back to the living room.

Ray was looking around in the bathroom as I called dispatch and notified them of the body. Then I took a set of digital pictures of the victim and the room. I had to struggle to breathe through my mouth because the smell of the congealed blood was playing havoc with my stomach.

When Ray came out of the bathroom, he was wearing rubber gloves and carrying a tub of Vicks VapoRub. "Fortunately Mr. O'Malley had a well-stocked medicine cabinet," he said. He handed me a pair of gloves, and then the open tub.

I smeared some on my upper lip. "Lemon," I said. I took a deep breath through my nose and felt a little better.

"We'll see if it works any better than the menthol."

We went back to the living room, where Malik Jefferson was waiting, looking sick and rubbing his stomach.

"We're going to need to see the tapes from your security system for the last twenty-four hours," Ray said. "Why don't you get started on that, and we'll call the medical examiner."

"This is a good building. Things like this aren't supposed to happen here."

"They happen everywhere." Ray put the VapoRub on the kitchen counter. "Go on, get the tapes," he told Jefferson, who backed out of the room and closed the door gently behind him.

"Turns out to be a good thing you came with me," I said. "I can imagine how it would look, me going to see some gay guy at his apartment, him ending up dead. People would think it was some kind of hook up."

"You don't know that."

"Just because *you're* cool doesn't mean the rest of the world is."

We searched the living room, but it was strangely impersonal— no family pictures or souvenirs from vacations. It was as if he'd rented the place furnished and never bothered to add any personal touches.

By the time we finished the ME's guys were there and the crime scene techs, and the apartment was buzzing with people and equipment. Ray pointed the techs toward a kitchen knife in the bathroom that had been wiped clean of prints; it looked like it was going to be our murder weapon. There was blood in the shower drain, perhaps the killer cleaning up before leaving.

Once the ME had taken the body away, we turned the AC on high, rubbed some more Vicks under our noses and started to search the room carefully. It still smelled pretty bad, but we managed. A T-shirt, jeans and bikini briefs were tossed over a chair by the bed, and we packed them up to check for fingerprints.

A mahogany jewelry box on O'Malley's dresser was empty, and we couldn't find a wallet anywhere. I assumed that a busy attorney would have a cell phone, a PDA and a laptop computer, but there were no personal electronics at all, though we found chargers for a couple of different pieces of equipment in the drawer of an antique roll-top desk along one wall of the bedroom.

We looked through the papers in the desk, but all we found were a few unpaid bills, an *Out* magazine still in its plastic wrapper and some unopened junk mail. In a box on the top shelf of the closet we found an old address book, from the time before digital contacts, along with some explicit gay comic books and erotica anthologies, including one called *Skater Boys*. I flipped through the books, and it was clear the kind of guys who turned O'Malley on. Hoodlums, thugs, skateboarders, soldiers, men with muscles and tattoos.

While we waited for the crime scene techs to finish, we went downstairs to Malik Jefferson, who led us into a back room set up with a bank of monitors and introduced us to the security guard there, a tough-looking haole with dark curly hair and a nose that had been broken at some time in the past.

"Carl can show you the tapes."

Carl shook our hands and then sat down and fast-forwarded through the grainy black and white footage, slowing down at a frame time-coded 5:38 PM. "That's Mr. O'Malley," he said, pointing. "Camera on the fourth floor of the garage. Mr. O'Malley parks in space 421."

O'Malley looked like an ordinary businessman, wearing a suit and carrying a leather satchel, his tie slightly askew. He approached the camera, which was focused on the elevator, stood there for a moment, then entered the elevator and exited the frame.

Carl turned a couple of knobs on the monitor and the footage zoomed ahead. Shortly after eleven at night, we saw O'Malley exit the garage elevator, this time dressed for clubbing, in the body-hugging black T-shirt and tight jeans we'd found strewn next to his bed.

"You only have cameras in the garage?" Ray asked.

"Each floor of the garage, by the elevator," Carl said. "We have a couple in the health club on the garage roof and another set in various parts of the building—mail room, card room and so on. Nothing in the main lobby; the concierge is always on duty there. So the only way to track Mr. O'Malley's movement is through the garage cameras or anything the concierge saw."

We both nodded, and Carl continued ahead to two a.m., when O'Malley walked back into the frame of the garage camera. He was accompanied by another guy, who was careful to avoid getting his face on the camera, always staying a bit behind O'Malley.

"I'm thinking he's been in this building before and knows where the cameras are," Ray said.

"Could be. Or he's the kind of guy who's accustomed to hiding," I said.

We could only make out he was a skinny haole in a white T-shirt and jeans, a few inches shorter than O'Malley, who was about five-ten. For a brief second we got a shot of the guy's tattooed lower right arm.

"Think that could be Dex?" I asked.

"Dex is straight, though, isn't he?" Ray asked. "He's got Leelee. What would he be doing picking up gay men in bars?"

"You'd be surprised," I said.

Once O'Malley and his visitor were in the elevator, we lost them. There were no cameras on the individual floors, so no way to see if the mystery man had been with O'Malley and gone into his apartment with him, or simply had been using him to get into the building.

"Mr. O'Malley often bring guys home?" I asked.

Carl shrugged. "We watch the cameras for suspicious activity, not to spy on the residents. I couldn't tell you who comes to see who. That's the concierge's job."

We went back out to the front and found Malik Jefferson behind his desk, a big semi-circle with a sign-in book for guests. We asked him the same question. "I don't usually work the late shift, and even if I do, I'm not always paying that close attention."

Gunter is the concierge at a fancy building in Waikīkī, and he knows everything that goes on—who gets packages from fancy stores, who has late-night visitors, who has an illegal cat. So I doubted that Jefferson was telling the truth.

"We can put you on the witness stand," I said. "You willing to go on record that you aren't paying attention to who comes and goes in this building? You think your boss, and the residents, will appreciate that?"

He looked down at his desk.

"The man is dead. Do you understand that? If he had a pattern of doing things like this, then that may help us find out who killed him. If he didn't, that sends our investigation in a different direction."

Finally, he said, "Sometimes, on Friday mornings, I see guys leaving, look like that guy there. Tough guys, not the kind you normally see in this building. The night man, he said sometimes Mr. O'Malley would bring them home. Sometimes they'd show up, late night, early morning, ask for him."

"That wasn't so hard, was it?" Ray asked. "Anything else you aren't saying?"

He shifted around in his seat. "Nope." I wasn't sure I believed him, but we had enough to start with.

As we rode back up to O'Malley's apartment, Ray said, "You think he picked up the guy in the bar for some rough sex, and it got out of hand?"

"I'd say slitting his throat is getting pretty far out of hand."

"You think Greg Oshiro could tell us anything?" Ray asked.

I was confused. "Greg? I don't know what kind of guys he likes."

"I wasn't asking that," Ray said patiently. "But didn't he say that he had dated O'Malley at some point?"

I nodded. My brain was moving slowly. I've seen a lot of dead bodies in my career, and they have some affect on me; I couldn't still be a cop if they didn't. But O'Malley's death had hit me hard. Despite the way his death looked I worried that scheduling the meeting with Ray and me had signed O'Malley's death warrant.

"You need to call up Greg and have a chat about sexual practices," Ray said. "I'm a liberated guy and all that, but I think this is a conversation you'd be more comfortable with."

I didn't want to do it, but I pulled out my cell and called Greg Oshiro. "Got a tip for you," I said. "Can you get over here pronto?"

I expected him to argue, but all he said was, "Give me the address." I gave it to him and then snapped the phone shut.

We waited for Greg in the Honolulu Sunset's fancy lobby. One of the other residents walked in with a couple of Foodland bags, and my stomach grumbled so loud that Ray looked over at me and laughed. I realized we'd worked non-stop since the morning. It was closing in on the end of our shift by then.

"I know this building," Greg said, walking in. "This is…"

"Yeah," I said. "It is. Or was."

Greg stepped backward, and his balance wobbled. "Jesus."

We led him over to a group of chairs in a quiet back corner of the lobby, out of casual earshot, and he settled into a big leather armchair. Ray and I sat down across from him.

"We need to know what you knew about O'Malley's interests. But first of all, you've got secrets, and there are details here we wouldn't want in the press. You protect us, and we'll protect you. Are we clear?"

Greg nodded. He took a deep breath and pulled out his notebook. "How did you guys get called here?"

"Right now, I'm asking the questions. Later, after we've got what we need, we'll take care of you."

He frowned. But he knew the drill.

"We had an appointment with O'Malley this morning," I said. "To follow up on the lead you gave us, that he was the attorney for KOH. Right now, we have no idea whether that's related to his death or just a coincidence. Evidence at the scene leads us to consider whether O'Malley might have picked up the wrong sort of guy. What do you know about his tastes?"

Greg looked sick. "You know The Garage?"

Ray was a bit confused, but I knew what Greg was talking about. "It's a gay bar. A converted garage. Kind of seamy."

"More than kind of," Greg said.

"You go there?"

He squirmed in his seat.

"Sorry. Wrong question. O'Malley went there?"

Greg nodded. "You have to understand, Adam had... issues. That conservative Irish Catholic background, sometimes he felt bad about the kind of things he liked."

"And he liked to be punished," I finished for him. The Garage was known as a haven for guys with a taste for unorthodox sexual practices.

"You think he could have picked somebody up at The Garage who killed him?" Greg asked.

"It's a possibility we're investigating."

I saw the calculation in his eyes, probably thinking about the big story he could get out of Adam's death, and then his body sagged and the corners of his mouth turned down.

"Poor guy," he said. "However it happened, I feel sorry for him."

THE GARAGE

My cell rang. Mike had reprogrammed it a few days before so that the ring tone assigned to him was the Baha Men singing "Who Let the Dogs Out." It reverberated around the high-ceilinged lobby of the Honolulu Sunset.

I grabbed the phone and flipped it open, standing up and stepping away from Ray and Greg.

"We having dinner tonight?" Mike asked. "Or are you going direct to the surveillance of that pai gow game your brother's in?"

"Ray and I have a couple of things to wrap up. But I can pencil you in for a dinner date."

"Sweet. I'll be the handsome guy playing with the cute dog."

I flipped the phone shut and came back to Ray and Greg. Ray had pulled out the list of questions we had for Adam O'Malley. "You know anything about accounting at KOH?" he asked Greg. "Based on the stories you've been writing about Hawaiian nationalism?"

"They use a small practice in a walk-up office in Chinatown. I spoke to the guy in charge, but he wouldn't give me any information." He pulled the firm's name and address from his notes and Ray copied it down.

We went over the rest of our questions, but Greg didn't have anything to say that he hadn't already given us. He left to write an obituary on Adam O'Malley, and we faced the fact that we had to call someone in O'Malley's family and notify them of his death.

"Rock-paper-scissors?" I asked.

We both shook our fists three times. I went with scissors, and Ray chose paper.

"That looks like the night concierge," I said, nodding toward the front door. "I'll talk to him while you make the call."

I left Ray dialing a number from O'Malley's address book and walked across the lobby. The night concierge was a middle-aged Chinese man with close-cropped hair and the same monogrammed aloha shirt as Malik Jefferson. His name tag read "Eli."

I introduced myself and asked, "Did you see Mr. O'Malley get home last night?"

"Yeah. It was around two, and he had a 'friend' with him."

I didn't like the way the guy put those imaginary quotes around the word, but it wasn't my business to be the language police. I had enough to do being the regular police.

"What do you mean by 'friend'?"

"He brought guys home every couple of weeks," he said. "On Thursday nights. Usually sleazy-looking men, not the kind of person who lives in this building. You ask me, it's not right. A man like that shouldn't be allowed to live here."

"That part of your job here, Eli? Deciding who should and shouldn't be allowed to live here?"

"You know what I mean, Detective. Not only was he a homosexual, he exposed the rest of the residents to a dangerous element."

"What made you think the guy with Mr. O'Malley was dangerous?" I asked, trying to keep my temper in check.

"I can tell what those people look like," he said. "Anyone can. They wear their depravity right there on their faces. I could tell they were going upstairs for something illegal, whether it was drugs or sex or both."

I took a deep breath. "Would you recognize the man with Mr. O'Malley again? Considering you took such a good look at his face that you could tell what he was going to do?"

Eli realized the trap he'd gotten himself into. "I didn't so much look at his face as his general attitude. The tight T-shirt, the torn jeans, the tattoos. I wouldn't recognize him again, though."

Ray joined us at the desk. "Spoke to O'Malley's father," he

said. "He wasn't exactly broken up over his son's death."

"I'm not surprised," Eli said. "Given the kind of man he was."

"That's enough. A man is dead, and if you had any sense of human decency you'd speak about him with respect. But then, you can probably see in my face that I'm a deviant, just like O'Malley was, so you won't care what I think."

"We done here?" Ray said, as Eli gaped at us.

"Yeah, we're done. I'll make sure that the building management hears what a high opinion you have of its residents, Eli." I turned and walked out, Ray on my heels.

"I'm not even going to ask what all that was about," Ray said, as we drove back to headquarters. "But I assume he didn't have anything to contribute."

"Nothing useful," I said.

We caught Lieutenant Sampson as he was packing up for the day and told him about O'Malley's death. "The bodies are piling up, Detectives," he said. "An elderly woman, a homeless guy, now an attorney."

"He wasn't homeless," I said. "He just looked that way."

Sampson glared at me. "I don't care if he lived in mansion in Kahala. He's dead and it's your case. Get it solved."

"Lieutenant, with Labor Day on Monday, we're not getting anything out of the medical examiner in a hurry," Ray said.

"Don't let that stand in your way." Sampson picked up his briefcase and walked out.

"Have a nice weekend," I called after him. Sampson turned around and glared, just in time to see Ray kick me in the shins.

"Keep him in line, will you, Donne?" Sampson asked, just before disappearing into the elevator.

"You have some kind of self-destruct button?" Ray asked me. "You kick into wise ass mode at the dumbest times."

"Yeah, yeah, yeah." I sat down at my desk and brought up the website for The Garage. "Look at this," I said, turning the monitor toward Ray. "Thursday night is Hard Hat night. Free well drinks to anybody in uniform or carrying a union card."

"Kinky," Ray said. "You ever go there?"

"They'd have to give me a lot more than free drinks to get me in my uniform," I said. "But that's why the concierge saw O'Malley bring guys home on Thursday nights."

"We've got a problem," Ray said. "You're going to need to hit that bar tonight, see if anyone saw who O'Malley left with. But at the same time we've got your brother's pai gow game."

"Shit." I was screwed, in more ways than one. Mike was going to have a jealous fit over my going to The Garage. But it wasn't the kind of assignment Ray could take. "I'll go to the bar early. Before it gets crazy. If I need to go back after the game, I will."

My stomach grumbled again, angry over our missed lunch. Ray laughed and said, "I called the KOH accountant's office and got a recording that the office is closed until Tuesday. So I'm going to go home, have dinner with my wife and then set up outside the Wing Wah to keep an eye on the FBI. You just get over there when you can."

"Will do." I called Mike and asked him to meet me at Raimundo's in Waikīkī, an old favorite restaurant from the days when we were dating. On my way there, I called Lui and told him the FBI was interested in the game that night. "I don't know if they're going to do anything. But they just want Tanaka. My contact swears they're not interested in the players."

"You can't bust Tung before the game?"

"Have to catch him in the act."

Lui grumbled, and I stopped paying attention, searching for a parking spot near Raimundo's. I finally got him to hang up just as I spotted a prime spot only a few blocks from the restaurant.

Mike and I were early enough to miss the dinner rush, and by six we were seated, tearing into garlic rolls and digging into an antipasto platter. I felt like I hadn't eaten for days.

"Slow down, tiger," Mike said. "They aren't taking the food

away from you. Jeez, you eat like Roby."

"You say the sweetest things." I smiled at him, glad once again that I was out of the sex and dating circuit that had been so dangerous for Adam O'Malley.

But that made me think about my case again and what I had ahead of me. When I had some food in my stomach, I felt ready to say, "The meeting I had this morning. It was with an attorney for Kingdom of Hawai'i. He said he had some information he didn't want to pass on in public, so Ray and I arranged to meet him at his apartment."

"So?"

"He was dead when we got there."

Mike nodded. "I'd say that's a complication."

"There's more, though. He was gay, this attorney. And he might have gotten killed by a guy he picked up at The Garage last night."

The waiter brought our entrees, and Mike didn't speak as he busied himself cutting his veal and tossing his pasta with the freshly grated parmesan.

"I should go over to The Garage tonight and see if anyone saw who this attorney was with," I said, looking down at my chicken piccata.

"And you were thinking that I would go with you," Mike said.

I looked up at him.

"Because I know you were not thinking you were going to that sleazy bar by yourself. You need adult supervision."

"Really?" I said, smiling. My foot brushed against his leg. "And are you my supervisor?"

"Well, for sure, I'm the responsible adult in this relationship." He smiled back at me. "I know I need to trust you more. You've never given me any doubt. But it makes me crazy to think of you going to a bar by yourself, flirting or fooling around with some other guy."

We ate in silence for a few minutes, both of us finishing our dishes, and then Mike said, "The Garage. You ever been there?"

"A couple of times, in the past. The Rod and Reel is more my speed."

"I went there once. They have that bar in the back where they show the videos."

"Mmm-hmm," I said.

"I might have gotten a little carried away, when I was drinking." Mike had gone on a couple of binges while we were apart, leading his father to believe he was an alcoholic, but I'd never pressed for details.

I speared the last piece of my chicken and pushed the empty plate away. "Carried away how?"

"Somehow I ended up naked, imitating Jennifer Beals in *Flashdance.*"

I burst out laughing. "Man, I wish I'd been there for that. There isn't a video on YouTube, is there?"

"Thankfully not. I could never go back after that, though."

"Gee, we'll have to see if anyone recognizes you tonight. Asks for an encore performance."

"I'm a private dancer now."

"You and Tina Turner. Ooh, strut that stuff, baby."

"Get out of here," he said, laughing and kicking my leg under the table.

We walked around Waikīkī for a while after dinner. The streets were packed with tourists and locals enjoying the holiday weekend. We strolled down Kalākaua toward Queen's Surf, the gay beach just before the aquarium, away from some of the neon and bustle from the strip. We held hands and sat on the curb overlooking the beach.

I wondered if I would have ended up like this, in love with Mike and settled down, if I hadn't been dragged out of the closet a few years before. Would I be like O'Malley, hiding my sexuality and picking up dangerous guys in bars? I'd done a few stupid things when I was single, despite my cop instincts and training, and I was lucky I'd never had any problems bigger than a couple of angry exes and a painful, though not deadly, visit to the emergency room.

The tide was coming in and the breeze smelled of salt and dead fish, but I was happy to be there with Mike. From the way he squeezed my hand, I had an inkling he felt the same way.

Shortly after eleven, we got up and walked back to where I'd parked my Jeep. I had a picture of O'Malley with me, one I'd picked up from his bureau, and I showed it to Mike as we drove to The Garage.

"Handsome guy," Mike said, and stretched his long frame back in the seat. "What kind of thing was he into?"

"We found him tied up, with a big black dildo sticking out of his ass," I said. "Creeped me out. Ray had to hold my hand for a while, metaphorically speaking."

Mike shook his head. "That guy is way too tolerant. I expect you to be trading blow job tips with him any day."

"Been there, done that." I laughed at how quickly Mike's head swiveled around. "Not."

"So was he the kind of guy you'd go for?" Mike asked. "This attorney?"

"You know my deal, sweetheart. I like sex a lot better when I'm with a guy I love. I love you. You're the first guy I can say that about. So sex with you is better than with anyone else. Ever."

"Good answer. Keep that in mind if anybody flirts with you tonight."

"Me?" I asked. "You're the big handsome firefighter stud with the sexy mustache. While I'm asking questions about a dead guy, you're the one the boys will be swarming over."

It was still early, so there was only a short line outside The Garage, the bouncer checking IDs. He waved us both in.

"Great, too old to be carded," I grumbled as we walked into

the darkened room, with neon wrapping the walls below the ceiling level. The place was decorated with gasoline memorabilia, with an old-fashioned gas pump along one wall. The floor was bare concrete, the DJ station behind glass windows as if it was where the clerk would stay.

Groups of two and three guys leaned against the walls and talked. A rap song pounded out through the sound system, and two men danced in the center of the room. There were two bartenders; I stepped up to talk to the cuter one while Mike went to order a beer from the other.

I palmed my shield and said, "Can I ask you some questions?"

The bartender was barely legal, a skinny haole in a tight tank top that showed his nipple rings. He had piercings in his eyebrow, his ears, his lip and who knew where else, though I could guess.

"What do you want to know?" he asked.

I showed him O'Malley's picture. "Recognize this guy?"

He took the picture from me, turned to the bar back where the light was better. When he handed the photo back to me he said, "Yeah. He comes in sometimes on Thursday nights."

"Was he here last night?"

The guy nodded.

"You see him leave with anyone?"

He might have looked brainless, but he wasn't. "Shit. Somebody hurt him?"

"Last night."

"Sometimes he leaves alone, sometimes he doesn't," the bartender said. "Last night, he left with this tough-looking dude, tats up and down his arms. He was making a play for your guy, for sure."

"Making a play how?"

"I saw him come up to your guy at the bar, start talking. Put his arm around him, that kind of thing. They didn't dance or anything, just hung out and drank and played around."

"You recognize him?"

"He's been in a couple of times before, but I don't know his name."

"If we find him, you think you could pick him out of a lineup?"

"I can try."

"Any other regulars who might have noticed something last night?"

"Thursday night's a specialized clientele," he said. "Hard hats night, you know. Tonight the promo's for younger guys. Different group entirely."

"I understand. Mahalo." I went down the bar and spoke to the other bartender, who hadn't noticed O'Malley or his mystery date.

I looked around at the interesting mix of guys. Older men, all races. A couple of middle-aged business types, looking scared. Some younger guys, the kind I might expect to see at a meeting of my gay teen group. And a guy like the one O'Malley had picked up the night before, with sunglasses propped on his head, as if he'd need them in the dim room. A sleeveless gray T-shirt showcased his beefy biceps. He wore loose athletic shorts that hung low on his hips and backless sandals.

He didn't have tattoos on his arms, though, so I gave up and scanned the crowd, looking for tall, dark and handsome. I spotted him in a corner, drinking a Bud and flirting with a young blond with a buzz cut.

I walked up and put my hand on Mike's shoulder. "Ready to go?" I asked.

"We're talking here," the blond said.

Mike looked amused. He drained the last of his beer and put the bottle down on a nearby table. Then he leaned back against the wall, his hands in his pockets, stretching his pants tight and displaying his ample endowment.

I turned to the blond. "Beat it. He's mine. I'm tougher than you are, I'm better in bed and I carry a gun. Get it?"

"Hey, fuck you," the blond said, but he turned away.

I wasn't exactly on duty, at least I wasn't going to put in an overtime sheet for this trip to the bar or for my unofficial surveillance later that night at the Wing Wah.

The DJ segued to a Lady Gaga song and turned the volume up high. "You want to hang around here for a while, or you want to go?" I yelled into Mike's ear.

"Neither." He shook his head. "I want to make out."

He grabbed me around the ass and pulled me toward him. His kiss was loose and beery, and I wondered if maybe he'd downed more than one bottle while waiting for me to finish questioning the bartenders.

But then I got caught up in the moment. Our bodies swayed in time to the music, and I felt his stiff dick grinding into my thigh. I got hard, too, and everything around us fell away as I kissed him, this man I loved.

We were putting on a show for the guys around us, who were on the prowl, after all, most of them strangers to each other.

After Mike and I had kissed and felt each other up for a while, he led me to the back bar, where an X-rated film was playing on a couple of plasma TVs. A guy in an obviously fake police uniform was getting his dick sucked by a punk.

Mike said, into my ear, "Cops. You know that excites me." He slid hand into the waistband of my jeans, teasing the tip of my dick with his index finger.

"You're bad," I said, leaning up against his ear. "You're going to make me come in my pants."

He leaned down and kissed me again.

I whispered in his ear, "Wish I could stick around, stud, but I've got another date. In Chinatown."

Winners and Losers

I dropped Mike back where he'd parked his truck and drove into Chinatown. It was the end of a long week, and I wanted nothing more than to relax and enjoy the Labor Day weekend. But I had a new murder on my plate and one more thing to do that night before I could go home and get some rest. I had to stake out the pai gow game, unofficially, and do my best to make sure nothing bad happened to my oldest brother.

I parked a couple of blocks from the Wing Wah and joined Ray in his Highlander shortly before midnight, where I told him what I'd learned at the bar. Even though the night was cool, I couldn't help sweating, waiting for the game to break up. Ray and I tried to figure out where the FBI guys were, but we couldn't make them.

Close to two a.m., two Ford sedans and a squad car drove up and parked right in front of the restaurant's side door. "Something's going down," Ray said.

Two uniforms stepped out of the squad, while five guys in FBI piled out of the Fords. I recognized Salinas as he walked up to the door and pounded on it.

"FBI! Open up!" we heard him yell.

There was no response from behind the door so he stepped aside and an agent holding a rammer stepped up. It was about forty pounds, basically a concrete tube with handles. The agent holding it smashed the door handle, destroying the lock, so that the door swung open. Then he stepped aside as the rest of the team streamed in. He dropped the rammer, swung his gun around and followed them in.

My heart rate accelerated as I watched. "My brother's probably pissing his pants right now."

The two uniforms pulled their weapons and led the way through the open door, with Salinas right behind them.

"I'm going to scoot over there and see what I can hear," I said, opening the Highlander's passenger door.

"No you're not." Ray grabbed my arm. "You'll only get in the way."

I sighed. "You're right." I closed the door. "But I hate sitting here waiting, not knowing what's going on."

"Trust Salinas."

"You obviously haven't worked with the FBI enough to know how dumb that statement sounds."

A man too thin and short to be my brother stepped through the door, stumbling in his haste to get away. He scurried down the street like a cockroach when you turn the lights on. A minute later, he was followed by another man, who behaved the same way.

"Jesus, what's going on?" I said.

"You know," Ray said. "You've been there. They're questioning each guy, searching them and then letting them go one by one."

I did know that, but it didn't make me feel any better about my brother. Two more men came out, and then Lui appeared, silhouetted in the light from the room behind him.

"I'm going after him. Can you hang around and see how things play out?"

"Sure."

I jumped out of the car and ran to my brother. "Lui! Hold up!"

He pivoted as I reached him, and he reached around and grabbed me in a big hug. I could smell liquor on his breath.

"What happened in there?" I asked, pulling back.

"I won, brah!" he crowed. "That fucker Tanaka made me the banker, trying to drive me even further into the hole, but I came out ahead."

I was so surprised at once again hearing my brother curse that it took me a minute to process. "So you didn't lose any of your inheritance?"

Lui laughed. "I didn't make back everything I owe Tanaka, but I walked away with a stack of bills. I didn't even count it yet. You know that song, 'you don't count your money as you're sitting at the table.'"

OK, Lui singing country songs was just too much for me. "What about the FBI? What happened when they blasted in?"

"Man, it was like something out of a movie. Cops and robbers, brah. They grabbed Tanaka and then started searching everybody for guns. At first I was scared shitless, but when they started letting everybody go, and I realized how much I'd won, I felt like I was the king of the world."

He spread his arms out and spun around, like Leonardo di Caprio in *Titanic*.

"Are you drunk, brah?"

"I'm high on life."

Oh, Jesus, I thought. "Come on, brah, I'll drive you home."

"I can drive, little bruddah. Only had two rumrunners. Don't worry about me."

I shook my head. I still had a lot to worry about—like would he be able to stop gambling, now he'd started again? I knew that winning that money would make him feel lucky again and make the temptation that much greater.

I decided I'd follow him up to St. Louis Heights, make sure he got home all right. "You drive safe, brah," I said, as we reached his car.

As I walked away, I heard him turning the radio up loud and starting to sing. I wished I'd had a video camera trained on him; might make good evidence the next time he was acting like a stuck-up prig.

I got in my Jeep and caught up to Lui, who was driving with exaggerated care. I stayed behind him until he pulled into his own driveway. As I was heading back downhill, Ray called.

"I'm outside the Kope Bean warehouse," he said. "The FBI brought Tanaka here for a search party."

"Very cool."

"Nothing more I can do here, though. I'll see you tomorrow morning."

When I got home, Roby was waiting for me by the front door, jumping up and down like a demented kangaroo. The rest of the house was quiet, so I figured Mike was already asleep. I grabbed the leash, and Roby and I went for a long walk, up and down hills, as I tried to decompress from the evening.

I hadn't realized how worried I'd been about my brother's safety until I saw him walk out of the restaurant. I was tired of feeling nervous about people; I'd spent a lot of energy worrying about Lui's gambling and my mother's work with Kingdom of Hawai'i.

Even the goofy golden retriever on the other end of the leash had suffered a loss and was recovering from the trauma of the fire that had destroyed his home and sent him away from the family who loved him. By the time Roby and I circled back to the house, I was pretty sure he had no more urine left in his bladder, and I was yawning and ready for bed.

Saturday morning I woke to find Mike's leg crossed over mine and his tongue tickling the outside of my ear.

"Missed you last night."

He ran his hand down my chest to my dick, which responded to his touch. We began carrying out the promises our bodies had made at The Garage the night before.

We were kissing and rubbing our bodies together when Roby's big golden head appeared over the side of the bed.

"Down, boy," Mike said. "This is not a participatory sport."

I laughed and pushed the dog away. He settled down on the floor next to the bed and had to wait until Mike and I had both had our fill of each other before I crawled out of bed, pulled on shorts and a T-shirt and took him for his walk, as Mike rolled over and went back to sleep.

I skipped breakfast in order to make it to headquarters and meet Ray just after eight. "I've been thinking about what you found out at the bar last night," he said, as I handed him a bodyboard-sized macadamia latte I'd picked up for him from the Kope Bean on my way in.

"Yeah?"

"What if O'Malley's death isn't related to the others at all— just a coincidence? You said that the bartender recognized the hustler had been in there before. He made a play for O'Malley, then went home with him. Both concierges confirmed that he often brought tough-looking guys home with him."

"But why kill O'Malley?" I asked. "He was already hog-tied. The hustler could have just picked up O'Malley's wallet and jewelry and walked out."

"Maybe O'Malley threatened him. Let me go, or I'll drag your ass into court."

"I don't think O'Malley could have been that stupid."

"Why stick the dildo up his ass?" Ray asked. "That's anger, don't you think? Like O'Malley did something to piss the guy off."

"Could be. Or it could be a red herring, the killer trying to make us think this was a sex thing."

I sipped my coffee and thought. "Besides, it's just too coincidental. He told me he was worried about people involved with KOH, that they were dangerous. I think his death has to be connected to our appointment with him."

"That's certainly one theory," Ray sipped his coffee, and sighed with pleasure, "but just to be thorough, let's see if there's anybody on duty in Vice who can tell us if there's someone out there committing similar crimes."

"They've probably all cut out for Labor Day," I said, but followed Ray down to the B1 level, where I was surprised to find Juanita Lum at her desk.

"Big sweep last night in Waikīkī," she said. "I had to come in this morning to help out. You know the lieutenant, he's lost without me."

"I heard that," Kee boomed from his office. He had a long, sad face like a Bassett hound and brush-cut black hair going gray at the sideburns. "What brings you gentlemen down to the bowels of the building?" he asked when we walked in.

I sketched out the details of O'Malley's murder. Kee frowned. "Let me see what we can dig up. Juanita! I need you in here."

He swiveled his computer keyboard around so that she could lean over the desk and type. "Get me all the crimes involving gay men and sexual violence."

"There's a course next week," she said, as she started to type. "Computers for Dummies. You should sign up for it."

"What do I need a course for when I've got you?"

"You want domestics, too, or just prostitutes?" she asked us.

"Nothing between long-term partners," I said. "But not just prostitutes, if you can do that."

"I keep this department running. I can do anything."

She typed for a bit, scanned the monitor and then typed some more. "Next time we need something, we can come to you, huh, Juanita?" Ray asked. "Bypass the lieutenant altogether."

"I'm not deaf, Detective," Kee said. "Just computer-challenged."

The printer on Kee's credenza started spitting papers, and Juanita went back to her desk. Kee picked them up and scanned them before handing them to us.

"Mostly it's the working boys who get hurt," he said, as Ray and I moved together to look at the sheets. "Customer realizes the goods aren't what he expected, he gets angry. That kind of thing."

He handed us another couple of sheets. "Every now and then you get a john who gets ripped off and calls us, though."

Two complaints stood out. The most important was one filed by Adam O'Malley over a year before.

"Guy sure didn't learn his lesson," Ray said, looking over my shoulder.

According to the police report, O'Malley had met a man at a bar, then gone to a secluded area of Kapiolani Park with him. The guy had pulled a knife and taken O'Malley's watch, wallet and college ring. I remembered being that desperate, long before, when I was still in the closet and picking up the occasional guy in a bar. I'd been lucky never to get in trouble, but I knew what it felt like to throw caution out the window when you were horny.

The other looked more promising. A tourist had gone to The Garage a couple of months before and picked up a man whose description fit the guy who'd left with O'Malley, in a very general way—skinny, white, tattoos.

According to the tourist, the skinny guy had picked him up and taken him to a cheap motel a few blocks away. Skinny had suggested that the tourist jump into the shower, promising to join him there. By the time the hot water had run out, the tourist figured something was wrong. When he stepped out of the shower, the skinny guy was gone, along with the tourist's watch, wallet and clothes. There was no phone in the room, so he'd had to walk down to the office wrapped only in his towel.

"You know anything about this guy?" I asked, pushing the paper back to Kee.

He picked it up and scanned it. "I remember this one," he said. "The tourist left, and then a couple of weeks later his gold Rolex showed up at a pawn shop. We pulled in Shakey Simons, but he swore he got the watch from another guy in exchange for some information. Of course, he didn't know the other guy's name or where to find him."

"Can we talk to Shakey?" I asked.

"Wish you could. He died a couple of weeks ago. HIV, complicated by ice."

"So it's unlikely he was at The Garage on Friday."

"That's what I like about working with you bruddahs from Homicide. Always so quick to pick things up."

"This is all you've got?" I asked.

"If that's all Juanita found, then that's all we've got."

"Which leaves us with nothing," Ray said, as we headed back to the elevator.

MEETING OLD FRIENDS

When we got back to our desks, Ray said, "We should look around for any similar MOs, guys picked up at that bar or others. You've got contacts. See if there's anyone who's been too embarrassed to report something."

Ray googled O'Malley, trying to guess what he might have known about Kingdom of Hawai'i. I flipped through the old address book I had found in O'Malley's closet, looking for familiar names. On the F page, I found one I knew: Gunter Franz.

"Jesus, Gunter," I muttered to myself. "Have you slept with every gay man on this island?"

It was just after ten, time to wake Gunter from his beauty sleep. "You have a few minutes to assist the police with their inquiries?" I asked, after he picked up.

"Are you buying breakfast?" I heard him yawn through the phone.

"Beachside Broiler in fifteen." I hung up and told Ray, "I'm taking a run over to Waikīkī. Be back in a while."

Gunter and I often ate breakfast at the Beachside Broiler when I lived in Waikīkī. It was a touristy buffet in one of the hotels on Hobron Lane, with an ocean view and pretty decent food. On my way inside I picked up one of the free magazines and found a two-for-one coupon. I was flipping through the magazine and looking at the ads for gay bars when Gunter came in, skinny as ever, his blond buzz cut newly shaved. He wore a skin-tight white tank top with a rampant dragon on it, flames from the dragon's mouth swirling all the way around to his back.

"So what's the occasion?" Gunter asked, as we loaded up our trays with macadamia nut pancakes, sausage patties, fluffy rolls and slices of fresh pineapple and papaya.

I waited until we were seated, in a quiet corner of the restaurant, before I asked, "You know a guy named Adam O'Malley?"

Gunter's forkful of hash browns stopped halfway to his mouth. "When you ask me about men, it usually means they're either under arrest or dead."

"Dead."

His fork clattered back to his plate. "Shit."

"So you did know him?"

"Yeah. Not that well. I tricked with him a couple of times, and then I gave him a client referral about a year ago. He took me out to a fancy dinner to say thanks."

"What kind of referral?"

"Guy I knew who was starting a business, needed some legal advice. What happened to Adam?"

I told him about finding O'Malley's body the day before. He just nodded, and we both ate in silence for a few minutes.

"That jive with what you knew about him?" I asked, pushing my half-finished plate away. I'd lost my appetite. "That he picked up the wrong kind of guy?"

"Yeah." He told me the same story I'd heard from Greg Oshiro—conflicted about his sexuality, O'Malley looked for men who'd treat him badly.

I shook my head. "Poor son of a bitch. You know any of his friends?"

"Not really. I'd just see him at bars now and then."

"You hear of anybody else who's gotten in trouble the same way Adam did? Picking up a guy and getting mugged?"

"Usually it's the tourists who get in trouble," Gunter said. "But if you want to ask around, this group I belong to, Māhū Nation, is sponsoring a picnic tomorrow afternoon. One of the guys there might be able to point you toward someone."

"Māhū Nation? What kind of group is that?"

"Just a bunch of guys. Once you abandoned me for domesticated life, I had to look for friends elsewhere."

"I can do without the drama queen routine. I get that from Mike."

"Yeah, he's so hot he has to wear asbestos underwear."

I'd seen Gunter get catty before, but there had always been an undercurrent of fun. That day, though, he didn't seem happy. Was he jealous that I'd moved in with Mike? Left him to his single life?

I remembered my purpose. "Thanks for the tip about the picnic. I'll talk to Mike about it. It might be a good way to find someone who saw my victim at The Garage."

When I got back to headquarters, Ray told me he had found O'Malley's name in conjunction with KOH in a couple of places online. Once he had been quoted in a *Star-Bulletin* article, and he'd been mentioned a few times as the attorney of record for KOH. But there was no indication of what kind of damaging information he might have had.

I tried the FBI, but the agent on duty informed me that Salinas was involved in a case and all the agent could do was take a message.

We hadn't released O'Malley's name to the press yet, and I wondered what kind of reaction we could get out of his coworkers. I called his office, and a human being answered the phone. I hung up without saying anything; I just wanted to see if anyone was there.

"It's a wonderful world, isn't it?" I said. "Hard-working attorneys piling up billable hours over the Labor Day holiday."

"Even better, it's your turn to drive," Ray said.

The Fields and Yamato office was in a high-rise tower overlooking the port of Honolulu. A teenaged Hawaiian boy sat at the reception desk, working at a computer monitor. "Aloha," he said. "How can I help you?"

I introduced myself and Ray and showed her our badges. "We need to ask some questions about Adam O'Malley."

"Mr. O'Malley isn't in today. Would you like to speak with his paralegal?"

"Sure."

He picked up the phone and punched in a couple of numbers. "Sarah, it's Akamu, out at the front desk. There are a couple of police officers who need to speak to someone about Mr. O'Malley."

He listened for a moment, then hung up. "She'll be right out."

"I'm surprised to see the office open on a Saturday," I said, as we waited.

"We're not officially open. Just a few of the attorneys and paralegals are here. I'm a student at U.H., and I'm interning here for the summer. I go back to school right after Labor Day, and I figured I would get a few more hours in while I can."

He was a cheerful kid in a light blue chambray shirt, and we chatted for a couple minutes until a stocky woman in an open-necked blouse, navy skirt and matching pumps came out to the lobby. I thought the bright red streak in her dark hair was an interesting touch in such a conservative environment.

"I'm Sarah Byrne," she said. "You have some questions for Mr. O'Malley? If it's important, I can call him." She had a crisp Australian accent.

I shook my head. "We need to speak to someone about him, and the cases he worked on here. Is there a place we can talk?"

She led us to a small conference room off the lobby. Floor to ceiling windows looked out at the port, where despite the holiday a crane was offloading containers from a big ship.

"I'm afraid we have some bad news for you," I said. "Mr. O'Malley was found dead in his apartment yesterday morning."

She reached out to one of the plush armchairs to steady herself. "Oh, my," she said, and she began to cry.

Ray poured her a glass of water from a pitcher on a side table, and I helped her sit in the big captain's chair.

"Do you know what happened?" she asked, once she'd

dabbed at her eyes and taken a sip of water. "Was it a heart attack or—was he killed?" Her eyes widened.

"We're still working on the details," I said. "That's why we're here."

She began to stand up. "I think you should speak to one of the associates."

"We will, soon. For now we just want to get some background on Mr. O'Malley."

"Where there any clients that you know of who were unhappy with his work?" Ray asked. "Anyone who might have threatened him?"

Sarah sat back down, clutching the tissue in her right hand. "We focus on corporate litigation," she said, shaking her head. "We don't handle criminal work at all. And Mr. O'Malley was a very quiet sort of a man—not the type to get into arguments, certainly not with clients."

"Was he upset about anything?" I asked. "Or did he seem worried, or unusually agitated?"

"Not at all. He had just come back from a business trip, and he said he was glad to be home."

"I understand he was in Washington, DC last week," I said. "Do you know what kind of case that was?"

"I can't give you any information about our clients or ongoing litigation," she said. "But I *can* tell you the case involved copyright infringement and both parties are large, well-known multinational corporations. Mr. O'Malley was in touch with various members of their in-house counsel, so there wasn't a specific individual who was involved in the case."

"Was it usual for him to take a Friday off?" I asked.

"Mr. O'Malley worked very hard," Sarah said. "I know he put in long hours when he was in Washington, because of the time difference. But when he did take a day off it was usually a Friday. I don't know why, because most of the time he'd be back in the office that weekend."

"How about his personal life?" Ray asked. "Can you tell us about any friends or activities?"

"He started at the same time I did, about five years ago," she said. "He went to college and law school in San Francisco and then worked for a firm there for a few years. I don't know very much about his private life." She paused. "He wasn't the kind of boss to get personal. I knew he wasn't married, because he didn't wear a wedding ring or have any pictures on his desk. But I don't even know if he had a girlfriend."

"Is there anyone here that he was friendly with?" I asked. "Any other attorney he might have confided in?"

She thought for a moment. "I know who you could talk to. I'll be right back." She hurried out of the room.

"She didn't even know if he had a girlfriend," Ray said, when she was gone.

"That's life in the closet."

While we waited for Sarah to return, we went back over what she had said, looking for anything we might have missed. Ray was facing the door, and said, "Here she comes."

I turned around. The first person through the door, though, wasn't O'Malley's paralegal—it was Peggy Kaneahe.

Peggy's dark hair, always down to her shoulders in the past, was now cut in a severe, yet fashionable bob. She was nearly 100% Hawaiian, and her skin had always been a rich olive-cocoa, a few shades darker than mine. Now, though, she appeared pale, as if she hadn't been out in the sun in months. There were a few more lines around her eyes than I'd seen before, and she had the attenuated, rail-thin aspect of a single woman who exercised too much.

She and I had a long history. Because of our last names, Kanapa'aka and Kaneahe, we always sat next to each other at Punahou. When we were sixteen I took her to our junior prom, and she was the first girl I ever kissed. She was the first I had sex with, too, one Saturday afternoon when her parents were at a christening on the North Shore. I broke up with her right after coming home from my first year in Santa Cruz, after I'd had my first sexual experience with another guy.

We dated again, briefly, when she returned to Honolulu after law school and was working in the DA's office. Since I'd come out of the closet, though, I'd been careful to avoid running into her.

She looked as surprised as I was. "Kimo," she said.

"Hi, Peggy. I didn't realize you'd left the DA's office."

"Two years ago."

She turned to Sarah Byrne. "I can take it from here, Sarah. Thanks." She looked at us. "Assuming you're done with Sarah?"

I nodded. "If we have any more questions, we'll get back to you."

Sarah left, and I introduced Peggy to Ray. "Peggy and I went to high school together," I said, leaving out the gory details.

We sat at the round table. Ray and I faced the water and the brilliant sun, while Peggy sat with her back to the light. I was sure it was some kind of attorney trick to put us at a disadvantage.

"You're working on Labor Day weekend," I said, to get the conversation started.

"I'm trying to make partner." She paused. "Sarah said this is about Adam O'Malley? I have to say, I'm not surprised that he's dead."

I sat back in my chair and looked at Peggy. "That's a pretty strong statement."

"Adam had a low self-image," she said. "I know it's a cliché, but he worked twice as hard because he didn't think he was smart enough, or a good enough lawyer, to become a partner here. But at the same time he desperately wanted the prestige that comes with that title, not to mention the money."

She sighed, and the corners of her mouth turned down. I wondered if she was talking about herself as well. She had always been a driven student in high school, not content with anything less than an A in every class. She was on a full scholarship at Punahou, always feeling inferior to our rich haole classmates despite her grades.

"From what I could tell, Adam's inferiority complex carried over to his personal life," Peggy said. "He never said so, but I knew he was gay. We were friends, and we were each other's date sometimes when we had to go to business dinners." She pursed her lips together and looked directly at me. "I seem to have a knack for attracting gay men."

I felt the sting of that dart but avoided acknowledging it. Fortunately Ray stepped in and asked, "He talked to you about his personal life?"

"Not in much detail. But I knew enough not to ask him who he went out with on the weekend or why some lucky girl hadn't snatched him up yet." She paused. "I had the feeling he was attracted to the wrong kind of guy. Once he told me that he'd been mugged and had his wallet stolen, and from how cagey he was about the details I thought it was a hook up. And another time I saw a bruise on his arm, and his explanation was lame."

I made a couple of notes, then looked back up at Peggy. "From what we've discovered, Mr. O'Malley went to a bar on Thursday night, where he met a man he took back to his apartment. That man is certainly someone we want to talk to, but we're trying to cover all our bases. Do you have any idea why someone would want to kill him?"

"I used to get death threats in the DA's office," Peggy said, picking unconsciously at one fingernail with another. "That's one of the reasons I left. I just got tired of the personal hassle. But here, we don't deal with real human beings and their problems. I like that. Nobody comes rampaging in, yelling at the receptionist. Nobody waves weapons at us or stalks us outside our houses." She looked up at us. "Adam was a very quiet guy, and this is a low-key practice."

"Ray and I had an appointment with O'Malley on Friday afternoon, to discuss some suspicions he had about one of his clients, which relate to two other murders we're investigating. He was threatened enough that he didn't want to discuss things in the office."

"Which client?" Peggy asked.

"Kingdom of Hawai'i. I understand he was the attorney of record for the group?"

"If there's any client who could have gotten Adam in trouble, they're the one. I encouraged him to get rid of them, but he didn't listen." Her voice cracked at the end of the sentence, and I could see her struggling to maintain control.

When we were in high school, our mothers were close friends, and her mother in particular was very proud of their Hawaiian lineage. I doubted Peggy would have let her mother volunteer for KOH. Even though my mother hadn't been hurt at the rally, I wished I'd been more aware of what was going on and tried to keep her away from what was turning out to be a very questionable group.

"What was it that you found suspicious?" I asked Peggy.

"Adam mentioned they took in a lot of cash donations," she said. "The man behind the group said that they had a lot of grassroots support among native Hawaiians, who didn't trust banks. But I knew that was bullshit. Most of my family is

Hawaiian, and we've all got Bankoh accounts."

"So you didn't believe him," I said. "But did Adam?"

"He believed what he wanted to. The non-profit and some allied corporations generated a lot of billable hours because of some kind of complicated corporate structure and interconnected transactions between companies. Adam was up for partner at the end of the year. He thought if he could hold on to them until then, the partners would see him as a rainmaker and make him an offer."

She bit her lower lip, and I remembered how she used to do that when she was uncomfortable. "How did he die?" she asked.

"He was killed in his apartment," I said. "It's possible that there was sexual activity involved or that the killer wanted to create a false impression. We just don't know yet."

"I was an ADA for years, Kimo. You don't need to sugarcoat for me."

"He was naked, tied to the bedposts, with a dildo stuck up his ass. His throat was slit."

As soon as I said it I felt bad, letting my anger and frustration and my discomfort at seeing Peggy again get the better of me.

She didn't even flinch, though. "And despite that situation you think there's a possibility that his death is connected to his work?"

"As I said, when I spoke to him on Thursday, he told me that he felt there were dangerous people connected with KOH and that he was frightened by them." I thought about what I wanted to say next. "You can see we don't have enough to show a judge. But we have a hunch that his death was more than just a hook up gone bad."

"And you want me to open up our confidential files to you," she said. "Without a warrant. On the strength of your hunch?"

I looked at Ray, then back at her. "That's about it."

Looking at Peggy's face, I figured she was running through her whole history with me. How many times had I dumped her for the chance to go surfing with Harry Ho? How many times had I disappointed her or hurt her? She had gotten in hot water at the DA's office over her attitude toward me. And here I was, asking her for a favor that could potentially damage her standing with Fields and Yamato.

Ray stepped in to rescue me. "We have more than just a hunch," he said. "Our investigation keeps leading us to a guy named Jun Tanaka, who runs the Kope Bean chain, and who's a big backer, through his various corporations, of Kingdom of Hawai'i. The FBI picked him up last night on suspicion of money laundering."

"The FBI?"

Ray continued, "Yup. They're probably filing subpoenas right now. They're not going to care about our murder victims, though. They'll get your files, they'll hold them up for a couple of years while they build their case." He paused. "You know how that works. We'll never get a conviction on any of these murders."

I watched Peggy's body language. Her back stiffened, and she stopped biting her lip. Ray had played her perfectly, without anything more than a gut instinct. He thought she would care about seeing Adam's killer brought to justice. And he was right.

She sighed. "I can't open up our files on my own. I'll have to talk to one of the partners."

"We can wait," I said.

Peggy led us to O'Malley's office. "Before you go, you guys must have some kind of program where you track billable hours, don't you?" I asked her.

"Why?"

"Our first victim, Edith Kapana, who was killed at the KOH rally, had O'Malley's business card. I'd like to know if she came in to speak with him and why."

She considered that. "I suppose we can look into that. I'll get Sarah to help you."

While we waited for O'Malley's paralegal, Ray and I prowled

the room, looking for evidence of O'Malley's life. Like his apartment, his office was impersonal. His college and law school diplomas had been framed and hung on one wall, along with various certificates from legal seminars. Another wall was taken up with bookshelves filled with thick volumes of legal codes. He hadn't even hung one of those ubiquitous landscapes or motivational posters.

It was sad to think that so much of his life had transpired in such settings. What mattered to him? What was he passionate about? I couldn't tell from anything around us. When we realized there was nothing else to see, we sat down in leather armchairs across from O'Malley's desk.

Sarah Byrne came in and went right to the computer. "Everything is online here," she said as it booted up. "The database is searchable by attorney and client."

"You have O'Malley's password?" I asked.

She shook her head. "I don't need it. Because I worked on cases with him, I have access to his client records."

As she typed her name and password into the database, she began to sing a little under her breath. I didn't recognize the song, but then, most of what I listen to comes with slack key guitar accompaniment. Ray did, though.

"Is that 'My Attorney Bernie'? I love that song," he said.

She blushed. "I'm sorry, I didn't realize I was doing that."

"No, you have a good voice," Ray said. "I'm a big Dave Frishberg fan. 'Bernie is a purist, not your polyester tourist,'" he sang. His voice was surprisingly good.

"I sing with a jazz group," Sarah said, hitting a couple of keys. "We do a lot of his songs. You should come by some time. You and your wife."

She was sharp, Sarah. I liked her.

She looked at us. "We're in. What are we searching for?"

"Edith Kapana," I said. "She was a volunteer for Kingdom of Hawai'i, and she had O'Malley's business card."

"The woman who was killed at the rally," Sarah said. "I read about that." She typed and hit a couple of keys, and a single record popped up.

"She met with him a couple of days before the rally," I said, pointing at the screen. "Any idea what it was about?"

She shook her head. "He has it coded new client consultation."

"Would there be a paper file? Maybe he dictated something about the meeting?"

"I can check. Anything else while we're in the database?"

"How about Kingdom of Hawai'i?" I asked.

"Isn't that the file Peggy went to get for you?"

"Yeah."

"Then I think we should wait until she gets back to look up his appointments with regard to them."

OK, maybe Sarah was a little too sharp. She wasn't going to let us do an end run around Peggy.

She looked through the file folders on his desk and in his drawers but couldn't find anything on Edith. By then Peggy returned to O'Malley's office, carrying a couple of heavy green hanging folders. "I had to get Mr. Yamato's permission, and he wasn't very happy. Attorney-client privilege doesn't end just because Adam is dead. Mr. Yamato gave me some latitude—if I think there's anything in the file you should see, I can show it to you. But if you need any copies I have to clear it with him first. And you can't use any of this in court."

"I know. And I appreciate this, Peggy," I said.

"I'm still an ADA at heart. I want you to find the bastard who killed Adam."

Peggy said it was all right for Sarah to pull up records of hours O'Malley spent on KOH and Kope Bean business, and the screen filled with a long list. "You weren't kidding when you said they generated a lot of work for him," I said.

It looked like O'Malley spent at least twenty hours a week

on Tanaka's business, mostly having to do with the Kope Bean and its intertwined companies. "I can see why he'd want to keep Tanaka as a client," Ray said. "Twenty hours is half his workload."

Peggy laughed. "You don't know much about how corporate lawyers work, do you?" she asked. "Twenty hours a week is just a drop in the bucket. We charge in fifteen-minute increments, so a good associate can generate at least five billable hours out of each hour of work. Make a two-minute phone call? That's a fifteen-minute charge. While you're on the phone, sign a set of documents for a different client. There's another fifteen-minute charge. If you're smart and you work hard, you can bill twenty-four hours a day."

We scrolled through the database with Sarah's help, but all it told us was that Adam O'Malley racked up the hours. Then we let Sarah go, and Peggy looked through the paper files. From the way she was flipping through pages, it didn't look like anything there could help us finger O'Malley's killer.

She was almost to the end of the folder as I started to wonder if maybe Ray was right. Suppose Adam O'Malley's death had just been a terrible accident, unconnected to our case. He had gone to The Garage and picked up the wrong guy.

"What's this?" Peggy asked, snapping me out of my reverie.

She was looking at two different sets of documents and moved them so we could look, too. Five pages, a list of handwritten names and dates, appeared to have been sliced from a book. The papers were very old, faded in some parts and water-stained in others. Without knowing what we were looking at, it was almost impossible to decipher.

The other set comprised records of intake and discharge at the Hawai'i State Hospital, for someone named Ezekiel Lopika. "Why would this be in the KOH file?" Peggy said, leaning over my shoulder. I could smell her perfume. If it wasn't the same one she'd worn in high school, it was a close match. "Who is Ezekiel Lopika?"

"Maybe these records really belong to Ezekiel Kapuāiwa,

who's the poster child for KOH," I said. "You know who he is, don't you, Peggy?"

"Yeah. I've seen him on TV a couple of times."

"If these are his records, they may be here because he's the person Kingdom of Hawai'i proposes should be king if the monarchy is restored. He might have been hospitalized under a different last name to keep people from realizing he was crazy."

"Like that would be easy," Ray said. "You said you've seen him, Peggy. Didn't he strike you as kind of squirrely?"

"There's a big difference between being eccentric and being crazy enough to be hospitalized," Peggy said. "And if these records really belong to him, it's a lousy attempt at camouflage. Why change his last name but not his first? Ezekiel's not a common name."

"I don't know. But maybe this is what O'Malley was concerned about." I looked over at Peggy. "Edith Kapana, the woman who was gunned down at the Kingdom of Hawai'i rally? She was from the same town on the Big Island as Ezekiel. She must have known him as a young man. People said she was his hanai tūtū."

I stood up and started pacing around the conference room. "Suppose she brought these records to O'Malley when she met with him," I continued. "Somebody could have killed her to keep her from making his hospitalization public."

"You're saying that's why she went up to the Ohana?" Ray asked. "But why go up there to ask about his medical records when she already had the paperwork?"

I stopped by the conference room door. "Maybe she was worried about Ezekiel, about the stress that being involved with KOH could cause him. She could have wanted to talk about that with David Currie, but he wouldn't discuss Ezekiel's condition with her."

Ray made me stop for a minute so he could fill Peggy in on Edith's visit to the Ohana Ola Kino. Even though I was worried that I was spinning a fantasy without any proof behind it, I couldn't help continuing my story once he'd finished.

"Maybe it wasn't even a threat. She might have thought that by releasing his records she was protecting him from another breakdown. But Jun Tanaka wouldn't feel the same way. Ezekiel's his main man when it comes to KOH."

My brain was racing so fast my mouth was having trouble keeping up. I had to start pacing around the conference room again just to slow myself down. "Somebody broke into Edith's room a couple of days after she was killed and stole a lot of papers and photos she had there," I said to Peggy. "Whoever it was could have been looking for these records, but she'd already given them to O'Malley."

"I'm confused," Peggy said. "I thought you said the FBI was investigating Tanaka for money laundering. How would these hospitalization records have any bearing on that case?"

"If Tanaka is using KOH as a front for the money laundering, then he'd want to do anything to protect his investment. If Edith's revelation threatened him he could have had her killed."

"If this is what he wanted to tell us about, why is this material here and not at O'Malley's apartment?" Ray asked. "We didn't find anything about KOH at there."

"Maybe he was going to bring us here. And if he did have copies with him at home, the killer would have taken them away."

Peggy said, "It's our firm's policy not to let original documents leave the office. He probably made copies to show you."

"See?" I asked Ray. "He couldn't bring the originals home with him."

"You have an answer for everything, don't you?" Ray said. "It would be nice if you had even a shred of proof to back any of this up."

Peggy stood up. "I'm glad I'm not an ADA any more. Life is a lot simpler here. I'll see if I can get copies of these for you." She took the papers and walked out.

While she was gone, Ray and I went back and forth. I felt like a big hot air balloon, struggling to take off, while he held down my guide rope. I knew that one of us had to be the rational one, but it was still frustrating.

"It's a motive," I insisted. "In addition to protecting his money laundering operation, Tanaka could be looking after his investment in KOH. Whoever controls KOH could be in line for a whole lot of money." I leaned forward. "You've got to admit it's starting to make sense. What if Dex told Tanaka that Edith went to the Ohana to research Ezekiel's hospitalization? Killing her at the rally could have been a diversionary tactic to keep us from learning the real motive."

Peggy came back to the conference room. "I spoke with Mr. Yamato. I can't give you copies of any of this material until he's had a chance to look at it himself and talk with the other partners on Tuesday."

I wanted to argue, pound the table, demand cooperation. But I knew I had no legal right and so I reined myself in.

While I was mastering my emotions, Ray said, "Thanks. You've already helped us a lot. More than we expected."

"I'll call you Tuesday," Peggy said.

We stood up to go. "It was good to see you again, Peggy," I said.

"You too, Kimo." She leaned up and kissed my cheek, and just for a moment I remembered kissing her in her parents' den and how much my life had changed since then.

The Old Swimming Hole

By the time we got back to the station after our visit to Fields and Yamato, it was the middle of Saturday afternoon, and our investigation had run out of juice. We wouldn't get the autopsy results until Tuesday, and we couldn't get the copies from Peggy until then, too. We had no new leads on Edith's shooting, Stuey's death or even the sniper attack on us at the Ohana. It was frustrating, and I didn't look forward to telling Sampson we had made no progress. I also didn't want to ship the cases to cold storage and move on.

But despite that desire, we called it quits for the rest of the weekend. Ray was on special duty on Sunday and Monday, picking up some extra cash toward a down payment for a house. "I'll swing by that Māhū Nation picnic tomorrow afternoon. See if any of those guys knew O'Malley or had the same kind of experience, picking up a guy at The Garage and having things go sour."

"Mike won't be happy about that," he said. "You going to a party full of gay guys."

"I'll just have to convince Mike to go with me."

"Good luck with that."

When I got home, Mike was vacuuming the living room and running a load of laundry. "How was your day?" I asked Mike, after a quick kiss hello. "You and Roby have fun?"

He shut off the machine, and Roby came running out from the bedroom.

"Nah. Just cleaned up and ran errands. How was yours?"

"Frustrating." I told him about all the dead ends we had run across. "And you won't believe this. I found Gunter's name in O'Malley's address book. So I had breakfast with him at the Beachfront Broiler. He confirmed that O'Malley liked rough trade."

"I believe Gunter's name is in the address book of most of the gay men on this island," Mike said. I couldn't tell if the tone of his voice implied disdain or envy.

"Gunter suggested I go up to this picnic tomorrow with this group of gay guys he belongs to called Māhū Nation. One of them might know about a guy picking up marks at The Garage and mugging them."

Mike crossed his arms over his chest, and I readied myself for a fight. "I've heard of them. They do these nudie swim things up in the hills. But neither of us are taking our clothes off."

"You're going?"

"Are you kidding? I'm not letting you go some place full of naked men by yourself."

That wasn't the fight I was expecting. Common sense told me to shut up, and for a change, I did. I kissed Mike's cheek, stripped down to my boxers, and started cleaning with him. We grilled some steaks for dinner and spent the evening on the sofa watching *Shock to the System*, a TV movie made from one of Richard Stevenson's gay mysteries.

Sunday morning I couldn't concentrate on the paper or the crossword puzzle. I took Roby out in the back yard and tossed the Frisbee to him, but he had forgotten the concept of "fetch." He grabbed it and settled down on the lawn to chew it. Once I wrestled it back from him and tossed it again, he took it and hid under the hibiscus hedge.

"You're not very cooperative." I wanted to ask Mike to go for a bike ride or run, anything to work off some nervous tension, but when I went back inside, he was napping on the bed, his white briefs a contrast to his tanned skin and black hair.

I put on a T-shirt and a pair of board shorts and drove down to Makapu'u Point, where I surfed until my arms and legs felt like jelly. As I was walking back up the beach with my board, I passed a shirtless twenty-something haole with long blond dreadlocks. He was waving a fist in the air and yelling at a woman with him.

I was worried he might be threatening her, so I stopped

nearby, planting my board in the sand and pretending to examine it for dings.

"See, that's the beauty," he told the woman, a petite blonde in a bikini that did little to cover her ample endowments. "We wait until no one's home. So there's no chance anybody gets hurt."

Oh, Jesus, I thought. What was this guy planning?

"I'm telling you, that's my dog," he said. "I'm getting that dog back no matter what."

I picked up my board and continued back to my Jeep. At least he wasn't threatening the woman or setting up a home invasion robbery, I thought. But people with crime on their mind should keep their voices down. That reminded me of Stuart McKinney, talking so loudly to Ray and me outside the Kope Bean warehouse. What if Dex, standing in the doorway waiting for him, had overheard him talking to us about the money Mr. T brought in at night? Could that have signed Stuey's death warrant? And could that be the connection we needed to make Stuey's murder fit into the story we were constructing?

I pushed thoughts of the case out of my head as I drove back up to Aiea. I called Gunter and got directions to the picnic, and an hour later, Mike and I followed them up Waimano Home Road, through the center of Pearl City and then up into the Ko'olaus. We parked on a cleared piece of land just off the road, along with a jumble of cars old and new, everything from gleaming luxury SUVs to beat-up Hondas and Nissans. I made sure my gun and badge were securely locked in my glove compartment before we left the Jeep.

A narrow, overgrown path led down the hill toward the natural pool at the bottom of the valley. The sound of Jason Mraz singing "I fell right through the cracks, and now I'm trying to get back," from the song *I'm Yours,* floated up toward us.

I felt really happy being there with Mike, as if both of us had come back from tough times and were lucky to be together. But maybe it was just the second-hand pakalolo smoke, mixed with the aroma of a charcoal grill.

The path opened up into a cleared area of about a quarter-acre. On the far hill, water gushed over a tiny waterfall into a stone pool about twice the size of the man-made one in my brother Lui's back yard.

A dense thatch of brown and dark green trees and vines climbed the slopes, and the place gave me the feel of a hidden paradise. A makeshift cabin stood next to the pool, with a small sandy beach leading into it. A half dozen guys were in the water, though I couldn't tell if they were wearing bathing suits.

Gunter came romping up, wearing a pink T-shirt that read Māhū Nation, with tiny white shorts and matching rubber slippers. He grabbed me in a big bear hug and kissed me on the lips—something I thought he did just to piss off Mike.

"I'm so glad you came," he said, looking like a giant six-foot-two pink puppy dog with a spiky blond buzz cut.

"Don't I get a kiss?" Mike grabbed Gunter and planted a big one on his lips.

I was astonished. Mike doesn't like public displays of affection, and he doesn't like Gunter either. But I guessed the big dogs were trying to show each other up. Gunter seemed surprised by the kiss and even more by Mike's hand squeezing his ass, but he rallied.

"I just might start to like you," he said.

He turned and introduced us to Ira, a balding man in his sixties with a fringe of graying hair like a medieval monk.

"Gunter said you might be coming. Welcome."

He hugged me and kissed me on both cheeks, but Mike short-circuited his own hug by sticking out his hand for a shake.

"I'm Mike. Kimo's partner."

"Great to meet you," Ira said. "Come on in. We've got hot dogs and burgers grilling over there, swimming in the pool. Dance if you want, or just hang out and enjoy the vibe."

Another group of guys, mostly in their twenties, were dancing, but most were standing around talking in small groups, drinking beer from a keg. We'd brought a tub of cookies from Costco, and we dropped them on a folding table already groaning with potato salad, chicken wings, rice and potato chips.

It looked more like a church social of the kind I'd gone to as a kid with my folks, though everyone was male and there were no children playing. Gunter was deep in conversation with a gray-haired guy in his fifties who was thin to the point of anorexia, so Mike and I got a couple of beers and started making the rounds.

"Not exactly a den of iniquity," I said to Mike.

A group of a half-dozen men, mixed ages, was standing near the cabin whispering to each other as we walked up. I figured they were gossiping about me, sharing the news that there was a cop on the property.

A forty-something guy with tousled brown hair stepped up as we got close. "Hey, Kimo, great to see you!" he said, enveloping me in another hug.

"Thanks. Ummm…."

"I'm Roy. We met a couple of years ago through the Hawai'i Gay Marriage Project."

"Oh yeah. Good to see you, too." I introduced Mike, and we met the rest of the guys.

"You're not here to bust us for a little pakalolo, are you," Roy asked, only half joking.

"Not my job. I won't join you, but I won't stop you, either."

A young guy in the group pulled a joint from behind his back and took a drag, and the crowd laughed. We all stood around for a while, talking about ordinary stuff—the weather, new movies and so on.

A Chinese guy discovered Mike was a fireman and wanted to hear all about his job. Mike told great stories, and quickly he had the whole group hanging on his every word.

I was happy to see Mike relaxed in a group of gay men. When we first met, he was so deep in the closet that he was uncomfortable around anyone who might be gay, afraid that something in his behavior would betray his secret. My high profile in the gay community was very tough for him back then, but he was getting more and more relaxed.

Mike and the Chinese guy went off to get some more beers for the crowd, and I thought the vibe with the group was comfortable enough to say, "I'm working on a case, and I was hoping somebody up here might be able to give me a lead. Any of you heard about a guy who picks men up at clubs like The Garage and then mugs them?"

"The Garage is sleazy," one guy said.

"And that's bad?" Roy said, laughing.

None of them knew anything concrete, though one guy said he'd heard some rumors. I gave him my card and asked him to get back to me if he heard anything more. Mike and the Chinese guy brought back the beers, and we all chatted for a few minutes more. Then I saw Gunter motioning me over.

"This is Simi," he said, introducing us to the thin guy with him, who looked Thai. "Tell Kimo what you were telling me."

Simi frowned and clutched his hands together.

"Anything you tell me stays confidential. And maybe with your help I can catch whoever's doing this and make it stop."

"I was at The Garage about six months ago." Simi pushed a tear from his eye with his right knuckle. "It's stupid. I was stupid. This guy picked me up, and I took him home with me. But before we could do anything, he hit me. I fell down and passed out for a couple of minutes."

Gunter reached around and hugged Simi. "This is good," he said. "Let it out."

"When I woke up, he was gone, and so was my wallet, all my jewelry, my laptop computer and my portable CD player."

"You make a police report?" I asked.

He shook his head. "I was too embarrassed. I cancelled my credit cards, got a new license. I just wanted to put it all behind me."

"Can you describe the guy?"

"Haole, maybe thirties, blue dragon tattooed on his right arm."

A blue dragon tattoo. Just like the one that Dexter Trale had. But I put that idea aside for a moment and focused on Simi.

"Anything more?"

"Very skinny," Simi said. "And very sexy. Very masculine, you know? The dominant type."

"You think you could recognize him again, if I showed you some mug shots?"

Simi pursed his lips together and nodded. "But I wouldn't have to see him again, would I?"

"I can't promise anything. But for now, you'd just look at pictures. And after that, we might ask you to pick him out of a lineup, but you'd be behind glass and he wouldn't see you."

He nodded again. I took down his full name, which was very long, and his contact information.

By the time we were finished with Simi, the smell of the hot dogs and hamburgers had made us all starving. Gunter, Mike and I filled up plates and sat on the grass.

"You had those guys eating out of your hand," I said to Mike. I turned to Gunter. "He loves anybody who'll listen to his stories."

Mike kicked me and we all laughed. As we were finishing, two older men came by, naked, running for the pool.

"Come on, Gunter," one called as they passed. "Everybody in the water!"

Gunter jumped up. "You don't have to ask me twice." He skinned off his T-shirt, kicked off his rubber slippers and dropped his tiny white shorts, then took off after them.

"Gunter can set a land speed record for getting out of his clothes." I looked over at Mike and saw his dick stiffening under his shorts. I smirked and asked, "You enjoying the view?" Gunter's naked body disappeared under the surface of the water, coming back up to romp with one of the younger guys.

Mike shifted his empty plate over his lap.

"You make a big show out of being straight-laced, but you're just like me," I said. "You have a dick, and you like to use it."

"I don't like being naked in public. It reminds me of the locker room in high school. I was always scared I'd get a boner in the shower, from all those naked guys around me."

"You were scared they'd know you were gay," I said, "but I've got a news flash for you. Everybody here knows. They knew it the minute you walked in and introduced yourself to Ira as my partner."

"Your point?"

"So what else are you scared of? Me? Are you scared if I get naked out here I'll end up making out or fucking some random guy?"

He looked away.

"That's it, isn't it? You still don't trust me."

It felt like the day had gotten a lot colder. I had struggled to trust Mike around alcohol; it still made me a little nervous to see him with a beer in his hand, knowing the trouble he'd had in the past. But I believed in him, and I knew it wouldn't help him to think I was watching every bottle he drank.

It had to work both ways. If he didn't trust my commitment, if he was going to get jealous every time I was around other gay men, that was going to be a big stumbling block.

He locked eyes with me. I didn't know what he was going to say, but I was scared. Suppose he admitted that he'd never trust me? What would I say? Could I live that way?

Very slowly, he reached down and pulled his T-shirt over his head. A drop of sweat glistened between his hairy pecs. He smiled and stood up.

"Come on, baby," he said. "Let's go for a swim."

BIG EAGER PUPPY

The guys in the pool hooted as we approached, both of us naked and hard and holding hands.

"Young love," Ira said, as we stepped into the water and submerged under the surface.

The water was cold, and as cold water does, it shrank the equipment quickly. We laughed and talked with the Māhū Nation guys, roughhousing a little, splashing and dunking.

"I see what you see in Mike now," Gunter whispered to me.

"You never saw him naked before?"

"How was I going to? You've never invited me for a threesome."

"And we never will," Mike said.

Gunter splashed the surface of the pool in mock petulance. We laughed, and Mike tackled him, dragging him under the water.

By the time we left the pool, we were both relaxed and happy. We had both bumped up against various naked body parts under the water, and our relationship had survived intact.

I remembered again that Mike was my best friend, not just my partner. We spent a couple of hours at the picnic, then climbed back to the Jeep late in the afternoon. By the time we pulled into the driveway, my body was still damp and clammy and I was worried that scum had penetrated some intimate parts.

"Feel like a shower, stud?" I asked, as I unlocked the front door.

Roby tackled both of as the door swung open.

"You beast," Mike said. "Get down!"

The shower had to wait a few minutes, until Roby had emptied his bladder and romped around the yard, but it was worth waiting for. Mike and I had an awesome connection; I already knew that.

But sex in the shower that evening was among the hottest we'd ever experienced, leaving us both drained and satisfied.

Lying in bed later, Mike on his back snoring gently next to me, I thought about how Mike had changed his mind and decided to go skinny-dipping—but there was more underneath that. It was like he'd relaxed somehow and come to trust me more. That was important, and it could only mean good things for our future together.

Roby padded into the bedroom, turned around a couple times on the floor next to my side of the bed and then settled to the ground. With my little ohana around me, I went to sleep, too.

My subconscious must have been telling me something, because I dreamed of dragons, and when I woke up on Labor Day morning I decided to follow a hunch and see if Dexter Trale, who had a dragon tattoo, was the guy who had picked up Simi at The Garage and then mugged him.

I was too antsy to wait until the next day to bring Simi in to headquarters to look at a photo array, though. If Dex was the guy who attacked Simi, then that made it more likely that Dex was the guy who'd picked up O'Malley the night he was killed. I thought it was a good idea to show that array to the bartender at The Garage, too, so I dug through my notes and found his name.

I left Mike playing with Roby and drove into headquarters, where I assembled a bunch of shots of Dex and similar-looking men. I tracked down both guys, going to Simi at his apartment in Pearl City first.

"That's him," he said immediately, pointing at Dexter. "How come you have his picture? Has he done this to other men?"

"Yeah. I think he has."

Sadly, I didn't think we could prosecute Dex for the attack on Simi. It had happened too long before, and he hadn't reported it at the time. But if we could nail Dex for O'Malley's murder, that would be put him away for a lot longer than a simple assault.

I drove over to the bartender's apartment next, but he couldn't give me a definite ID.

"Sorry," he said, shrugging. "It's dark in the bar, and I'm usually swamped." He put three of the photos in a single line and looked at them again. "It could be any one of these three." He did include Dex in that trio, but that wasn't something I could take to a judge.

By the time I got back home, Mike was waiting, ready to go out to an afternoon movie and an early dinner, and it wasn't until we were about to walk out the door that he said, "I asked my mom and dad to come with us. I hope that's okay."

It wasn't okay—but I had dragged Mike to dinner with Terri and Levi, to my parents' even to the Māhū Nation picnic, and it was time for me to do something for him. I could suffer an afternoon of his father's frosty disdain and his mother's aloofness if I had to.

So I said, "Fine with me, sweetheart."

When we walked outside, his father was picking a few tiny weeds from the pikake bed in front of their side of the house. Fragrant white flowers were dotted among the lustrous green vines, which Dr. Riccardi had trained to grow on a wooden frame. He was meticulous about pruning and fertilizing them—as he was about everything. I thought it was evidence of his controlling temperament, but Mike insisted it was just a nice hobby.

His father is almost as tall as Mike, with the same black hair and dark eyes. But Mike's face has been tempered by the Korean influence of his mother. His father's face is narrow and angular, his cheekbones sharp. Mike's chin is rounder than his father's, and his thick black mustache contrasts his father's clean shave.

Dr. Riccardi stood up and wiped his hands on a moistened wipe that Mike's mother handed him. Mike kissed his mom, leaving me and his father facing each other awkwardly.

"Hi, Dr. Riccardi." I reached out to shake his hand.

He shook my hand, his palm still damp, and then we switched and I kissed Mrs. Riccardi's cheek. She had a heart-shaped face, with her own dark hair pulled back. I'd seen pictures of her as a young woman, when she was strikingly beautiful, and even over fifty she was still lovely. Mike came from good genes.

"We've been thinking, Kimo," Dr. Riccardi said, as he unlocked the Mercedes sedan. "Soon-O and I know you have your own parents, so we wouldn't expect you to call us Mom and Dad. But we were hoping you could call us by our first names."

I looked at Mike, my eyebrows raised. He gave his shoulders a slight shrug. I guessed that Mike had been working on his parents to be warmer to me. I appreciated the effort, and knew I'd have to meet it.

"I'd like that. Dominic. Soon-O."

Their names sounded strange on my tongue, but I figured I'd get accustomed to it. And I was pleased that we were able to move on from all the drama of the past to a new, warmer relationship. We climbed into the car, Soon-O and Dominic in the front, me and Mike in the back like a pair of high schoolers being chauffeured.

Soon-O turned around to face us and said, "I've been trying to convince Mike that he needs to take that dog in for obedience training. He's a little wild."

I resisted the urge to say that Mike could use some training, too. Instead I said, "He has a good heart. He just needs a firm hand on the leash."

"Does he obey you?"

I wasn't sure by then if we were talking about Roby or Mike, but I said, "He knows the basic commands: sit, down and so on. He's housebroken, and though he likes to chew on socks he hasn't caused any major damage yet. But if it looks like he needs it, I don't mind taking him in for lessons."

We talked all the way to the Pearlridge multiplex, and for the first time since I met Mike I felt relaxed around his parents, like I was part of their family. We saw a romantic comedy that made us all laugh, and that good feeling carried over through dinner at a barbecue joint where we sat at a big wooden picnic table and shared big platters of ribs, chicken, biscuits and fries.

"We used to come here all the time when Mike was a boy," Dominic said. "You should have seen him attack a platter of ribs."

"And you complain about the way I eat," I said to Mike, elbowing him.

I remembered something that my brother Haoa had told me, years before, soon after he married Tatiana and met her parents and her many brothers and sisters.

"You don't just marry the person, you marry their whole family," he'd said.

Mike was an only child, and his parents' relatives spanned the globe, from Long Island to Seoul. I'd always focused mostly on integrating him into my family, and I was glad it seemed like I was becoming a part of his, too.

By the time we got home we were stuffed and tired, but we motivated ourselves to take Roby for a long walk around the neighborhood, savoring the last moments of our time off together. We spent the evening slumped together on the sofa, watching mindless TV with Roby sleeping on the carpet, his spine curled so his head met his back feet.

≈≈≈

Tuesday morning I drove to work so eager to tell Ray what I'd learned over the weekend that I felt like Roby, a big eager puppy with a bone to share. As soon as he came in, I explained about meeting Simi and getting him to identify Dex's picture.

"But if the bartender can't say for sure it was Dex who left with O'Malley we don't have a connection," Ray said. "And the concierge at the Honolulu Sunset didn't see the guy who came in with O'Malley."

"We can run Dex's prints. See if they show up at O'Malley's."

Thanh Nguyen, the fingerprint tech, was backed up because of the holiday weekend, as was the ME's office. I wanted to go out and shake somebody, because I felt like we were so close to understanding. "I think you've been drinking too much coffee on this case," Ray said. "Calm down. We'll get everything figured out."

Sampson called us in to his office as I was pacing around Ray's desk.

"Where are you with the lawyer's murder?" he asked, as we sat down across from him. He'd gotten the haircut he needed over the weekend and a little sun, too. There were red patches on his cheeks and forehead, and his nose was peeling. I thought that his maroon polo shirt was a good choice that morning, because of the sunburn, but instead of commenting on it I plunged into a status update.

"I found a guy who picked up a trick at The Garage who mugged him. The victim pulled Dexter Trale's photo out of an array and fingered Dex as his attacker. Dex lived with Edith Kapana and worked with Stuart McKinney, so we think that now we can connect him to all three murders. We're waiting on a fingerprint comparison with the prints we found in O'Malley's apartment. And we're waiting for the autopsy results. Both offices are backed up because of the Labor Day holiday."

"Death doesn't take a day off," Sampson said. "What's your plan?"

"If we get something from either the prints or the autopsy that implicates Trale, we'll pick him up," Ray said. "Otherwise we'll just keep looking for evidence."

"Not exactly the kind of plan I was hoping you'd have. But it'll have to do. Let me know what you find. And remember, Donne, you're responsible for keeping Kanapa'aka from breaking too many laws."

Ray gave Sampson a two-fingered salute and said, "Will do, chief."

"Let's call Salinas," I said to Ray as we left Sampson's office. "I want to know what he pulled out of that game on Friday night. See if we can figure out how Dex and Tanaka work together."

Salinas's secretary said that he was in court but would be back by two. I asked her to leave him a message that my partner and I would be there then to see him. Then I called Peggy, and she said that the partners were meeting to discuss our request.

"We'll come over," I told her, knowing it's always harder to refuse a cop something to his face than it is over the phone.

Faded Documents

"You think Peggy will come through with those documents?" Ray asked, as I scooted through a traffic light that started out yellow. "And that was a red light, you know."

"You're taking the job of being my conscience seriously, aren't you?" I said. "I don't know. I don't even know if they're relevant to our case."

Peggy met us in the reception area and said, "The partners have agreed to let you have the copies. Sarah is putting them together now." She led us back into the conference room and sat down across from us. "The partners are going to want to know if these files are related to Adam's death. You know lawyers. They're worried about liability."

"Right now we're just developing our case." I sketched in our thoughts about Tanaka as Sarah Byrne brought in the copies of the hospitalization records and the originals of the other sheets we had found in the folder.

"These old pages are too old and faded to get decent copies," she said, showing them to me.

"Can we take the originals?" I asked Peggy. "We'll get them back to you, I promise."

"I'll ask Mr. Yamato." She walked out, and Sarah stayed behind.

"Did you have something else you wanted to tell us?" I asked her.

She pursed her lips, deliberating. "I saw that these materials relate to the Kingdom of Hawai'i, and I wondered if you spoke to Akamu when you were here on Saturday."

"Akamu?"

"Our student intern. I know he's a volunteer with KOH."

I looked at Ray, my eyebrows raised. "No, we didn't speak to him," he said. "Is he here now?"

"It's his last day. I think he's in the law library."

Peggy came back in then. "Who's in the library?" she asked.

"You have a student intern here who's also a volunteer with KOH?" I asked.

She looked from me to Sarah. "Yes. Akamu Hastings. But he doesn't have access to any case files."

"Even so," I said. "We'd like to talk to him."

Peggy nodded toward Sarah. "Can you ask him to come in here? But don't tell him why."

Sarah left. "You think Akamu is connected to Adam's death?" Peggy asked.

"I don't know, Peggy. But it's certainly an interesting coincidence, don't you think? O'Malley agrees to meet me and talk about KOH, and then he's killed. And you have somebody in your office who volunteers for KOH."

Peggy was about to argue when Akamu came to the door. I could tell from his eyes that he recognized us as the cops from Saturday.

"You wanted to speak to me, Miss Kaneahe?"

"Come in and sit down," she said, pulling out a chair for him.

I could only imagine what she was thinking then. Adam O'Malley had been her friend, and he was dead, and it was possible that this kid was involved somehow. I wondered whether she'd revert to her prosecutor stance or be the kid's advocate, as a representative of Fields and Yamato.

She introduced Ray and me. "The detectives have some questions for you about your involvement with Kingdom of Hawai'i," she said. "I want you to be honest with them, okay?"

He nodded. I could see his right hand shaking a little on the big wooden table.

"It's okay, Akamu," I said. "Nobody's in trouble here. We just want to ask you a couple of questions, all right? Peggy said you've been volunteering with KOH. What kind of stuff have you done?"

"Nothing major," he said. "Mostly I'm like a gofer, kind of like I am here. I run errands, I help out at rallies and stuff."

"That's good. It's important. My mom volunteers for KOH sometimes too."

"Oh, yeah, Mrs. Kanapa'aka. I know her. She's really smart."

"Thanks. I'll tell her you said so. So is that how you got the internship here? Through KOH?"

"Sorta. A couple of times I drove around Mr. Kapuāiwa, and through him I met Mr. Tanaka. I told him I wanted to be a lawyer, and he said maybe he could help me out."

I looked at Ray and Peggy. Ray kept a poker face, but I could see Peggy's mouth setting into a grim line.

"Mr. Tanaka, huh?" I asked. "Jun Tanaka? From the Kope Bean?"

"Yeah. He's super nice. He's taken a real interest in me. He's always calling me up and asking how things are going. A couple of times he even took me out to dinner."

"I guess you heard about what happened to Mr. O'Malley," I said. "How he was murdered last week."

"Oh, man, I felt so bad. He was a nice guy. I was talking about him to Mr. Tanaka just the other day, how Mr. O seemed really committed to helping out KOH."

Suddenly his mouth dropped open. "Oh my God," he said.

"What?"

"Oh my God, oh my God." He started shaking. "It was his meeting. The meeting he was talking about."

Peggy reached over and took the kid's right hand and squeezed. "It's going to be okay. But you have to tell us what you know."

He took a deep breath, his teeth chattering a little. "It was Thursday afternoon. Right after lunch. I was walking past Mr. O'Malley's office, and I heard him on the phone. He was talking about meeting someone the next day to talk about KOH stuff. I thought that was so amazing of him, you know? I mean, he just got back from this big case on the mainland, and he was going to have some meeting about KOH on his day off."

He looked from me to Ray. "That must have been who killed him, right? That person he was meeting with."

I shook my head. "He was supposed to meet with us, Akamu. But when we got to his apartment he was dead."

"With you? With cops? But that's not what… oh my God."

"What?"

"Mr. Tanaka called me Thursday afternoon, just kind of to say that he had heard I did a really good job this summer, and he wanted to keep in touch with me in the fall. I think I… I mean, I didn't even think about it, you know?"

"You think you what?"

"I told Mr. Tanaka that Mr. O was having a meeting the next day about KOH stuff." He looked from me to Ray and back again. "I didn't know he was meeting with you or that there was anything strange going on. I just thought it was great of him to do it on his day off, you know?"

The pieces clicked in place. Tanaka knew that Adam O'Malley was meeting with someone on his day off, to discuss KOH business. Even if Tanaka didn't know Adam was meeting with the cops, he'd have been right to be suspicious. And maybe even to have ordered his attorney's death.

We got Akamu's contact information, and he left the conference room. "Tanaka has to be connected to Adam's death," Peggy said.

"Looks like it," I said.

"If you find out anything that compromises Fields and Yamato, will you give me a heads up? As a favor to an old friend?"

"Of course."

I signed a receipt for the old faded documents Sarah had been unable to photocopy, and we left the law firm.

"Harry might be able to do something with these," I said to Ray. "Mind if we swing by his place?"

"No prob." As the elevator doors closed, he said, "So how long did you date her?"

"What?"

"The attorney. Peggy. You did date her, didn't you?"

"How did you know?"

"I'm a detective, dude. I look at the way people interact with each other. And you two have failed booty call all over you."

"I guess you could call it that."

We reached the ground floor, and I called Harry and said we were on our way over. We walked back to my Jeep, and I told Ray the whole sad story, from those make-out sessions in Peggy's bedroom to the way she had tried to screw me after I came out of the closet.

"And all that time, you didn't know?" Ray asked. "My cousin Joey, he couldn't even talk about sex with girls. He'd get this weirded-out look on his face and squinch up his nose like he smelled something bad."

"I was clueless, what can I tell you?" We got in the Jeep, and I backed out of the parking space and turned onto the street. "I look back at it now and wonder what I was thinking, but at the time, I thought everybody felt the way I did. That everybody was, you know, bi to some extent. I figured once I met the right girl I'd stop thinking about guys."

"Do you still think about girls?" he asked. "Seeing Peggy again, that do anything for you?"

I thought about it as we waited at a red light. "I look at her now, and there's so many things going on, you know? I remember high school and stuff we did. But it doesn't make me want to get in her panties again. Not at all."

"Other women?"

"I can appreciate a good-looking woman. And if you want to know the truth, I could probably have sex with a woman again, if I wanted to. I just don't anymore."

Ray nodded. "Joey and I used to talk about this all the time. We finally decided we were just wired differently. He'd talk about how cute some guy was, and I'd see it but not in the way he did." He turned toward me. "I guess I had this idea of you, being like Joey. And then seeing you with Peggy, it was kind of like, whoa. You don't mind that I get so personal, do you?"

"I spend more hours in a day with you than I do with Mike. If we didn't get personal with each other life would be pretty dull."

It started to pour as we got on the H1, gray clouds scudding across the sky and palm trees tossing restlessly in the wind. The battered old Toyota in front of us threw up rooster tails that splattered my windshield. We passed a pickup truck festooned with plastic leis in every color, so many that you couldn't see the rails, with a battered statue of King Kamehameha propped up in the back.

"Dex worked for Tanaka at the Kope Bean," I said, the wipers sloshing against the windshield. "Could he have sent Dex to The Garage that night to find Adam and kill him?"

"Why would Tanaka think Dex could be a killer, though? As far as we know right now, he's just a dude who works at the warehouse, who plays in the pai gow game. And even if he did hire Dex, how would Dex know that O'Malley would be at the bar that night?"

"Maybe Dex staked out O'Malley's apartment. Followed him to the bar, saw his chance."

"That part works," Ray said. "But I still don't know why Tanaka would look to Dex. He has those yakuza connections. Why not just call in a professional hit?"

We both mulled that over as the rain eased and we switched to the Moanalua Freeway. By the time we began climbing Aiea Heights Road, the sun was back out. That's Hawai'i weather. If you don't like it, hold your breath for a minute, and it'll change.

Arleen answered the door and led us to Harry's office, where I handed him the documents. "Can you do anything to enhance these?"

Harry held up one of the pages, which had writing back and front. I could just make out the lines and the margins of the original paper. But all the writing had been done by hand, and the ink had faded almost completely. Arleen came in as we were peering down at them, with glasses filled with pink-orange liquid.

"Pineapple orange guava," she said. "It's all Brandon will drink these days."

Harry had adopted Arleen's son Brandon when he married her and both had changed their last name from Nakamura to Ho. Brandon had asked if he could change his middle name to Tally, but both Harry and Arleen had refused. Brandon had turned nine the previous spring, a smart kid who had blossomed under Harry's supervision.

"I went through a phase like that." I flashed back to my childhood, drinking juice and flipping pogs with Harry.

Harry held up one of the pages to the light. "These look like church records to me." He had been brought up in the First Chinese Church of Christ, though like me, he wasn't big on organized religion. "We had an old book like this at my church, where they wrote all the births and deaths and baptisms."

He found a big plastic magnifying screen, and laid it down over the first page. With the magnification we could make out the words "Opihi Baptist Church" on the top line, printed in a strong hand with ink that had remained dark. The rest of the lines were in a mix of cursive and print writing, from many different hands, and it hurt my eyes to look at them for too long.

A quick Internet search showed us the Opihi Baptist Church had been destroyed when the lava surrounded Opihi and Kalapana on the Big Island.

"Why would old church records be in the file on Kingdom of Hawai'i?" Ray asked.

"The book at my church tells you when people are born

and died," Harry said. "And who their parents are and their godparents and so on."

"It's like a family tree," I said. "Telling us if Ezekiel really is descended from Kamehameha."

Harry said, "Let me play around with some image enhancement tools and see what I can do with these pages."

"We need it ASAP, brah."

"Hey, why not? Anything else you need while I'm working for you? Want me to pick up your laundry? Walk your dog?"

"I might take you up on the dog thing," I said.

Ray and I walked out to the Jeep. "Salinas is supposed to be back from court by now," I said, looking at my watch. "Suppose we pay him a visit and see what he's willing to share about Tanaka."

We grabbed a quick lunch and got to the FBI office on Ala Moana just as Salinas was walking up to the front door. The sun was directly overhead and bounced off car windshields in harsh shards. I hailed Salinas and said, "Got a lot to talk to you about."

"You can talk. I'll listen."

"Can you ask Tanaka about Dexter Trale?"

"Slow down, Kimo," Ray said. "Say hello to the nice G-Man. Hi, Francisco, how are you today?"

Salinas laughed. "I'm good, Ray. What's new in the world of Honolulu homicide?"

He led us up to his office, chatting in the elevator about the weather and a new energy drink he'd found that gave you a boost without caffeine. He took us directly into a small conference room off the lobby, and I couldn't help comparing the simple round, wooden table and metal chairs to the furnishings at Fields and Yamato. The walls were hung with government directives in plain frames instead of original landscapes of Honolulu and the North Shore.

"What can you tell us about Jun Tanaka?" I asked, when we were sitting.

"He's the subject of an ongoing investigation."

"Yeah, I got that part. Has your investigation turned up anything that ties him to any of our homicides—Edith Kapana, Stuart McKinney or Adam O'Malley? We have a witness who says he told Tanaka that O'Malley was having a meeting on his day off about KOH business. On Thursday afternoon, just a few hours before O'Malley was killed."

He shook his head. "None of those names has come up."

"Can we talk to Tanaka?"

"Nope. Not till we're finished."

"When do you think that will be?"

"We're the government, Kimo. We take the time we need." He leaned back in his chair. "You might want to practice your surveillance techniques," he said, smiling. "You guys stood out like a sore thumb in Chinatown on Friday night."

"Sometimes that's the point." We stood up. "Thanks for the cooperation, Francisco. I'll remember it the next time you need something."

He was still smiling when we walked out.

"We shouldn't have told him about Tanaka's connection to our homicides," Ray said. "I feel like a teenage girl who puts out and then gets slapped for her trouble."

"That's something else you need to take up with your wife."

After that productive little meeting, we went back to headquarters, where O'Malley's autopsy report was waiting for us. It indicated that the cause of death was exsanguination, which means loss of blood. The method of death was a "necklace incision" across his throat, in which both his carotid arteries and his jugular vein had been cut.

Doc Takayama had noted, in clinical language, that the extra large black dildo in O'Malley's butt had caused damage to the anal walls, but the fact that no blood was present indicated that the device had been inserted there post-mortem.

"Kinky," Ray said.

"Or a red herring. The killer wanted to make sure we thought it was a sex thing."

"He's doing a good job of it."

Sampson called us in as we were packing up to leave for the day, no closer to finding our killer than we had been that morning.

"Do you like this guy Tanaka for your murders?" Sampson

asked, when we'd laid out our progress. "The one the FBI has in custody?"

"We think he's pulling the strings," Ray said. "But we have nothing that ties him to the weapons, and only theories that connect him to the victims. Once the FBI makes their case for money laundering, we might get a shot at Tanaka."

"I'm putting you back in the rotation tomorrow. There's no use chasing your tails until the Feds are finished."

Sampson was right; we knew Tanaka was involved in the murders and we would have to wait for Francisco Salinas to let us talk to him.

When I opened the front door, Roby was delighted to see me, and I took him for a long walk around the neighborhood. I couldn't stop thinking about Adam O'Malley, though. Was his death a random sex crime? Or was it connected to our case? Did Tanaka have an alibi for Thursday night, when O'Malley had been killed? What about for the other killings? He was Japanese, but in the dark he could have passed for haole. Did he have the kind of tattoos we had seen in the video of the man following O'Malley into the Honolulu Sunset? Or had he simply hired Dex to do his dirty work? And what would have made him think a warehouse worker like Dex could function as a hired killer?

By the time we circled back to the house, my head was so full of questions that I didn't know what was real and what was speculation. When we walked in the house, Mike was in the living room, unbuttoning his shirt. Roby raced across the floor to jump up and nose his crotch. He pushed the dog away, laughing, and we kissed.

"I'm really antsy," I said. "You want to go for a run?"

"Yeah. I could use a run. Spent most of the day behind a desk, and I'm feeling stiff."

"Stiffness we can deal with when we get back," I said, smiling at him.

He laughed. "I might hold you to that."

We changed into T-shirts and running shorts and took off up the hill. Mike's legs are longer than mine, but I kept up with him as we ran. We stopped high up on Aiea Heights Road, looking back down at Pearl Harbor and the Ford Island Bridge. The sky was turning from lavender to black, and street lights were coming on. In the far distance I saw the neon dragon that glowed over a Chinese restaurant at the boom of the street. Dragons again. I remembered Dex's tattoo, and his pai gow name, Lan Long, which meant blue dragon. It was time to do some research on Dex and see if we could connect him to the murders and to Jun Tanaka.

We turned around and went back down the hill toward our home and our dog, and I pushed thoughts of murder out of my head and focused on enjoying the evening with Mike.

The next morning, while we waited for a new case, Ray and I plunged into researching Dexter Trale. I called Karen Gold at Social Security and had her run Dex's work record, and Ray called his Army contact and discovered that Dex had served two tours in Iraq.

Dex's employment records started coming through the fax, and I pulled them out to review. Ray and I were looking them over when Harry walked in.

"Hey, brah, howzit?" I said. "You do something with those faded pages?"

"Didn't get a chance to yet. But I couldn't sleep last night and I was fiddling around online. I remembered that guy you asked about, Dexter Trale, and thought I'd look him up and see what I could find." He pulled out his iPhone and started typing. "I'm sending you a link now."

"For what?" I asked.

"Just open your e-mail."

I turned to my computer and opened Harry's message, then clicked on the embedded URL. I got a big warning message that said the material was suitable only for adults.

"Ray, look away," I said, as I clicked through.

He gave me the finger, and I gave him a *shaka* back, the Hawaiian hand salute with the thumb extended, and the two middle fingers bent over, the others erect. We both laughed, and the two of them clustered around me as the page opened.

"That's Dex," I said, pointing at the photo of a naked skinny haole guy on the screen. Dex was standing in what looked like the living room of the house he shared with Leelee. He was flexing his arms, which were covered with tattoos, and his stiff dick, which was only average-sized, jutted out from his body. There was another man, naked, on all fours on the floor, presenting his butt to Dex. The other guy's face wasn't visible.

"Hello," Ray said. "Guess Dex isn't so straight after all."

"I believe the term is 'gay for pay,'" Harry said.

"Are there more like this?" I asked.

"You can't see them without a membership. You have one?"

"Hey, I've got a boyfriend. I don't need to go looking for one online."

"Go ask Lieutenant Sampson if he'll authorize the fee," Ray said, poking me in the side. "I want to see what he says."

"I was only kidding," Harry said. "Other guys might need a membership, but not me."

I looked at Ray as Harry's fingers danced across the keyboard. Before we could start to argue about hacking, though, a whole portfolio of pictures of Dexter Trale opened up. In some cases he was alone, touching himself and looking provocatively at the camera. In others he was either fucking or getting sucked.

Despite knowing what a scumbag Dex was, and the fact that Mike and I were fucking like bunnies every time we could, I still found myself getting hard. I wondered if all guys were wired like that. I guess that's why porn is such a big business. I was glad I was sitting behind my desk so I didn't have to make any adjustments.

"He get paid for this?" Ray asked.

"Looking to pick up some extra cash?" Harry asked.

"Dex is the kind of guy who doesn't do anything for free," I said. "But interesting as this is, I don't see how it relates to our case."

"Between this, and what your witness said about meeting Dex at The Garage, Dex could be the guy who picked up O'Malley," Ray said. "I'll bet he needs cash, too. You saw that place where they live. Leelee sure doesn't work. With the uncle gone and Edith dead, he could be doing anything he can to pick up a few bucks."

"Including a little sharpshooting," I said. "But the person who shot Edith Kapana had damn good aim, and Dex's hand shook when he was lighting his cigarette."

"Think it was a military injury?" Ray asked.

"Wonder if he's getting any treatment at Tripler?" I asked. That was the Army medical hospital in Honolulu where Mike's parents worked, but I didn't think I could ask either of them to pry into Dex's records.

"Actually I have something that might relate to that," Harry said, showing us a printout from a pharmacy a few blocks from the Kope Bean warehouse.

I groaned. "I don't even want to look," I said, but I looked anyway. "You know, you're making Ray and me crazy with this. It is so illegal to go into someone's medical records without a court order."

"Yeah, yeah," he said. "So forget for the moment how I might or might not have gotten hold of this information. He has prescriptions for propranolol and primidone. I was curious to see what those are for, so I did some research. Propanolol is a beta blocker; doctors prescribe it in conjunction with primidone when a patient has a condition called Essential Tremor, ET."

"Phone home," Ray said, holding an imaginary phone to his ear.

"This ET condition would explain why his hands shook?" I asked.

Harry sat back in his chair. "Yeah. And taking his meds would block adrenaline in his system, calm him down enough so that he could shoot."

"Tanaka has the motive for all three killings—to protect Ezekiel's position as the KOH figurehead, because KOH is essential to the money laundering operation. And now we can see that he had the means—Dex."

I got up and started pacing around, just like I'd done back at Fields and Yamato. For some reason that helped me think.

"Dex was in the military, so we could get a subpoena to determine if he was qualified on the M16A4 rifle with sniper scope," I continued. "Which would give him the training to kill Aunty Edith and shoot at us outside the Ohana. And as long as he took his medication, his hand wouldn't shake and he should be able to fire a rifle accurately."

"And cut Adam O'Malley's throat," Ray said.

I looked through the paperwork on my desk until I found the images we'd captured from the video at the Honolulu Sunset. The face of the guy with O'Malley never showed, but there was one good shot of the guy's lower left arm, with a tattoo of a grinning skull there. It matched the skull tattoo we could see on Dex's arm in the porno pictures.

"Suppose we go out to the Kope Bean warehouse and talk to Dex about his extracurricular activities?" I asked.

"Fine with me," Ray said. "But if he starts striking poses I'm leaving the conversation up to you."

Harry left, and Ray and I went in to see Sampson. Fortunately we still hadn't gotten a new case handed to us.

"Everything we've found in the three murders we're investigating ties back to Jun Tanaka," I said. "He was the biggest backer of Kingdom of Hawai'i, which he used as a conduit for money laundering. The figurehead for KOH is Ezekiel Kapuāiwa, and we believe that Edith Kapana, the first victim, was going to expose Ezekiel's hospitalization."

I showed him the copies of Ezekiel's records. "She gave these pages to Adam O'Malley. That made them both a threat to Tanaka's investment in KOH. Stuart McKinney was a witness to the large amounts of cash passing through the Kope Bean warehouse. Tanaka couldn't afford to have that information get out."

"And Trale connects how?"

"He played in Tanaka's card games," Ray said. "He worked for Tanaka at the Kope Bean and also did other jobs for him, like driving Ezekiel around."

I continued, "He lived with Edith Kapana, the first victim. He worked with Stuart McKinney, the second victim. He fits the description of the man who went home with Adam O'Malley, the third victim."

"Means?" Sampson asked.

"Dex served in the military," I said, handing him a printout of what Ray's friend had e-mailed. Sampson knocked the miniature cannon on his desk back and forth a couple of times as he thought.

Ray jumped in. "We have a witness who will testify that Dex picked him up at a gay bar called The Garage, then mugged him. We think we can make Dex as the guy who left The Garage with O'Malley the night he was killed."

"Opportunity?" Sampson asked.

"We're waiting on fingerprint comparison to see if we can place Dex in O'Malley's apartment," I said. "We're going to find Dex and talk to him, see if he has an alibi for the times of the three killings."

"Okay," Sampson said. "If Trale doesn't have an alibi, I think you've got enough to pull him in."

I walked back to our desks with Ray, who held out his hand for a fist bump, and I knocked my hand against his. "You and me, brah," I said. "You and me against the world."

"Okay, quoting Helen Reddy is just a little too gay, even for me," Ray said, and we both started laughing.

We drove to the warehouse under cloudless skies the color of the light-blue porcelain floor tiles in my parents' kitchen. My mother used to say that when she was stuck in the kitchen cooking for her husband and three sons, at least she could feel like she was outside, walking on air.

The white pickup registered to Dex wasn't in the Kope Bean parking lot, but we still made a circuit of the property, looking for Dex on the loading dock, before we went inside.

Tuli was at her computer, taking orders, when we walked in, but Dex wasn't there.

"He was supposed to be here Labor Day and yesterday," she said, taking off her headset. "People don't stop drinking coffee just because it's a holiday, you know. But he didn't show up." She shook her head. "First Stuart McKinney, now Dexter Trale. It's hard to get good help these days."

"You haven't heard from him?" I asked.

"Not since he left on Friday afternoon."

We thanked her and drove out to the house in Papakolea where he'd been living with Leelee and her family. She answered the door, the baby attached as always to her hip. Her right eye had been blackened a few days before; the skin around it had turned yellow and purple. Her hair hung in greasy strands around her face.

"We need to see Dex," I said.

She started to cry. "He *wen bag.*"

"Left," I whispered to Ray.

"Friday. He fed up wid the keiki crying, *hana hou, hana hou.*" She was wearing a shapeless T-shirt with what looked like baby vomit on it, a pair of shorts and rubber slippers. She looked so young and vulnerable, and I felt bad for her, stuck in such an awful situation without anyone to help her. Her shoulders shook. "I don't know why the keiki cry. Aunty Edith only one who make him *pau.*"

I dug a tissue from my pocket and gave it to her. Ray took the baby, who was crying, too. "I'm going to get him fixed up," he said.

Leelee led me into the kitchen. She hadn't been cleaning up for a couple of days; dirty dishes and baby bottles were stacked in the sink, and ants crawled over an open package of crackers on the counter.

I felt out of my depth. Ray babysat as a teenager, so at least he had a handle on how to look after the keiki. I may be in my mid-thirties, but in some circumstances the first thing I think to do is to call my parents.

Leelee sat on the sofa, looking dejected. I walked into the kitchen and called my mother. "Mom, you remember Leelee," I said, when she answered.

"Oh, no. What's happened to her?"

I started washing the dishes, holding my cell phone against my shoulder as I gave her the quick rundown.

"You can't call Social Services," my mother said. "You know the first thing they want to do is take away the baby. Your father and I will come over now and help get things cleaned up."

"Thanks, Mom."

"We're all ohana," she said.

By the time I finished washing the dishes, Leelee had calmed down. "Dex come home Friday from work," she said, when I found her back in the living room. "Maybe six, seven o'clock, in bad mood. I say, 'Kay den, Dex, no make like dat.'"

She blew her nose. "He get all stink on me. He start grab his stuff, I was all like, wat doing? No leave me! Dat when he hit me."

"You know where he went?" I asked.

She shook her head. She had gone to look for him on Saturday, walking all over the neighborhood, but no one had seen him. Or at least, no one would tell her if they had. After that, she'd stayed home, hoping he would show up. But she hadn't been able to do much more than get out of bed and heat up some bottles of formula for the baby.

Ray came back in with the baby; he'd given him a quick bath and changed his diapers. "Not exactly what they'd call police work back at the academy," he said, handing the baby to her.

"Keiki smell so *ono*!" Leelee said, snuggling her nose into the boy's chest, and he giggled.

"Any chance Dex is going to come back here?" I asked Leelee.

She started to cry again. "He say he no come back, evah."

Ray put out a BOLO on Dex's license plate, warning that he might be armed and dangerous, while I called my brother.

"Hey, Lui, your buddy Lan Long did a runner. You know if he was friendly with any of the guys in your pai gow game?"

"Don't think so. Tung was the only guy he ever really talked to. Though he bragged a lot to us about his time in the army, all his shooting skill and so on."

I made a mental note of that. Dex really could shoot, and Tanaka knew it.

"You hear anything from the FBI after the raid?" Lui asked.

"Nothing. Listen, brah, you call me ASAP if Dexter Trale contacts you. Lan Long, that is. He's very dangerous."

"You don't have to tell me that," Lui said.

Ray sat on the sofa next to Leelee and asked if there was any place she thought Dex might go. "He have any friends? Family? A place he could hide out?"

"I never met no family. He said his parents die long time ago."

"Where did he live before he moved in here?" Ray asked.

She looked as if we'd asked her one of those analogy questions from the SAT, the kind that used to boggle my mind. "Don't know."

"Come on, Leelee, you've got to give us something," I said.

She started to cry again. "Don't know. He just show up. I think he work with Uncle Amos on some job. He come over one day, and then he move in."

I heard my mother's car in the driveway and went to meet her. "Your father's pressure is up so I left him at home," she said, kissing my cheek. "How's Leelee?"

"Getting better." I led her into the kitchen, where she looked around.

"At least she has some diapers and some formula. So things haven't fallen apart completely." She shook her head. "After we get organized I'll see if I can talk to the neighbors about helping her."

"Thanks, Mom," I said, leaning down to kiss her cheek.

Ray and I drove around the neighborhood looking for information on Dexter Trale. Everybody we found, though, was glad that he was gone. One old lady at the community center called him a *pilau moke*, a dirty crook.

"Is he why nobody helps Leelee?" I asked.

"Dat girl babooze to stay wid him. But now he gone, I make her some sticky rice."

"That would be very nice of you, Aunty."

I figured it was up to us to make sure that Dexter stayed gone.

"Sticky rice," I said, as we walked away from the old lady and climbed into the Jeep. My stomach grumbled. "What do you say we stop for some lunch on our way back to work?"

Ray was all for that plan, so I swung past a Zippy's, where we both ordered bowls of chili. We stood around in the tiled lobby of the restaurant, hovering like everyone else until the server called our numbers.

"Edith Kapana was a nosy old woman," I said. "She knew about Ezekiel's stay at the mental hospital, and that could destroy the foundation of KOH. Who's going to choose a crazy man as king of Hawai'i?"

"Dex worked for Tanaka at the Kope Bean. He told Tanaka about Edith, and Tanaka hired him to kill Edith, to protect his investment in KOH. And when Stuey started talking to us about the money being sorted at the warehouse, Dex killed him, too."

The server called our numbers, and we carried our food to a table by the window.

"A skinny guy with tattooed arms picked up Adam O'Malley at The Garage," I continued as we sat down. "That was Dexter Trale. Dex has been picking up extra cash posing for naked pictures and rolling gay men he picks up in bars. He went home with O'Malley, slit his throat, then staged the scene to make us think it was a sex crime."

Ray sighed. "We still don't have any concrete proof we could take to a DA."

"We need to connect Dex to Jun Tanaka, because Tanaka is the one who benefits from the murders," I admitted. "It's not enough that Dex worked for him and that my brother heard Dex talking about his marksmanship skills at the pai gow game. But with Dex in the wind and Tanaka with the FBI, we don't have any place to go."

My phone rang as we were leaving the restaurant. I looked at the display and saw it was my mother's cell. "Hi, Mom, what's up?"

She didn't answer. Instead, I heard voices in the background, as if she'd dialed my number accidentally and I was overhearing her conversations.

I was about to hang up when I heard someone say, "Please, Dex." It sounded like Leelee's voice.

I turned the phone so Ray could listen. We walked to a shady spot by the side of the building, away from the noise of traffic.

"Stupid damn bitch," a man's voice said.

The idea that Dex was anywhere near my mother was pretty scary. The sound faded, and I pressed the phone to my ear, trying to hear more. Ray handed me his phone and mouthed, "Call your father. Where's your mother?"

He took my phone from me and walked a few steps away.

My father answered, yawning as if I'd woken him.

"Dad, where's Mom?"

"Still at that girl's house, I guess. My blood pressure was up this morning so she made me stay home. What's up?"

"Nothing, Dad. I'll call her cell."

"You and Mike should come by for dinner," he said.

"Yeah, Dad, we will. Gotta go. Bye."

I switched phones with Ray. Still nothing on my mom's end. "My mom's at Leelee's" I whispered.

"I'll call for backup. Let's roll."

We ran for my Jeep. I popped the flashing light up on my roof and burned rubber. It was a good thing I excelled at the defensive driving class at the police academy, because I used every trick I knew to swerve around slow-moving cars, take curves at high speed and generally drive like a maniac for the next twenty minutes.

I lost the connection to my mother's cell phone when we went through a dead zone, and I didn't want to call her back because I didn't know what was going on at the house.

I turned onto Wyllie, narrowly missing a soccer mom in a minivan plastered with decals of kids dancing and playing soccer. "Watch the flashing lights, asshole!" I said as I slewed around her.

"Take it easy, Kimo," Ray said, grabbing the passenger door. "It won't help if we smash up on our way there."

"Yeah, yeah," I said, jumping onto the Pali Highway and accelerating. We were lucky that there wasn't much traffic; I was able to dart around the slower-moving cars. We took the first exit we could and climbed the narrow streets to Leelee's house in record time, blasting the horn at a convertible full of clueless tourists and narrowly missing a garbage can that I swear jumped out at us as we passed.

One thing you've got to say about our SWAT teams, they mobilize fast. A block from Leelee's house. I pulled up beside a black SUV I knew belonged to one of the SWAT team leaders, a crusty Nisei named Yamashita. He stood in front of it, with three other guys in bullet-proof vests checking various pieces of weaponry.

All around us I saw neighborhood residents clustered on porches and lawns, watching the action. "We passed a white pickup going fast as we were heading up here," Yamashita said. "The license plate was covered with dirt, so we couldn't get a clear ID on it and didn't want to initiate a chase without knowing what was going on in the house."

"Did it have one of those "Welcome to Hawai'i—Now Go Home" bumper stickers on it?"

"Yeah. I saw that."

"That's Dexter Trale's vehicle. Any passengers in the truck?"

Yamashita shook his head. "Not that we could see."

"I'll call you as soon as I know what's going on," I said, and drove on, pulling up in front of Leelee's ramshackle house.

I jumped out and raced up to the front door, Ray right behind me. My mother was sitting on the sofa with her arm around Leelee when I burst inside. Leelee held the baby on her lap. I hurried over and kissed my mother's cheek.

"I'm sorry I got you caught up in this," I said.

Her black hair was still perfect in its black bouffant, her white sleeveless blouse a crisp contrast to her tanned skin. With her pink cotton skirt and black ballet-slipper flats, she could have been on her way to lunch with one of her friends, instead of confronting a man who might have killed three people. She shivered, but then she smiled and hugged Leelee.

"It's okay. He just left. That boy, that Dexter." Her voice was shaky. "Leelee was very brave."

"He was so mad," Leelee said. Tears stained her cheeks, but she had combed her hair and was wearing a clean T-shirt and a pair of denim cutoffs.

Ray called dispatch and put out an APB—an all points bulletin—for Dexter Trale, and I tried to calm down, so I wouldn't show my mother how upset I'd been. It was one thing to worry about a witness or a hostage in a dangerous situation—and another thing entirely when it was your own mother.

Between them, my mother and Leelee told us what had happened. "I think he might be on drugs," my mother said to me in a low voice. "He looked crazy."

Dex had ranted and raved, yelling at Leelee, while he had packed up some of his belongings. That's when my mother dialed my number, keeping the phone in her pocket.

"That was very smart, Mom. You've got a cool head in a crisis. Maybe you should have been the cop, not me."

"No, thank you. I nearly fainted when Dexter started waving his gun and yelling at Leelee. She stood up to him, and he hit her in the mouth." She took a couple of deep breaths. "He wanted all the money Leelee had in the house, which wasn't much, and then he took the cash from my wallet."

The anger kept bubbling up inside me, and I struggled to rein it in. Nobody messes with my family—especially not my mother.

"Did you notice what kind of gun it was?" I asked.

"It looked like your father's Glock. But I'm not sure."

My father had raised us all around handguns; his favorite was the Glock 9 millimeter. He had given us each one when we graduated from college. I still kept mine oiled and polished, in case he ever asked to see it. I didn't want to endure a tongue-lashing about the care of firearms. I realized a couple of years into my career that everything I'd learned as a cop was just reinforcement of what my father had taught me. And that goes for a lot more than weapons.

"When he left, he took a rifle with him too," my mother said, balancing the baby on her hip as if he was one of her own grandchildren. "There are some neighbors outside, I'm going to go out and talk to them." She patted Leelee's shoulder. "You'll see, things will be better now."

"Where do you think Dex might have gone?" I asked Leelee.

By then she was calmer, drinking some herb tea. "He say he want money. He say Ezekiel know where there lots from that group, da kine KOH."

"Ezekiel Kapuāiwa?"

"Yeah, he used to drive him places."

The front door opened, and soon the living room was filled with women comforting Leelee and offering her help. It seemed like Leelee's ohana was finally pitching in now that Dex was gone. A police car was going to sit outside the house, in case Dexter came back, and it was time for Ray and me to get moving.

I walked my mother out to her car. "Dex didn't take your wallet, did he? Or any of your ID?"

She shook her head.

"Good. So he doesn't know who you are or where you live."

She beeped open the door of her car, and I could see in her

eyes that she was glad to be going home.

"I don't think we should tell Dad about this," I said, "if his blood pressure's up. But you should stay away from Leelee until we know that Dexter's in custody."

"That poor girl," she said, shaking her head.

"Mom."

"I know, I know. I just hope those women will help her."

"You saw how they were talking. Like you always say, it's ohana."

We drove the few blocks to the house where I'd seen Tanaka drop off Ezekiel, but no one was home. Ray called Maile Kanuha to see if he was with her.

"Ezekiel doesn't carry cash," he said to me, after he hung up. "But she admitted that there's a safe deposit box with some cash in it, though she wouldn't tell me where the cash came from."

"Where's the box?"

"A bank called Hawaiian People's. Apparently there's only one branch."

"I know it. Let's get a car out there."

We started back down the twisting, narrow streets. I drove a lot slower now that my mother was out of danger and no garbage cans or other obstructions jumped in our way. We were about halfway to the Hawaiian People's Bank when dispatch called.

"We have a radio car at Hawaiian People's Bank that reports a truck there matching the description you put out," the dispatcher said.

"On our way. Make sure all units know the suspect is armed and dangerous."

The bank was on Iolani Avenue at the foot of Tantalus, and we were there a few minutes later. When we pulled up in front of the single-story whitewashed building, Jimmy Chang and Kitty Cardozo were directing traffic away from the bank. It was late afternoon, and the sky was the color of a purple bruise behind the looming mass of the mountains.

"Sorry, the bank is temporarily closed," I heard Kitty tell a woman in a pickup.

"I just saw someone come out," the woman argued. "It's only 3:40."

"Please move along, ma'am," Kitty said. Standing there in her uniform, hands on hips, she had a "don't fuck with me" attitude, and the woman, grumbling, continued on past the bank.

I figured about forty-five minutes had passed since Dex left his house for Ezekiel's, giving him enough time to pick Ezekiel up and drive down the hill to the bank.

The SWAT team was assembling again. Yamashita had one hand on the gun in his belt holster and was communicating by headset with someone when Ray and I walked up. He held up his index finger while whoever it was finished talking.

"There's a disturbance in the vault," he said to us. "Apparently there wasn't any cash in that safe deposit box."

"I didn't think Tanaka would give Ezekiel a key to a box full of cash," I said.

Yamashita listened again. "They're coming out." He positioned his sharpshooters around the parking lot. Into his microphone he said, "Suspect about to exit the building with a hostage. Hold fire unless you have a clear shot."

Ezekiel walked out first, with Dex right behind him. "Dexter Trale!" Yamashita's voice boomed through a megaphone. "Put your hands up."

Dex grabbed Ezekiel and held him as a shield. "I've got a gun!" he shouted. He took off at a run, dragging Ezekiel with him.

"That's his truck," I said to Yamashita, pointing to the white pickup a few hundred feet away. I felt impotent standing there— this was my case, and I couldn't do anything more than watch the SWAT team and see how things would play out.

"Take out the white truck," Yamashita said into his headset.

Almost immediately, a series of shots rang out. I looked at the truck and saw the tires on the side facing us start to deflate. Dex made it to the truck, though, using its body as a shield. As he ducked in, Ezekiel pulled away from him. Instead of running away, though, Ezekiel remained at the side of the truck, peering in the window. We couldn't see what Dex was doing.

"He took a rifle with him when he left the house," I said to Yamashita, as the barrel of the rifle poked out the driver's side, Dex staying low.

Ray and I both had our hands on our guns, though at such long range neither of us would have a decent shot. It was instinct, I guess.

"Why doesn't Ezekiel get out of there?" Ray asked. "Is he that stupid?"

"According to all reports."

Dex fired the rifle and a blast shattered the window of Jimmy Chang's police cruiser.

"Does anybody have a shot?" Yamashita asked, the frustration evident in his voice.

Jimmy Chang was at the front door of the bank, keeping the patrons from spilling out onto the sidewalk. There were SWAT officers poised behind vehicles and one on the roof of the bank. A couple of EMTs from the fire station down the street were on hand in case there were injuries.

Kitty Cardozo was in the middle of Iolani Avenue, yelling at people on the street to get down and motioning cars to move away. It looked like she was so busy doing her job that she didn't realize that she was right in the line of fire. But she was a rookie, after all; this was probably the first real police action she'd been involved with.

I didn't want to call attention to her by yelling her name, and I didn't have her cell phone number. But I knew someone who did: her stepfather.

I pulled out my cell and pressed the speed dial for Lieutenant Sampson. When he answered I said, "Call Kitty right now and tell her to get out of the street." One thing I love about working for Jim Sampson is that he has the innate ability to react in a crisis. He disconnected from my call, and I slapped my phone shut. Then I watched.

I could hear sirens of other patrol cars approaching. I figured Dex could, too, because he took out the windshield of a Lexus parked close to the street entrance. I watched as Kitty reached down to her belt and picked up her cell phone. She scanned the display, then popped the phone open.

She stood there frozen. It was clear that Sampson had gotten through to her—but she didn't know what to do. I couldn't blame her; most cops don't get into serious trouble while they're still in the FTEP. The point of the training program is to get them some street knowledge under the supervision of a seasoned officer. Unfortunately, Jimmy Chang was too far from her to get her out of the way.

Dex kept shooting, blasting at cars passing by on the street. Suddenly I saw Kitty grab her upper arm and fall to the ground on the median strip. A few feet from her, there was a hibiscus hedge that could shelter her from further fire—if she could get there. But she wasn't moving.

"Shit. I've got to get her out of the way," I said to Ray. "Sampson will kill us both if anything happens to her."

Ray pulled his Glock and assumed a shooting stance, focused on Dex in the truck. "I'll cover you."

"What the fuck are you doing?" Yamashita yelled, as I took

off across the open parking lot.

I heard Ray start shooting toward Dex, hoping to distract him. I sprinted as fast as I could, pumping my arms. I reached Kitty, lying on the grass clutching her arm, with her face turned toward me, her mouth open in surprise. I grabbed her under the arms and dragged her behind the hibiscus. I collapsed on the ground beside her, one of the bright red blossoms in my face.

The air was filled with the sound of gunfire, but I couldn't tell if it was aimed at us or just distracting Dex. I was panting and my heart was racing. I felt sweat beginning to drip down my forehead.

Kitty began crying, and I put my arm around her. "It's okay," I said. "We're okay." The hedge didn't provide us with much shelter, and if Dex wanted, he could get a direct bead on us through the shrubbery. But I didn't want Kitty to know that.

"I froze," she said. "Jim told me to get out of the way, and when I realized how vulnerable I was, I just couldn't move."

Her whole body shook with sobs. "Today was my last day in the FTEP. But I froze. How can I be a cop if I can't handle the pressure?"

She was clutching her upper left arm, and I could see blood seeping out between her fingers. "Remind me sometime, and I'll tell you a few of the stupid things I did when I was on patrol," I said, unbuttoning my aloha shirt. I pulled it off and made a rough tourniquet for her arm. "Right now, though, you've got to pull together. All right? I know you can do that, Kitty."

She looked at me. "You're right," she said, wiping her hand across her eyes. "I can do that. What should I do?"

Kitty's phone buzzed. "For starters, answer the phone, and tell your dad you're okay."

She started to cry again. I took the phone from her and popped it open. Sampson was not only my boss, but also a man I respected. He had taken a chance on me when no one else in the department would, and I owed him. I couldn't help feeling that I had disappointed him by letting Kitty get hurt. Yeah, he was a cop, and so was she. Both of them knew the risks of the job. But Kitty was more to me than just my boss's stepdaughter; she was a friend, a mentee, another gay person traveling the same road I was.

I took a deep breath. "I'm with Kitty," I said into the phone. "She took a hit to her upper arm, but we've controlled the bleeding. As soon as the shooter is contained we'll get her medical attention."

"I'm on my way," Sampson said and disconnected the call.

I snapped the phone shut and handed it back to Kitty, then looked over at Dex's pickup. From the street angle, I could see the passenger side.

"Jesus, Ezekiel, what the fuck are you still doing there?" I muttered, watching him staring into the passenger window like he was at the aquarium watching the sharks.

Then he opened the door and reached in.

My phone had stayed clamped to my belt through my run and dive. It buzzed, and I flipped it open. "Can you see what's going on?" Ray asked.

"Ezekiel's grabbing for something in the truck."

"The rifle's pulled back inside," Ray said. "What the fuck is going on?"

"He's got Dex's foot. He's pulling him out of the truck."

I heard Ray relaying the news to Yamashita. "Jesus, the guy's an idiot," I said. Ezekiel kept backing up, dragging on Dex's leg, as Dex kicked at him. Two of the SWAT cops rushed toward the truck.

Dex was too close to Ezekiel to turn the rifle on him, but he had his Glock, too. If he got hold of it he could shoot Ezekiel and the SWAT cops. But the cops converged on the truck before Dex could get a shot off. One of them pushed Ezekiel out of the way as the other grabbed Dex. Within seconds, they had Dex on the ground in handcuffs.

A pair of beat officers helped me and Kitty up. The cool

breeze felt good on my bare skin, though I was a little embarrassed to be walking around a crime scene without a shirt.

Other cops surrounded Dex, and still others converged on the front door of the bank to help Jimmy control the crowd from the inside. The whole area around the bank was blocked with cars and flashing blue lights.

"Come on, let's get you fixed up," I said to Kitty, leading her toward the fire truck where the EMTs waited. "Can you walk okay?"

"I'm good." She put a hand on my arm. "Thanks, Kimo. For everything."

"You're going to make a great cop, Kitty."

I led her to the wagon, where one of the EMTs pulled off my bloody shirt and began cleaning her wound. The other guy looked at me and said, "You look familiar. Aren't you Mike Riccardi's partner?"

My mouth opened, but I didn't say anything. Mike had always been so careful at work—how did this guy know he was gay? Would I be outing him by saying anything? Then I caught a look at the guy's face, and I knew it was okay.

"Yeah." I shook his hand. "I'm Kimo."

"Nice to meet you. You and Mike are doing good things for all of us." He reached back into the wagon and handed me T-shirt with the Honolulu Fire Department logo on the front and the saying "Firemen do it with big hoses" on the back.

I pulled it on as Lieutenant Sampson rolled up, the blue light on his car blazing in the bright sun. I could see him holding back, though, walking, not running, toward us.

"Everything under control here?" he asked us.

"The scene has been secured, sir," Kitty said to him. She had a bruise on her cheek and some smudges of dirt on her uniform, but otherwise, she looked just like she was—a good cop, who'd gone through her first trial by fire.

"You joining the Fire Department, Kimo?" Sampson asked

me, half smiling.

"Detective Kanapa'aka used his shirt as a tourniquet," Kitty said. "I'll owe you a shirt, Kimo."

"I'll give you a tip, Kitty. Mix a little laundry soap with some hydrogen peroxide and blot the blood before washing," I said. "This won't be the first time you get blood on your clothes."

I left Kitty and Sampson at the EMT wagon and walked over to Ray. The SWAT guys had Dex in cuffs, and Ray and I arranged to have a pair of uniforms deliver him to a holding cell at headquarters while we conducted interviews at the bank. I was glad that the incident had been resolved without anyone else getting killed, but I knew that our work wasn't over yet. We still had to nail Dex for the three murders, using evidence that would hold up in court. That wasn't going to be a slam dunk.

Too Bad He Was Crazy

Sampson took Kitty to Queen's Medical Center to get her arm checked out, and I called Mike and let him know I was going to be home late. It was after six by the time Ray and I set up at the manager's desk inside the bank and began taking statements from customers and employees.

Outside, a couple of uniforms managed the traffic on Iolani Street. The SWAT team cleared up, including having the damaged cruiser and Lexus towed away. Ryan Kainoa and another evidence tech showed up to collect the bullets and casings, in case we needed proof of who shot where and when.

Our next-to-last statement came from the manager, a sallow-faced Indian named Pradeep Singh. "Mr. Kapuāiwa is one of the registered signers on a box rented by his organization, the Kingdom of Hawai'i. He had his key with him, so I had him sign our log, and I opened the vault for him."

"Did you recognize the man with him?" Ray asked.

Singh shook his head. "But Mr. Kapuāiwa always has someone with him when he comes to the bank. As I understand it, he doesn't drive."

"As you've probably heard, the man with Mr. Kapuāiwa was Dexter Trale, who is under suspicion for numerous crimes. Did Mr. Kapuāiwa appear to be under any pressure from Mr. Trale?" I asked.

"It is not really my business to pay attention to such things," Singh said. "I opened the vault and used my key to unlock the box, after Mr. Kapuāiwa had inserted his. Then I returned here, to my desk."

"And what happened next?" Ray asked.

"This Mr. Trale began yelling," Singh said. "Things like, 'where's the money?' He was very loud, and I got up to ask him to be more quiet. When I reached the door to the vault I saw that he had a handgun, and I backed away before he saw me."

He took a breath, and his teeth chattered a little. "I was very frightened, but I came back to my desk and pressed the emergency alert, just as I have been trained and according to bank policy. I notified the tellers and the other bank officers, and we were beginning to escort the customers from the lobby when Mr. Kapuāiwa and Mr. Trale came out of the vault." Singh's breath was coming in short bursts, and I worried that he might have some kind of attack.

He pulled an inhaler out of his jacket pocket and used it, then relaxed. "I'm sorry," he said, between pants. "I have asthma."

"Take your time," I said.

"Mr. Trale began waving his gun and yelling. We were all very frightened. But Mr. Kapuāiwa spoke to him, and then suddenly Mr. Trale took his arm and yanked him toward the front door. That is when I looked outside and saw the police."

We asked a few more questions, clarifying details, then thanked Singh for his time and told him he could go. "Oh, no," he said. "I must remain to lock up the bank."

"We'll try and get out of your way soon, then," I said. We nodded to Jimmy, who came over and escorted Singh back out to the lobby.

We left Ezekiel for last. "You were quite a hero today, Mr. Kapuāiwa," I said, as Jimmy returned with him.

"Oh, no," he said, sitting down.

"Sure you were," Ray said. "You pulled Dex out of the truck, kept him from hurting anybody else."

"I had to do it. It is in my blood, you see. The blood of the kings of Hawai'i. I am responsible for my ohana."

I nodded. Ezekiel was so earnest, it was clear that he believed his own publicity. Too bad he was crazy; he might have made a great king.

He didn't look half as squirrely as he had the day Maile Kanuha brought him to headquarters, and I wondered if his behavior was controlled by medication—or just affected by being around Maile.

"Why don't you tell us what happened today?" I asked.

"I was at my home when Dexter came to visit," he said.

It was an odd choice of words for the appearance of a guy with a gun, but that was Ezekiel. "You knew him?"

"Of course," he said. "I often visited Aunty Edith at the home she shared with Dexter and Leelee. And sometimes Mr. Tanaka asked Dexter to drive me to events. I do not drive myself, you know."

I nodded.

"Dexter said he needed money very quickly. I only had a few dollars to offer him, and that made him angry. He hit me in the head with his handgun and demanded that I come with him, here, to to this bank."

"So he already knew about the safe deposit box?" Ray asked.

"Yes. I tried to explain that the box was only used to protect important papers, but he would not listen. He believed there was much money here."

"What happened when he found there was no money in the box?" I asked.

"He began speaking of robbing the bank. I knew that would be a terrible thing. Many Hawaiian people trust this bank with their money. So I told him that he should not do such a thing, that we could go and speak with Mr. Tanaka, and he would give Dexter the money he wanted."

"That was good thinking," Ray said.

I disagreed; if we hadn't gotten to the bank when we did, Dex and Ezekiel could have slipped away. Ezekiel would still be in danger, and Dex would still be on the loose. But I didn't say anything.

We went back over Ezekiel's statement, confirming the time Dex had arrived at his house. It was only a few minutes after he had left my mother, Leelee and the baby at his own home and made sense when compared to the time he and Ezekiel arrived at the bank.

By the time Maile Kanuha arrived to take Ezekiel home, the sun had set, and the crime scene techs and SWAT team were gone. Jimmy stayed behind until Pradeep Singh could lock the bank up, and Ray and I grabbed some fast food on our way back to the station.

The blood had dried on my aloha shirt, and I put it back on before we went into the interrogation room with Dex, who'd waived his rights to an attorney. Sampson and Francisco Salinas watched from behind a two-way mirror as Dex explained how it had all started.

"That nosy old Aunty Edith. She had these records showed Ezekiel had been in the mental hospital. She was bragging about it to me and Leelee one night. I knew that the boss was backing Ezekiel, so I told him about it."

"The boss?" I asked.

"Mr. T. Mr. Tanaka."

"That would be Jun Tanaka?" I showed him a photo of Tanaka and he nodded.

"For the tape, could you please identify this picture?"

"That's him. Mr. T. My boss."

He said that Tanaka had paid him ten grand to kill Aunty Edith. It was Dex's idea to do it at the rally, making it look random, like one of the other groups was trying to disrupt KOH. "He never gave me no money, though," Dex said. "I owed him from the pai gow game."

He explained that periodically Tanaka would send him to retrieve cash from the video poker machines in the warehouse off River Street or other fan tan or pai gow games. Then, while Stuey stood guard, thinking he was just watching the coffee beans, Tanaka would divide up the cash into separate deposits for each Kope Bean store and prepare a bag of cash for his safe deposit box. Dex had heard Ezekiel talk about a box once, and he figured Ezekiel had access to the box that Tanaka had been using.

"But there was nothing in the one at Hawaiian People's," Dex said. "Nothing but a bunch of papers."

We asked him about Stuart McKinney. "Screwy Stuey," Dex said, shaking his head. "He started to mouth off about the money that Mr. T sorted at the back of the warehouse. I told Mr. T, and he paid me another ten grand to take care of things. That paid off the last of what I owed from pai gow. I even had a little extra, picked up some fine pakalolo from the Campbell brothers."

He smiled, and then his eyebrows went up. "Hey, maybe I can do a deal with you guys. Be one of those informant types. I could get you the Campbell brothers easy."

"We'll talk about that later," I said. "What about Adam O'Malley? How'd you know he was going to be at that bar?"

"Mr. T, he told me about this lawyer, said he had some papers he shouldn't have. He told me to get hold of the guy and collect the papers. He showed me the dude's picture, and I recognized his face, knew I'd seen him at this māhū bar, The Garage, on hard hat nights."

He leaned back in his chair. "Some of these māhūs, they're like shooting pigeons at the park," he said, shaking his head. "When I need cash I go to The Garage on Thursdays. The guys there love me. The tattoos really turn them on." He leaned forward again. "Only on Thursdays, though. The rest of the week it's more of a pansy crowd."

He told us about picking up guys at The Garage, letting them suck him off, sometimes tying them up or hitting them, then stealing their cash and jewelry. "So it was real lucky it was Thursday afternoon when Mr. T came over to the warehouse, 'cause I was pretty sure this O'Malley guy would be at The Garage that night."

Not so lucky for Adam O'Malley, I thought.

Dex flexed his shoulders like a rooster strutting. "I went over there looking for him, and sure as shit, he was right there at the bar."

Ray and I shared a glance. Premeditation was always good to have on the record.

"I went up to the bar, chatted him up," Dex continued. "He was all over me. It was easy as pie to get him back to his place. And once we were inside, he was all mine."

Dex grinned broadly, remembering. "I made him take all his clothes off, and I tied his wrists and ankles to the bed. The dude was squirming, he was so eager for it. But I told him he was going to have to cooperate with me if he wanted my dick."

"Cooperate how?" I asked.

"I told him I needed those papers for Mr. T. That if he was a good boy and gave me what I wanted, I'd give him what he wanted. But he got all crazy on me. Said I didn't know who I was messing with, that he'd drag my ass to jail."

"That must have pissed you off," I said.

"You bet. I went into the kitchen and got a knife from the drawer, and when I came back I held it to his balls. He caved like a little baby. Told me all the papers I wanted were in a folder on his desk."

He looked at us. "After that, I couldn't just let him go. I mean, what if he did try to drag me to court? Mr. T wouldn't be happy about that. So I grabbed him by the hair and sliced his throat."

Well, there went our premeditation. But it was still murder.

"I mean, if he'd cooperated, I'd have fucked his ass, grabbed the papers and walked out. But not after those threats. Anyway, I was pissed by then. So I dug around his drawers and found that big black dildo, and I rammed it up his ass so you guys would think it was just a sex thing."

I felt bile rising in the back of my throat. I wanted to see Dex get locked up for a good long time, preferably with a big tough cellmate who'd make Dex his bitch.

It took us hours to get everything down on tape and to get the warrants issued for Dex and Tanaka for all three murders.

We booked Dex, but Tanaka remained in federal custody while Salinas assembled his money laundering case.

It was after midnight by the time I got home. I was exhausted, and I wanted nothing more than to climb into bed and go to sleep. Mike, however, had other plans.

When I came in he was sitting at the kitchen table with a pad of paper, making lists. Roby was sprawled at his feet and barely looked up at me as I walked in.

"What happened? Where's that blood from?" Mike said, looking at my shirt.

"Don't worry, it's not mine." I thought it was pretty cool to have someone to come home to who cared about me. I leaned down and kissed his stubbled cheek.

He sniffed. "Smells like shit. Take it off."

I smiled. "There's a surprise for you underneath."

I unbuttoned the shirt, showing off the fire department T-shirt, and Mike burst out laughing. "You're joining my team."

"Speaking of your team." I told him about the EMT who knew I was his partner.

I was worried he'd freak out. But instead he said, "Yeah, I know him. Cool guy."

Maybe I was just too tired. That didn't sound like Mike. But instead of starting an argument, I sunk into the chair across from him and motioned to the pages on the kitchen table. "What's all that?"

"I want to have a housewarming party."

I yawned. "You've been in this house for years."

"Yeah, but you just moved in. Look at this list of people I want to invite."

He pushed a sheet of paper across the table to me. He'd included my parents and his, my brothers and their families, Terri and Levi, Harry and Arleen, Ray and Julie and a bunch of other people I didn't know. I recognized some names as his coworkers and friends.

"You want to have this many?"

"I want to make a big luau. Haoa can dig the *imu* for us, right?"

An imu is a big pit in the back yard where you roast a pig.

"We have to make sure Roby doesn't dig it up," I said. Roby looked up from the floor as if my mentioning his name indicated there was a treat in his future. When he saw nothing coming, he slumped back to the tile.

"Yeah, dogs," Mike said. "Everybody has to bring their dogs." He made a note on another piece of paper. "And the Greshams. They'll want to see how Roby is doing."

The only way I could drag him away from the kitchen was to start stripping, there in front of him. I had the fire department T-shirt and my pants off, my dick poking out of the slit in my boxers, before he finally got the hint.

After Mike and I had licked and sucked and rubbed each other to orgasm, he went right to sleep, but I lay there in bed next to him for a few minutes, relishing the feeling, once again, of bringing down the bad guys and making things right with the world, even if only for a little while.

The next morning, Ray and I were back in the rotation, but we made time, over the next few days, to pull together all the details. Once Dex was in jail, Leelee confessed that she thought Dex had done something with her uncle Amos. Dex and Amos had fought a lot, especially when Amos was drunk and Dex was high.

One day Amos didn't come home, and Edith and Leelee had both been too frightened of Dex to say anything—not to mention the consequences from the Office of Hawaiian Affairs if the ownership of the property had to change to Leelee, who didn't have the 50 percent Hawaiian blood to qualify to stay. Edith had the blood but didn't want the responsibility. So neither had done anything.

Though the pressure let up at work, as Ray and I handled a stream of simpler cases, it only got worse at home. When Mike got his mind on something, I couldn't distract him. He spent the weekend making luau plans and fixing little things that had broken over the years. We argued and fought and then had make up sex, and I started wishing for an emergency to call me back to work. I was relieved when Monday morning came.

We recruited my mother, his mother and both my sisters-in-law to help us cook, and every day that week someone was ferrying foodstuffs over to our house. We filled up the extra refrigerator-freezer in the garage with fruits, vegetables and platters and spent our spare time cleaning the house from top to bottom. My mother even sent us her maid to scrub down the kitchen and the bathrooms and polish the furniture.

Mike and I both took Friday off from work. Haoa and his crew showed up to dig the imu shortly after 7:00 a.m., rousing us out of bed and sending Roby into a frenzy of barking, especially as the earthmover rolled down off the back of the pickup.

The imu had to be about 2' by 4', with sloping sides. Haoa

brought a lot of twigs and other combustible material he'd been gathering from work sites for the last week, and Mike and I helped him and his guys place the kindling at the bottom of the pit. There was a separate pile of banana leaves, ti leaves and palm fronds, or *hali'i*, to put on top of the pig and the other food once the fire was going.

Mike and I positioned some big logs on top of the kindling, then a tier of stones on top of the logs. My parents arrived around nine, bringing with them a bunch of old woven *lauhala* mats and *tapa* cloths that we would use the next day, once the pig was in place, to cover the whole mess.

Tatiana and Liliha came over while their kids were in school to help set up the rest of the yard, putting up tables and chairs. Mike hung decorative Japanese lanterns from the tree branches, and I kept busy running stuff back and forth.

Everybody left halfway through the afternoon, and Mike and I took a break with a couple of beers, sitting in the back yard with Roby at our feet, nibbling bits of roast chicken that Mike fed him when he thought I wasn't looking.

"I never thought I could have this," Mike said.

"A luau?"

"This," he said, waving his beer to encompass the yard and all the preparations. "You. Me. Roby. A big luau like this with all our family and friends."

"I thought I could," I said. "But I always thought there'd be a wife and kids involved." I sipped my beer. "When we first graduated from the academy, Akoni was dating this divorced woman, a few years older than us, with a couple of kids. I remember asking him how he would feel about raising somebody else's kids. He said they weren't that serious, they were just dating."

I stretched my legs and leaned back in my chair. "I couldn't understand that, dating a woman for fun. I thought the only reason to date somebody was so that you could get married eventually."

Mike laughed. "That why you dated so many women? You

wanted to marry them all?"

"I kept hoping things would be different," I said. "That I'd really, I don't know, like it, you know? That I would feel that thing I felt when I looked at guys." I reached over and squeezed his hand. "That thing I feel with you."

We got up and finished the preparations, nibbling on the platters for dinner, trying to artfully rearrange the cold salads so that it didn't look like we'd been at them. We spent the evening hanging out, Mike watching reruns on TV and me playing a computer surfing game that alternated between fun and frustration.

We were up at six lighting the fire, and it was ready by the time Mike's father got back from the butcher in Ewa Beach with the pig, which would take about eight hours to cook. Roby was so excited he kept dancing around the car and then us.

As Mike and I dragged the pig out of the car, Haoa showed up to supervise. "More hali'i," he said, from the sidelines, as Mike and I piled on the banana leaves. "You want the pig to steam, not to burn."

We were both sweaty and tired by the time we had the pig in the pit, the hali'i piled on top, then the lauhala mats over it all, covered with a layer of dirt. Haoa left, and we took the opportunity to take showers and eat some breakfast before the next wave of people showed up.

Our kitchen was commandeered by my mother, working with Tatiana, while Liliha went next door and helped Mike's mother. They prepared platters of chicken long rice, poi, shark-fin soup, sweet and sour spareribs and Portuguese sausage and beans. There were Korean dishes, Chinese ones, even a boat load of Russian pierogies from Tatiana's mother's recipe.

My mother and Tatiana had been baking cakes and pies and cookies all week, which they piled on the tables along with platters of fruit, tubs of mango sherbet and chocolate ice cream in coolers and about ten different types of crack seed.

The smell of the pig roasting began rising from the pit, and

Roby positioned himself right at the edge, alternately leaning forward to sniff and backing away from the heat. By noon, the yard was full of kids and dogs. Roby pretended to be the big shot, barking at every newcomer then jumping up to be petted and adored. We set up speakers in the yard and played The Makaha Sons, Keola Beamer and Mark Keali'i Ho'omalu and the Kamehameha School Children's Chorus singing *Hawaiian Roller Coaster Ride*. It was just like something out of *Lilo and Stich*, only without the space alien.

I worried about the different groups of people we invited. Would the cops, like Ray, Kitty and Lieutenant Sampson mingle with my gay friends from the North Shore? How about Gunter, who brought a couple of guys from Māhū Nation? I had spoken with Peggy Kaneahe and invited her, and she'd asked if she could bring some attorneys and paralegals from her firm, who wanted to thank me for arresting Adam O'Malley's killer. Would they get along with everyone else?

My fears were unfounded. When Mike's old boyfriend, the one who worked at the Halekulani, arrived with his new sweetheart, they bonded with Harry and Arleen. Greg Oshiro showed up with his two-year-old twins, and every mom in the place gathered to coo over them. Peggy and a male lawyer from her firm played croquet with Jimmy Ah Wang, a kid I had met on a case years before, and a college friend of his from Chicago. The Gresham kids played with Roby and my nieces and nephews.

By the time we opened up the pit and pulled out the pig, the party was in full swing. My cousin Ben was the focus of an adoring group of kids who realized that they had a champion surfer in their midst. Uncle Kimo, usually the fountain of all surf wisdom, was relegated to the sidelines. My mother and Aunt Pua, Ben's mom, were getting along, the two of them talking story in a corner of the yard with their other sisters. Miscellaneous cousins renewed old friendships and feuds, with Lui's son Jeffrey and Haoa's daughter Ashley organizing a touch football game that ended with the ball on our roof and Mike climbing up there to retrieve it.

My dad and Mike's were turning into fast friends, regaling each other with stories of how badly each of us had behaved as keikis. Gunter and Jimmy began planning a Māhū Nation party at the U.H. campus, in conjunction with the GLBT group there. It was much more than just a luau; it was a meeting of worlds, and just as Rodney King would have wanted, we were all just getting along.

Late in the afternoon, Harry came over to me carrying a manila folder. "I managed to enhance those birth records you gave me. Want to take a look?"

"Sure." I called over Ray and Lieutenant Sampson, and we added Peggy Kaneahe and Sarah Byrne since the materials had come to us through Fields and Yamato. I explained that to Sampson as the six of us sat down at the picnic table.

Starting with the most recent page, I traced my finger down the list. "Look here," I said. "1968. Ezekiel Kapuāiwa Lopika. Parents Alfred and Leilani Lopika."

"Ezekiel Lopika," Peggy said. "That's the guy whose hospitalization records we found."

"So it looks like those records do belong to Ezekiel Kapuāiwa," I said. "He must have dropped his last name after he got out of the mental hospital."

"King Kamehameha's birth name was Lot Kapuāiwa," Peggy said. "We learned what Kapuāiwa meant in Hawaiian school, didn't we, Kimo?"

I struggled to recall anything I'd learned in those open-air classrooms, washed in memories of Peggy and me as little kids learning the Hawaiian language and the legends of the gods.

We usually think of *kapu* as something forbidden—but really it means something sacred, restricted only to royalty. Tossing that idea in my head, I tried to put *kapu* together with *āiwa*, which means mysterious or strange. Then it came back to me in a flash.

"Yeah. Something like a sacred one protected by supernatural powers."

"Something sure protected Ezekiel at the bank," Ray said. "The way he was able to pull Dex out of that truck without getting himself killed."

"So maybe Ezekiel really is a descendant of Kamehameha," Peggy said excitedly. "And Tanaka convinced Ezekiel to drop Lopika in order to focus on the connection. Didn't you say you found some big koa bowls somewhere?"

"That's right. My mother said bowls that big were reserved for royalty. Edith was Ezekiel's hanai tūtū, so she may have been holding them for him."

"Let's not get ahead of ourselves," Ray said. "We have the records right here. Let's see what we can find."

We hunted backward until we found Alfred's birth record, in 1925. No father's name was given, but his mother was Victoria Lopika. In 1906, we found the birth of a baby girl by that name. I struggled to remember the details Maile Kanuha had given us. "Victoria's father is supposed to be Moses Kapuāiwa, who was the grandson of Kamehameha V."

"Kamehameha?" Sampson said. "I'm no expert on Hawaiian history, but I thought he never had any children. Isn't that when Hawai'i started electing kings, after he died?"

"The story that Kingdom of Hawai'i tells is that Kamehameha had an illegitimate son named Ulumaheihei, maybe with one of the girls who was at the Royal School with him, who dropped out and got married quickly. That his advisors would never let him recognize the boy, and that's why he refused to name a successor. Ulumaheihei died when Moses was young, and the family never came forward until now."

"Let's look for Moses, then," Peggy said.

But there was no Moses, no one designated to lead his people out of slavery. Victoria's parents were John and Apikela Lopika. The records didn't go back far enough to track John Lopika's birth, but I was willing to bet he wasn't related to Moses Kapuāiwa, if such a person existed.

"If it's true, then Ezekiel isn't descended from Kamehameha, and he has no more right to a restored throne than you or me," I said.

"Speak for yourself," Peggy said. "My great-grandmother insisted she was a distant cousin of Queen Lili'uokalani."

"It would destroy the foundation of KOH, though," I said. "If Jun Tanaka was betting on Ezekiel and then he discovered his horse was out of the running, he might do whatever he could to keep the information from getting out."

"So what do we do with this material?" Peggy asked. "It shuts down KOH."

"I think KOH is going down anyway," I said. "Without Tanaka's money, without him pulling the strings, you've got Ezekiel. And everyone who knows him admits he's a little squirrely. He did act like a hero at the bank, though."

I sat back in my chair. "Ezekiel said something to me. That he believed it was in his blood to protect the people of Hawai'i. That they were his ohana. And who knows, maybe those big bowls Aunty Edith had really did come down through his family and that means he has royal connections somewhere."

"He may be nuts, but he's a good guy," Ray said. "If he hadn't pulled Dex out of the truck, Dex could have killed more people."

We were agreed. The secrets of Ezekiel's parentage and hospitalization would stay between us, at least until there was some reason to make them public. The Bishop Museum had contacted Leelee about buying the bowls from her, and Peggy had agreed to look after Leelee's interests in the deal. Some of the money would go to get her settled off homestead land, and some would be put away in trust for the baby.

The CDs had all ended by then, and no one had gotten up to put new ones on. "I think we need a little live music," Peggy said. "To cap off a great luau. Sarah, you want to sing something for us?"

"Oh, no, I couldn't," Sarah said. "Not without a band behind me."

"You have a great voice," Ray said. "You know Frishberg's song *I'm Home*? The one Al Jarreau sings? It's a great song for a housewarming."

After a little more persuading, Sarah stood up, and we shushed the crowd. When she sang, "I knew that I'd found what's at the end of the rainbow... There's no place on earth I'd rather be than stayin' right here with you," I looked around for Mike.

He was standing at the back door, where two steps led up into the house. He looked so handsome, in his Honolulu Fire Department T-shirt and geometric-print board shorts. A smile curled out from beneath his mustache. I had this powerful desire to be with him—the kind of magnetic attraction I'd seen between Haoa and Tatiana, where neither of them looked complete without the other. I'd always envied that about them, and now I knew what it felt like from the inside.

I climbed up there with him, and we listened the music and looked at everyone enjoying themselves, celebrating a union that neither of us had ever dreamed we could enjoy.

Sarah finished the song, and everyone applauded. Then, holding hands, Mike and I stepped down to take our places in our *ohana*.

About the Author

NEIL PLAKCY is the author of *Mahu, Mahu Surfer, Mahu Fire, Mahu Vice,* and *Mahu Men,* about openly gay Honolulu homicide detective Kimo Kanapa'aka. His other books are *Three Wrong Turns in the Desert, Dancing with the Tide, The Outhouse Gang, In Dog We Trust, Invasion of the Blatnicks,* and *GayLife.com.* He edited *Paws & Reflect: A Special Bond Between Man and Dog* and the gay erotic anthologies *Hard Hats, Surfer Boys* and *Skater Boys.* His website is www.mahubooks.com.

The author acknowledges the trademark status and trademark owners of the following wordmarks mentioned in this work of fiction:

Bankoh: Bank of Hawaii

Billabong: GSM (Operations) Pty LTD

Bluetooth: Bluetooth Sig Inc.

CHiPs: Turner Entertainment

Colt Python: Colt Manufacturing Company

Disney Store: Disney Enterprises, Inc.

Dodge: Daimler Chrysler Group LLC

Flashdance: Paramount Pictures

Foodland: Foodland Super Market, Ltd.

Frisbee: Wham-O Mfg. Co.

Gamblers Anonymous:

Glock: Glock Inc.

Google: Google Inc.

Hawaii Five-O: CBS Productions and Leonard Freeman Productions

Hawaiian Airlines: Hawaiian Airlines

Highlander: Toyota Motor Company

Honda: The Honda Motor Company

Honolulu Advertiser: Honolulu Star-Advertiser

Indianapolis Speedway: Brickyard Trademarks, Inc.

iPhone: Apple Inc.

Jeep: Chrysler Group LLC

Kona Fire Rock Ale: Kona Brewery LLC

Lexus: Toyota Motor Company

Lilo and Stitch: Disney Enterprises, Inc.

Longboard Lager: Kona Brewery LLC

Mercedes: DaimlerChrysler

Mickey Mouse: Disney Enterprises, Inc.

Mont Blanc: Montblanc-Simplo GmbH

Nintendo Wii: Nintendo of America Inc.

Nissan: Nissan Jidosha Kabushiki Kaisha TA Nissan Motor Co., Ltd.

Out magazine: Here Media Inc.

Primidone: AstraZeneca

Propranolol: AstraZeneca and Wyeth

Shirokiya: Shirokiya International

Shock to the System: Richard Stevenson

Starbucks: Starbucks Corporation

Star-Bulletin: Honolulu Star-Advertiser

The A Team: Universal Television and 20th Century Fox

TheBus: Oahu Transit Services Inc.

Titanic: 20th Century Fox, Paramount Pictures and Lightstorm Entertainment

Vicks VapoRub: Proctor & Gamble

YouTube: Google, Inc.

Zippy's: Zippy's Inc.

CPSIA information can be obtained at www.ICGtesting.com
234671LV00001B/11/P